SPANISH CROSSING

Jed spends his summers drifting between cow outfits, and his winters hunting wolves. One season, he encounters the coyote he dubs "the Grinner" — small, sly, and seemingly unkillable. As the constant solitude begins to fray Jed's mind, his fevered pursuit of the Grinner tips over into a dangerous obsession . . . When Old Man Coffee hears Lije Evers has been murdered by Tommy Beckwith, the man who'd accused him of cheating at cards, he has no reason to disbelieve it. But local biscuit shooter Lynda Clayton claims Tommy has been set up, and enlists Coffee in her quest for the truth . . . Sheriff Lon Stevens and Joan Carter, cook at the Tinplate ranch, harbour a mutual affection — but, as a lawman's daughter, she swears she will never marry him while he wears the star. Then Lon receives information that a killer is making his way straight to the Tinplate. . .

SPANISH CROSSING

ALAN LEMAY

SAGEBRUSH
Large Print Westerns

First published in Great Britain by Gunsmoke
First published in the United States by Five Star

First Isis Edition
published 2015
by arrangement with
Golden West Literary Agency

A catalogue record for this book is available
from the British Library.

ISBN 978–1–78541–013–0 (pb)

Published by
F. A. Thorpe (Publishing)
Anstey, Leicestershire

Set by Words & Graphics Ltd.
Anstey, Leicestershire
Printed and bound in Great Britain by
T. J. International Ltd., Padstow, Cornwall

This book is printed on acid-free paper

Table of Contents

Foreword

Alan LeMay; my father, the writer, was born June 3, 1899. If anyone was ever born to write, it was Alan LeMay. He sold his first story at the age of twenty: "Circles in the Sky." It was published as a short novel in the December 30, 1919 issue of Street & Smith's *Detective Story Magazine*. Anyone who has papered his den with rejection slips will appreciate that accomplishment. But ahead of the writing had come a zest for life and an appreciation of history and heritage that might best be illustrated by the following excerpt from *Adventure* magazine, September 1, 1927 when he was an established author, experienced and well traveled, and had just turned twenty-eight.

Although Alan LeMay, whose serial of the Mississippi begins in this issue, is by no means new to our pages, he rises to tell us something about himself.
"I was born in Indianapolis. My forefathers are a good deal more interesting than myself. One of my great-grandfathers was killed by Indians at Deer Creek, Indiana, when he left the besieged blockhouse in an attempt to fetch water. Another was lost off the Horn in

his own full-rigged ship, the *Eagle*. One of my grandfathers was wounded in the battle of Kenesaw Mountain; there were six of the family in that fight. My other grandfather was killed by a buffalo on the Kansas plains. One of them made a fortune in cattle, and lost it again. Four of the family, one a captain, fought at Bunker Hill; five were engaged in the French and Indian War — two on the French side of the fence, three on the other. A LeMay built the first edifice — a trapper's hut — where Chicago stands today.

"I am a graduate of the University of Chicago. I have acted as horse wrangler in Colorado, swamper in Wisconsin, fisherman off Florida, super-cargo on a schooner in the Caribbean, geologist in the Colombian coast jungles, sparring partner for a welterweight in Chicago. During the war I was a shavetail in the infantry at eighteen, but didn't get over. Since then I have been a first lieutenant, horse and reconnaissance, in the 124th Field Artillery, Illinois National Guard. I've also tried several other things, none of them for very long, but each, I was told, for long enough."

His pride in his pioneer heritage also shows in the dedication he wrote for THE SEARCHERS (Harper, 1954): "To my grandfather, Oliver LeMay, who died on the prairie, and to my grandmother, Karen Jensen LeMay, to whom he left three sons under seven."

From the start writing was what he did. The rest was for the experience. His wild odyssey of strange jobs and exotic travels was scarcely interrupted when he married Esther Skinner on August 9, 1922. They put off having

2

kids, and kept moving. A writer is not tied to his employer's location, so he could live where he liked. Dad liked variety. My sister, Joan, was born in Aurora, Illinois, in 1926, but within six months the family moved to the French Quarter of New Orleans, and I was born in LaJolla, California, three years later.

The move to New Orleans immersed Dad in the Mississippi River scene for his research on PELICAN COAST (Doubleday, Doran, 1929) and other stories about river boats. The subsequent move West was to get closer to Western ranch atmosphere. He felt that he had to live within the culture that he wrote about, to learn the jargon, the mores, and the ambiance so important to authenticity. It also gave him the opportunity to live the action life he loved and wrote about.

During the late 'Twenties and early 'Thirties Dad sold a story about every two to four weeks to *Adventure*, Street & Smith's *Western Story Magazine*, *Short Stories*, *Collier's*, *The Saturday Evening Post*, *Cosmopolitan*, or *McCall's*. That was before television — people read stories, instead.

In the early 'Thirties we lived in San Diego while Dad explored the ranches in the outback, and got to know the local cowboys and Indians — San Diego County has more Indian tribes than any other county in the U. S. He also became a member of the Padres Writers' Club. This was where young hungry writers gave each other free criticism and encouragement. It was formed in 1925 and still exists today. Members included Stuart Lake, the writer who popularized Wyatt Earp.

During this same period, Dad's output of short stories started tapering off, and he wrote more serials and books. Early books included PAINTED PONIES (Doubleday, Doran, 1928), OLD FATHER OF WATERS (Doubleday, Doran, 1928), PELICAN COAST, and ONE OF US IS A MURDERER (Doubleday, Doran, 1930). He considered all of these to be Westerns, although many had neither cowboys nor Indians. They have the action style that characterizes "Westerns." (Paul-Loup Sulitzer, author of MONEY, and France's most widely read contemporary author, calls his own books "financial Westerns," because they are fast-paced stories where the good guys make mind-boggling fortunes by whipping the bad guys into bankruptcy.)

When not sitting at his typewriter or dictating to his long-time secretary (a petite little woman who liked to be called "Gus"), he played hard at high-risk sports. Most things he played at were things where you could get killed, such as amateur boxing, light airplane flying, polo, and sports car road racing.

Movies were too expensive during the Depression, so people bought lots of pulp fiction for escape. My father's stories sold well, but not without a lot of late nights. I can still hear my mother saying: "We can't get that until Daddy sells a story." But overall we prospered. Dad loved horses, and in 1935 he bought Lula H (the "H" was for horse) and took up polo. The game had been quite popular since the 'Twenties, and there were teams all over Southern California: Coronado, Lakeside, Riverside, and Mission Valley —

the last of which was the team that he joined. They usually had no spares; everyone played the whole game. The team was always listed as "undefeated" because every time they lost, they disbanded and re-formed under a new name. They were variously known as the Mission Valley Maniacs, the Sidewinders, Overholt's Outcasts, and the Rattlesnakes.

In 1935 he bought a ranch in Santee, ripped out the peach orchard, and put in a private polo field. The polo action moved there when the floods of 1937 covered the Mission Valley polo field (and all of the valley where the malls are today) with wall-to-wall river. Every Sunday afternoon there was a game at our ranch, usually locals, but occasionally the Riviera Club (Hollywood), which included Hal Roach and Darryl F. Zanuck. Once we entertained a team from Argentina, and another time a British Naval team.

Dad had been an amateur boxer, and Roberto Lovell, the Argentine welterweight champion, trained at the ranch before his U. S. match in San Diego. I think of these times when I read F. Scott Fitzgerald: the surreal visitors, the lavish barbecues, and those Sunday polo parties at the ranch.

In 1939 Dad learned to fly, flew across the country and back alone in a single-engine light plane, and wrote a series of airplane stories. By 1941 he had had about two hundred titles published and was called to Hollywood to write for Cecil B. DeMille. Dad had divorced in 1937, and remarried just before going to Hollywood. He spent his honeymoon on DeMille's yacht, discussing scripts. The bride was not invited along.

His first picture for DeMille was NORTHWEST MOUNTED POLICE (Paramount, 1940), starring Gary Cooper, Paulette Goddard, Madeleine Carroll, and Robert Preston. This was an original screenplay for which he won Paramount's "Best Picture of the Year" award. Also with DeMille he did the screenplays for REAP THE WILD WIND (Paramount, 1942) with John Wayne, Ray Milland, and Paulette Goddard, and THE STORY OF DR. WASSELL (Paramount, 1944) with Gary Cooper, Madeleine Carroll, and Signe Hasso.

His work ethic somewhat clashed with Hollywood's. He was used to working long hours. Most Hollywood writers spent more time in story conferences, at lunch, or on the golf course than they did in lone contemplation at a typewriter. So Dad would arrive early at Paramount, rewrite yesterday's pages before the moguls arrived for the morning story conference, take a midday break in the studio gym, and have lunch before settling in to the second shift until evening. It took at least a twelve-hour day to get in his usual eight hours of concentrated writing.

Long hours of writing can be a grind, and his acrobatic mind needed a frequent change of pace. "No pace without a change of pace" he always said. He designed gadgets, remodeled every house he lived in, and even invented a game that was patented and sold well until the patent ran out. Called FotoElectric Football (patent 2,260,467), it showed dynamic trails of players dodging the defenses down the field as a slide was pulled out of a light box.

Moving to Warner Bros. he did the screenplay for TAP ROOTS (Universal, 1948) with Susan Hayward and Ray Milland, and an original screenplay for Errol Flynn. The treatment for that one was called GHOST MOUNTAIN, but the movie was, instead, called ROCKY MOUNTAIN (Warner, 1950). Other Errol Flynn films he wrote while at Warner Bros. included SAN ANTONIO (Warner, 1945) and CHEYENNE (Warner, 1947). Another couple of Westerns featured Randolph Scott: THE GUNFIGHTERS (Columbia, 1947), based on Zane Grey's TWIN SOMBREROS, and THE WALKING HILLS (Columbia, 1949). Dad always called the Zane Grey adaptation TWIN HATS. He also did THE ADVENTURES OF MARK TWAIN (Warner, 1944) starring Frederick March and Alexis Smith.

In a brief stint with Republic — a company whose slogan was: "Always a good seat at a Republic Picture." — he did FLIGHT NURSE (Republic, 1953) and I DREAM OF JEANNIE (Republic, 1952) which was about Stephen Foster.

He and Dink Templeton then formed LeMay-Templeton Productions and did a quick series of three original screenplays: HIGH LONESOME (Eagle Lion, 1950), THE SUN-DOWNERS (Eagle Lion, 1950), and QUEBEC (Paramount, 1951). On two of these he was writer/producer and on THE SUNDOWNERS writer/director. THE SUNDOWNERS featured Robert Preston and Robert Sterling and was the most successful. The other two introduced John Barrymore, Jr., who never quite lived up to the Barrymore image. This experience was about as much Hollywood as Dad felt anyone needed in his lifetime, so he went back to writing books.

Returning to real life, he took up road racing at the age of fifty-five, racing in both the S C C A and Cal Club road races. He first drove an M G, then a stock Jaguar X K-120, then a Lotus Offenhauser, and finally a Ferrari Monza. We spent weekends road racing at Pebble Beach, Torrey Pines, Salinas, Hansen Dam, Porter Ranch, Palm Springs, Santa Barbara, Willow Springs, Stockton, March Field, and on and on. There wasn't time for much else.

He had sandwiched in a book called USELESS COWBOY (Farrar and Rinehart, 1943) between pictures. Nunnaly Johnson bought the screen rights and made it into a movie called ALONG CAME JONES (RKO, 1945) with Gary Cooper, Loretta Young, and Dan Duryea. Dad wrote THE SEARCHERS in 1954, THE UNFORGIVEN in 1957, and his last book, BY DIM AND FLARING LAMPS, in 1962. THE UNFORGIVEN was made into a John Huston film, starring Audrey Hepburn, Burt Lancaster, Lillian Gish, and, of course, Chill Wills, who was in most of the films listed above. John Ford made THE SEARCHERS. I shall have more to say on that.

Not everything he wrote was published. Three things come to mind. One was a short story called "A Gift from Korea" that he wrote during the Korean War. To research it, he talked his way into a trip with the military to the front lines. He finished the story as the war ended. His agent liked it, but said the country was sick of that war, and didn't want to read about it. Another was a book, TEN NIGHTS OVER A BARROOM: THE STORY OF FORTY GIRLS WHO WENT WEST. It is notable for the tremendous research that went into discovering the true nature of Calamity Jane, Rowdie Kate, Virginia Slade, Cattle Kate Maxwell, Little Breeches, Big Nose Kate Fisher, Prairie Rose, Poker Alice, Faro Nell, Molly b'Dam', and other Western women who became legends.

The third piece, never intended for publication, was a poignant letter Dad wrote to his parents in anticipation of their first trip West on an airliner in December, 1936. He explained to them how the aeroplane might feel like it was bouncing around a little, but that was normal, so don't be alarmed. The letter was sent air mail; it arrived six months later with an understated rubber stamp on the cover: "Delayed Due To Service Interruption At Salt Lake City." The mail plane had crashed, killing all aboard, and the letter had spent a cold winter on some Wasatch mountain peak. The plane his parents were on, fortunately, fared better than the mail plane.

In 1963 Dad lived in Pacific Palisades with his wife, Arlene, and was at the top of his form. He had an office two miles away in the village. He would walk or jog there at dawn, write for four hours, work out at the nearby gym or meet a friend for tennis, take a nap, and then wake up for the afternoon's four hours of writing. He felt that he was in the best shape of his life. Then

9

one day his right hand didn't work. He had brain cancer. They said they had to operate. They weren't very good at it in 1963, and Dad knew it. His last unsedated words were a defiant: "O K, pull the trigger." He died April 28, 1964.

I have always regretted that his early death kept him from enjoying two later developments. The first was computer word-processors. He wrote with everything but stone tablets and a chisel. He typed. He dictated, both live to Gus and mechanically on an old Dictaphone with a bakelite cylinder that had to be shaved with a lathe tool to erase. He wrote longhand. He said that some days a pencil worked, and other days only a pen would do. But a word processor, with its freedom of editing, would to him have been a discovery more profound than fire or the wheel.

The other development that he missed was the classic status achieved by one of his last novels. THE SEARCHERS had been adapted as a screenplay by Frank S. Nugent in 1956. It was well received at the time, but its greater recognition came two decades later. In the March 5, 1979 *New York Magazine*, Stuart Byron wrote an article entitled "THE SEARCHERS: Cult Movie of the New Hollywood." The gist was that the film had become a classic as rated by industry insiders, if not by the public.

Stuart Byron quoted Ernest Hemingway as having once said: "All modern American literature comes from one book by Mark Twain called HUCKLEBERRY FINN." Byron claimed that in the same broad sense it can be said that all recent American cinema derives from John Ford's THE SEARCHERS (Warner, 1956). Throughout this article Byron gives total credit to John Ford, and only passing acknowledgment to the novel by Alan LeMay. A second opinion was written by Gary Arnold in "Heroes' Welcome for THE SEARCHERS" in the September 23, 1979 *Washington Post.* Recognizing Byron's treatment, Arnold said: "The admiring reassessments of THE SEARCHERS seem to preclude recognition of the seminal, utterly indispensable importance of Alan LeMay's original novel. This neglect illustrates the disparity in status between superior Western fiction and superior Western filmmaking. Ironically, LeMay, who died in 1964 of a brain tumor at the age of sixty-four, was once a prominent screenwriter. Recruited by Cecil B. DeMille, LeMay set aside a prolific early writing career, mainly Western fiction, to collaborate on the scripts of . . ." and then he went on to recite highlights of the Hollywood chapter. Gary Arnold further commented on the lack of recognition given to writers:

A critical anthology called FAVORITE MOVIES includes an appreciation of THE SEARCHERS by Jay Cocks, who refers to Nugent's 'superb script' without mentioning that it happens to be an effective distillation and modification of a novel that was itself exceptionally effective. Indeed, the filmmakers felt impelled to sacrifice certain elements whose loss you profoundly regret once you become aware of them. LeMay devised stunning climactic and concluding episodes. They leave emotional reverberations that the movie never quite equals, despite the combined eloquence of Ford's pictorial genius and Wayne's towering physical presence at the fadeout.

When the film's final portal image closes, it appears to exclude Ethan Edwards from the society he has struggled to revenge, protect, and restore. The movie ends with a lingering impression of Wayne's Ethan Edwards beyond the threshold, a proud, lonely man. But there's also an unseen, forgotten man lingering out there in the cinematic ether: the storyteller who imagined THE SEARCHERS in the first place.

That sounds like something Dad might have said.

Dan B. LeMay
Fallbrook, California

The Wolf Hunter

During the third winter of his wolf hunting on the open range Jed began talking to his horse; he soon gave it up, however, since it was apparent that the horse never listened. At the first word the animal always flicked back a hairy ear, but as Jed's nasal voice droned ahead without command the ear relaxed again, and the horse jogged on unnoticing.

It was a colorless sort of horse, anyway, a dirty gray-white, shaggy, and always round barreled, for it was a good keeper; the only horse that Jed had ever thought of as "it." The name it recognized was "Hey!" Though Jed also addressed it as "Here, you!"

Jed never thought of wolf hunting as a job. Its hardships were the same as those of paid winter riding, but, because nobody was telling him what to do, Jed thought he was idling — just drifting around, and meantime piecing out by taking wolf scalps for bounty.

He meant to go back to work by and by to "get somewhere." The trouble was that he never rode for a cow outfit for long without concluding that everybody in the spread was down on him. Since he was uncommunicative, a methodical man with an unkindled

eye, no one ordinarily thought anything about him —
but Jed believed differently. Presently some small
dispute would arise, over a rope or some such matter,
and Jed would recognize the old story — universal
enmity breaking out again.

As a wolf hunter he found that the few cents each
scalp brought was enough for his needs. He almost
never had to buy food; that was supplied by the cow
camps to which necessity periodically drove him. This
liberality, accorded by the ranchers to the wolf hunter
as a valuable, almost self-sacrificing citizen, was a
mystery to Jed. He could neither imagine himself
publicly useful nor believe in anyone's friendliness. The
generosity remained unexplained. Jed took it as an
ominous sign.

Summers he grub-tested, moving on from camp to
camp, working stock satisfactorily but very little; but
through the long winters he wandered alone with his
strychnine bottles. He would ride a twenty-mile circle,
leisurely scattering wolf bait, then slowly traverse the
circle again, looking for dead wolves. He found plenty.
Sometimes he shot a steer, for meat and bait; that was
another thing the ranchers thought nothing of.

Each year he grew more solitary, avoiding chance
meetings shamefacedly, almost like a hunted man. As
he grew more solitary, he grew more careless of his own
comfort. He would go for days without making coffee
or cooking food, subsisting by perpetually chewing raw
corn meal, like tobacco. Since he did not count raw
corn meal as food, he thought he was a man who could
go for days without eating. He had worked himself into

14

a singularly bleak rut by the time the Grinner took him up.

The grinning varmint was an undersized but unusually shaggy coyote of the race that formed the bulk of Jed's catch. They were commonly accepted under the law as prairie wolves, drawing a bounty somewhat less than that for timber wolves or grays. When Jed first saw him, the Grinner was sitting in the open a hundred yards away, watching Jed make his perfunctory camp. Jed upped his rifle, but lowered it again, for the coyote flicked out of line and merged with the sage. The wolf hunter went about frying a steak from a chunk of beef he was packing, the coyote out of his mind.

The steak had no more than sizzled in the pan than the coyote appeared in another quarter, again sitting on his haunches, his tongue lolling. This time Jed pretended not to see. Casually he lay down, as if intending sleep, worked the rifle out in the coyote's direction, slowly rolled on his belly, upped sights, and — the coyote was not there.

Not until he had sat up, rifle in hand, did he see the coyote sitting in another place, looking exactly as before. This time he made a snap shot of it, and the dirt jumped where the mark had been. But the animal had disappeared.

Jed was not surprised; it had happened before. Only one scare was generally enough for one coyote. This time he was surely gone for good. A faint sift of snow was beginning to settle, and Jed, who had made almost a fetish of his rifle, wrapped the weapon in a blanket.

When this was done, and the steak turned, the coyote appeared again.

The wolf hunter took a better look at him — meanly small, foolishly furry, with the usual slanting, close-set eyes. Some coyotes have a wrinkle between the eyes, giving them a sharp look, and this one had that. The frown gave that tongue-lolling laughter a peculiarly personal, irritating turn.

Jed's lips formed unfriendly names. There was still plenty of light — long hours formed no part of Jed's resumé. With deliberate motions he unwrapped his rifle. When he looked up again and found, as he had expected, that the beast was gone, he sat down to wait the coyote out.

The long minutes passed. The steak scorched, was jerked off the fire, and slowly cooled to rigidity. Jed sat twisting his neck, watching for the coyote to reappear. Dusk settled with the snow that was frosting his sheepskin collar. It was almost too dark for a shot when he decided that the coyote was gone for good. He thumbed his nose in two directions.

"Go to hell!" he shouted, so that Hey!, the indeterminate horse, raised a simple head.

He wrapped the rifle in the blanket once more. When he raised his eyes, there sat the coyote, scarcely fifty yards away.

That night the Grinner stole his beef.

All the next day the coyote followed him, not pointedly, but casually, as if merely trotting about its business. Twice Jed fired at it. As he slowly scattered his

16

baits, he was thinking that he would pick up the ears of that coyote on his next round.

During the night a coyote howled surprisingly close to the ashes of his fire, a shrill, yammering, nickering scurl of sound fit for twelve animals of that size — *Hee-ee yipipipip, ah-ah-yapapapapapa-o-o-o* — dying away at last in a mournful dree. And in the morning when he found that his saddlebags had been dragged off, rifled, and their non-edible contents defiled, the same meanly sized, over-furry coyote was sitting in a hummock two hundred yards away, his tongue lolling in that foxy laughter.

"You damned Grinner," Jed shouted. "I'll fix your clock works fer that!"

From then on he thought of the coyote as *he* instead of *it*.

At his next camp he poisoned a bit of meat, and left it close by his dead fire, and took care that nothing else stealable was left around.

Daybreak showed the bait gone, but the coyote in the middle distance, scratching fleas. Jed was mystified and exasperated.

"Oh, you *copper-lined* son-of-a-gun!" he yelled at the animal. He thought that by some slip he had failed to poison the bait.

At the next opportunity he slit a good-size hunk of wolf haunch and loaded into it enough poison to stretch out half the wolves on the open range. When in the morning the bait was gone and the Grinner still on deck, he took advantage of a light snowfall to trace the imprinted diagram of the coyote's theft. He found the

17

remains of his bait skillfully nibbled, but with the heavy drench of poison untouched. Jed grunted. Three times more that day he tried to bring the coyote down by rifle.

So it went for another week, while Jed's circling carried him from the slopes to the flats and back to the rock-bound slopes again. Soon after midday he would begin looking for a good place to camp. Unless he was seeking water, the prairie was a vast blank, with no point of focus, no logical place to stop. This induced an indecision that used up most of his afternoon.

But once the fire was built, all that was changed. His fire had a way of seeming the center of the universe, a permanent living thing that had always been destined to be just there. It was a bright landmark, reducing everything to relationship with itself.

And by the time the darkness had closed in about the fire, the grinning coyote was there. Jed got so he paid no attention to him. After all, he was not trying to get all the coyote ears in the world — only the easy ones. If the Grinner didn't want his baits, Jed didn't give a whoop. Thus the wolf hunter and the coyote, along with that unconsidered horse, slowly trailed a great circle and got back to the place where the Grinner had first baffled Jed's gun.

Now a new element came in, changing their relationship. For the first time in three years Jed rode along a day's line of baits without finding a dead wolf. At first, Jed thought only that wolves were getting scarce, but when, the next day, he still found no wolves, he inquired into causes. He rediscovered his baits with some trouble, but, when he had found a few, the difficulty became clear.

Systematically the Grinner had nosed out Jed's baits, nibbled what he could of each without poisoning himself, and so defiled the remainder that no animal would touch it.

A fury steamed up in Jed, making his eyes watery pale against the red of his face. He shook knobby fists over his head, calling upon heaven to witness that he would get even with that varmint if it were the last thing he did. When he had cooled, he began to scheme, matching his resources against the coyote's nose.

From day to day he rode on, in short stages now, spending most of his hours in preparation. He no longer rode back over his baited lines, for the continuing company of the coyote discouraged him. Instead, he put out only clever baits, pointed for the Grinner alone.

He made grooved sticks and crammed the grooves with poisoned tallow. These the Grinner spoiled, but would not touch. He poisoned tiny, hashed pellets of meat and set them aside to freeze, to kill the scent, hid the pellets in small chunks, and froze them, and finally wrapped the chunks in fresh meat, forming baits still so small that a coyote should take each at a gulp. The Grinner gnawed off the outside wrappers, and the ruse failed.

For a week he experimented with marrow bones, making short tubes of them, with poison in the middle and pure marrow in both ends. This failed, too. He made snares with his lariat, cunningly contrived and baited with non-poisoned meat. The Grinner scratched in underneath, and stole the bait. He also tried a deadfall, when once materials lay at hand, but that night the ground thawed. The Grinner, tunneling under, escaped uncrushed, and after that would not steal from beneath logs again.

Stopping at a ranch for provisions, Jed borrowed a string of wolf traps, very cumbersome to carry with no pack horse. These failed him, as had everything else. He cached them in a gully and never remembered to take them back to their owner.

Jed wandered on, his marches lengthening. He made only half-hearted efforts now to poison the beast. Instead, he burned his scraps of food in an attempt to starve the coyote out, but there were as many resources along Jed's trail as anywhere else, and the coyote stuck. The wolf hunter brooded sourly over this thing that was "just his luck."

Jed's unplanning routine, calling for little thought or attention, had served as a comfortable oblivion. Through the slow days his mind wandered woolgathering over his past. As he relived each remembered scene, he improved it, putting into his own mouth bold and witty remarks, confusing and over-bearing his persecutors. He reënacted his battles, letting inconclusive outcomes flower into triumphs. "A mite quicker, an' I'd 'a' had him by the throat. Now, blast you, I guess you'll . . ."

But the Grinner broke into his meanderings like a persistent fly on the face of a man who is trying to sleep. A dozen times a day Jed's hand stole toward his rifle. In the night he sat watching for the Grinner's green eyes, like phosphorous balls hung in black frost. He roused from sleep at the Grinner's howls, cursing and hoping for a shot. When the coyote was long out of sight, which occurred every day, Jed's eyes forever searched the sage, so that the brute's absence was no relief.

Sometimes, as he lay looking at the pulsing dance of the rocks behind his fire's heat column, he thought of women he had known and certain others he had only seen. His wandering mind glorified himself and them so that for a while he forgot the cold snow cake of the prairie, and walked in a world of music, warmth, and light, admired by women's eyes. His vision caressed contouring silk, round white arms. Then nearby would go up that long falsetto devil-yell: *Hee-ee yipipipipip* . . . . And out of his blankets would start the actual Jed, the man with sourly furrowed face and hands grimed and gnarled, cursing so as to shatter any dream past all recall.

One day, in a paroxysm of helpless wrath, he turned the dirty-gray horse toward the coyote, and with spur and quirt set out to run the animal down. For two miles the Grinner led him up slope and down, then, tiring of the pursuit, went into an easy sprint and was lost in a long reef of sage.

The horse stumbled to a walk, then stopped of his own accord, head down. Jed, getting off to tighten the cinch, noticed how lean the animal was. It was weeks since the horse had tasted grain. A poor keeper would have been out from under him long ago.

In the saddle again Jed mumbled endless curses at the forlorn sage. He sat thinking for a long time, sometimes turning the wad of cornmeal in his cheek.

"All right," he said at last. "You win. I'm leavin' this whole damned range to you. Take it an' keep it. I ain't wantin' it no more."

He turned Hey!'s head north. "I guess you can go it three days more," he decided.

That day he covered a long distance steadily north through a rising blow. Gray noon found him at the foot of Long Ridge, which divided that part of the free range, the north from the south. He was heading over for the Crazy K country. "The varmints have their ranges, same as a man," he was telling himself. "They won't noways cross out of 'em if they ain't terrible pushed."

Late in the day the toiling horse reached the saddle notch in Long Ridge's backbone, and Jed stopped. A slashing gale was rearing through the gap, swaying him in the saddle. It carried with it a whip of hard, dry snow. He turned sidewise, looking back. "I ain't through with you," he promised. "I'll come back and do fer you yet."

A furlong down the trail he twisted his head to look back through the thin, racing snow. On a boulder he saw a small, blurred projection, like a vague pin. It disappeared, and a gray wisp, like a shadow, drifted tangent-wise down slope across a drift of snow. The Grinner was following Jed through.

Hollow eyed and bitter lipped, Jed pushed on down the slope with the sting of the wind in his face. The darkness closed in an hour earlier than usual, under a moaning sky already hidden by level-driving flakes. The gray horse tried to turn tail to the wind and quit, but Jed forced it to go on. For an hour more they drifted with the barren slope, head down into the storm, until at last the flattening way suggested the foot of Long Ridge, and Jed swung down.

Moving clumsily on saddle-cramped legs, Jed sought a windbreak behind which a man in blankets could live through the night. He clung stubbornly to the idea that since here he had stopped, here he would camp; yet, as rod after rod showed only wind-scoured hollows and windward drifts, he was forced to admit that only a fool would have crossed to the windward side of Long Ridge in such circumstances.

The storm was growing worse. The sage shrilled, and the sky was alive with a vast moaning, the rushing of great winds high above. Shamefacedly he resigned himself to pushing on twelve miles to the Crazy K.

He hurried back, searching for Hey! in the dark. When he reached the place where he had left the horse, it was gone.

A stark terror — the first he had known in years — came into Jed like rising water, slowly at first, then with a wild rush like the scouring wind. Panic urged him to go rushing and plunging ahead. For an instant he almost yielded, and his bedroll slid from his shoulder to the snow.

Then the plainsman's experience took the upper hand, and, instead of abandoning his bedroll, he sat down on it. He sucked at the cornmeal in his cheek, seeking half by reason, half by instinct, to divine in which direction the gray horse should be sought.

At first, while he still thought his horse could be found, he searched keenly and wisely. Later, as successive sorties gained him nothing, he searched obstinately still, but with an increasingly fearsome despair. He lost account of his position and hence of the probable position of the horse.

There could be no limit to that groping under the blizzard, other than that set quite as much by the grip of despair as by the numbing of his limbs. He went on with the dogged hunt until his feet were like clubs and the dree of the wind was dulling in his ears. His purposes were becoming blurred.

Jed did not believe it possible for a man to lie down on that wind-planed slope and live through the night. To roll in his blankets meant to him to die, caught in the closing trap of the cold. Yet, partly because the shelter of his blankets offered that last slender hope, he at last resigned himself to it.

He fumbled the strap from his bedroll. The wind tore at the loosened blankets, almost snatching them from his grasp, but his numbed hands held on to them with the grip of fear, and he managed to roll himself into them, like a mummy or like a worm in a cocoon. He lay in a bitter snow, nose down in the blanket, breathing hard.

Swiftly the snow salted over the blanket roll. Within it, the nightmare of conscious existence was slowly seeking numbed oblivion. Yet, when the Grinner yelled,

Jed heard the yammering voice through the growl of the wind, and his mind was drawn back.

He thought: *No coyote howls in a blizzard.* And then: *It ain't right he don't get froze.*

The Grinner howled again, that long falsetto nicker: *Yipipipip, hee-ee-yapapapapap* . . . . An insane fury brought him to his elbow, fumbling his Colt free. He dragged the blanket away from his face, and the salt snow whipped against his mouth. In the faint gray luminosity of the snow he thought he made out a moving blur, a close circling form.

He leveled the gun, elbow grounded, and fired.

The dark blur became a fallen, frantically kicking swirl. He heard the Grinner's thin yip, and fired four times more into that swirl, until the hammer snapped on an empty cylinder. Then he drew back into the tube of his blankets, better fixed — as he thought — to die.

Jed was mistaken. He was not dying, or anything near it.

He woke in misery, every joint filled with cold pain. A faint seepage of light showed on the nap of the blanket an inch before his eyes, and presently he stiffly raised himself. A douse of snow dropped across his face like feathers, for half a foot of it lay over his bedroll. He blinked his eyes across a morning gray and still. The gray horse was huddled dejectedly a few feet away.

The circumstances of the night returned to him slowly. Their force was dulled, even when they were complete. He was a little chagrined that he had overestimated his danger, a little pleased that he was mainly unharmed. But his underlying emotion was a flat one — merely the wretched sense of ill-being that goes with stiff joints and a cold dawn. Then his loose Colt reminded him of the Grinner.

He hardly believed, even when he had kicked the stiffened coyote out of the snow, that the Grinner was really dead. The animal in death looked more meanly small than before, more mangy, more fleabitten, less furry. His rigid tongue, sticking sidewise out of his jaws, was bright with frozen blood. Only the crease between his eyes gave him a resemblance to the immortal grinning varmint that had spoiled Jed's wanderings for so long.

What would have been a grand triumph under other circumstances was reduced to only a faint ironic satisfaction as Jed opened his big knife and haggled off the Grinner's scalp.

Jed stopped only three days at the Crazy K. During that time he cooked, and they wanted him to stay on in that job. But as soon as he was warm clear through, and tired of eating, he judged that the gray horse had downed enough grain to move on. He was anxious to prove to himself that he was as good a wolf hunter as ever, now that the Grinner was dead.

For the first week he had little luck, for the Crazy K had been fighting wolves on its own account, but, as he came into new territory, things began to improve. For a week or two he heartily enjoyed the discovery of gray carcasses near his baits.

Then he began to notice that something was lacking. Once more he futilely attempted conversation with Hey! Often, as he rested by his fire, he would catch himself listening; not naturally, as he habitually listened, but tensely, waiting. If a coyote yelled far off, he would stir, brightening almost, with the fresh breath of animosity that the Grinner had earned. Then his interest would fade out again, leaving the prairie more bleak than before, peopled only with the foolish brutes that ate his baits.

Sometimes a voice almost exactly like that of the Grinner would sound not far away, and for an instant he would forget that the Grinner was dead. Even after he had remembered, he would lie listening to the yapping voice, pretending, half convincing himself that it was the same.

Often he amused himself by thinking how he would out-smart the Grinner, if the brute were still alive. There was not much to that, though; there was so little he had not tried.

Perpetually, as he loafed in his makeshift camp, while the gray horse grazed, his eyes wandered to sweep the snow-floored sage. The brush was a salty gray; its twigs worked faintly in the wind, with a whispering voice indescribably desolate.

Once as his eyes roved from his fire, his nerves leaped to action; for a coyote was watching him, seated in plain sight ninety yards away, as the Grinner had sat. His rifle came up cautiously, for he expected the animal to disappear. When he had shot the coyote through the head, he lacked the spirit to walk out and get the ears; he let it go until the next day, when he was ready to move on.

A month passed in that way. The winter had grown old, but there were still six weeks of it left.

Late in a gray afternoon, after a dinner of fried mush, Jed got the ears of the Grinner out of his bounty sack, and put them on a rock behind a bush, a hundred yards from his camp. They made the rock look a good deal like the Grinner in the failing light. He meant to use them as a mark to shoot at, but, instead, he played for half an hour with an elaborate calculation of how he was going to shoot the Grinner this time and get around that disappearing trick.

Suddenly he was shocked by his own childishness. With a grumble of oaths he turned his back and tried to go to sleep, but his awareness of those taunting ears out there behind the sage would not let him. On an impulse he resaddled his horse and rode away, leaving the ears behind. Three miles farther on he decided he wanted them, after all, and rode back.

Then, as he sat his horse, staring down at that pair of ears in the twilight, a sense of his own folly overwhelmed him. He sat pulling at his lower lip with gloved fingers, gazing vacantly at those ears — two shabby triangles on a hardened bar of hide.

He was wishing he were a granger, eating a frosty winesap apple by a hot stove, with a family of kids around him. It seemed to him that if he could only have a decent job again, away from the stark loneliness of that vast vacant prairie, he would never want anything else. Those accursed ears kept pulling his attention back.

"Gosh," he muttered, "I can't go this no more."

28

He turned the gray horse, and they went lumbering off into the dark.

Once, a long time after, he found himself on that prairie again, while he was driving the cook wagon for the Crazy K. Cooking had turned out a good job for Jed. Cooks were supposed to be crotchety and queer; the riders made allowances for that. Men in hopes of coffee at odd hours spoke pleasantly to him, and, if they joked over him, they put in elaborate winks and grins. He felt foolish when, as the trail passed near the rock where he had left the Grinner's ears, he turned off to see if they were still there. They were gone, of course. Something hungry had carried them away.

Just a Horse of Mine

So this, thought Tip Roddy, swinging down from his saddle without being invited, *is High Wind MacDowell — himself.*

About all Roddy knew about MacDowell, except that his cattle were the best range stock in the Southwest, consisted of a rumor picked up in Redregon to the effect that old High Wind was going to have a concrete statue made of himself, and set up at the Dog Wolf water hole that he had fought over for so long.

Redregon was wasting its time debating what the statue was going to look like, and whether it would be in natural colors, gold leaf, or just plain, buckwheat-batter cement.

The town was split, some thinking the effigy would resemble a white-face steer looking through a Joshua bush, and others expecting it to look more like a balloon. But all agreed that it would not stand out there in the cactus very long before taking on a likeness to the Spirit of Smallpox, so many Redregon riders were going to throw lead at it — men that had always wanted to jump High Wind MacDowell in person, but never worked up to it.

Of course, the concrete business had nothing to do with Tip Roddy, except that Roddy, now that he was meeting old High Wind for the first time, thought he saw new light on several aspects of the statue rumor. MacDowell had grown portly in his advancing years, but his short, grizzled beard still bristled like nobody's business, his eye could kindle faster than the powder in a gun, and he had a voice like thunder up the gulch.

"What horse is that?" demanded High Wind bluntly.

"Just a horse of mine. My name is Roddy, and I'm from . . ."

"So you want to see me, do you?" High Wind blared with no marked cordiality. "Oh, you do? Hold on now! Don't get talkative yet. Answer me this, young man. How many cows can a calf have in one year?"

"How many cows can a calf . . . I don't get you, mister," said Roddy.

"I said," roared MacDowell, "how many calves can a cow . . . ?"

"Oh," said Roddy. "That's different. Looks like you had your feet tangled up in your rope for a minute there, Mister MacDowell. Well, they tell me that on some ranges, and providing they have the right brand, a cow is liable to come in with two or three calves . . . and maybe a couple of colts," he answered.

"Just fresher than a steam laundry in hell, aren't you?" rumbled MacDowell. "You had a peach of a nerve, riding the front half of your horse right up into the step of my verandy. Still, riders is scarce this fall, and you seem to have the right basic idee." He ran a slow eye over Tip Roddy, from Stetson hat and smooth-shaved jaw to worn chaps and time-polished rowels. "Yeah, I can use you, I guess."

"You don't mean to tell me," said Tip Roddy. "And what for?"

"Ain't you been looking for a job with me?"

"Not by a long spit," Roddy told him. "I'm looking around to buy fifty, sixty head of two-year-old bulls for a spread I've got over in Moon Pan Basin. And now, my short friend, since you never asked me to step down, I'll step right back up again. I'm right sorry my horse set foot on your porch step . . . he must have mistook this for a ranch house, such as he's always been welcome at before. Thank you kindly, good bye, and go to the devil," said Roddy, and prepared to mount.

For a moment High Wind's jaw slacked, but immediately his short beard spread in an unaccustomed grin, and he chuckled.

"Wait a minute," he said more genially. "I mis-assumed you for one of these darned student-cowboys, at first, but I see plain where I got my saddle on wrong end to. The drinks are on me, Mister . . . Rocky, was it? . . . and I'll take it as a kindness if you'll step down and have something to eat."

Tip Roddy was not surprised. He had learned by this time that it is only secretly uncertain men who like to do business with crawlers. Still, High Wind's apology sounded overdone to Roddy, so that he suspected sarcasm; and he would have replied that he wouldn't choose anything, thank you just the same, if Kit MacDowell had not come to the door just then.

32

Roddy took off his hat, dropped it, picked it up, and stood pulling the brim around and around through his fingers. Even from his first sight of the girl, Tip knew that he was done for. It came on him in a sort of dazed, sinking sensation, as if he knew he was up against his manifest destiny, and that any minute it might find him short of powder.

A friendly, understanding sort of girl Kit MacDowell was, with a merry mouth, and sober, comprehending gray eyes. She was golden tanned, and her soft chestnut hair was sun-burned where it curled about her ears, and you knew by the general look of her that she could ride any old horse, any old time. And at the same time she was so beautifully clear cut and all, like a racing filly, or a flower . . .

"It just does seem like I've seen that horse before," High Wind mused. "Would you mind saying where you got him, Mister Rocky?"

"Gave an Indian five bucks for him, three, four years back. He's old, but I like him."

It was kind of awkward, Roddy felt, that High Wind MacDowell did not introduce him to the girl. Roddy turned on her a sort of confused look, and she smiled at him, as if she understood and felt the same way about it, and at that Tip dropped his hat again.

"May I hold that for you?" she said.

"Ma'am?"

"You've dropped your hat twice."

Just so almighty competent and cool, thought Roddy. *And so almighty sweet, too.* His knees went watery on him, and he turned red as he mumbled some fool answer. At that, all this confusion was something new to Roddy, who had always been considered to have a free-handed way with girls.

"This here is my niece, Kit," High Wind came to earth. "She's from Montana. Her paw and maw died on her . . . that makes her my niece. Kit, this here is Mister Rocky. He . . ."

"Roddy," Tip corrected.

"Roddy? Not Tip Roddy? Well, I'll be darned! I remember now, we wrote some letters back and forth this spring, about them same bulls. Sure enough . . . I remember hearing you'd set up a right nice little lay, over in the Moon Pan. Kit, Mister Roddy. He's stopping by with us a few days . . . he's got one of the prettiest little spreads over in the Moon Pan . . ."

"Pleased to meet you," mumbled Roddy, looking it.

"Mister Roddy is liable to succeed," said High Wind expansively. "He tells me he guesses a cow can be got to bring in three, four calves a year, with right handlin'."

"I said, I've heard they do on some ranges," Roddy corrected him, looking MacDowell over as cool as be damned. "In the Moon Pan we think an eighty per cent calving is mighty good, and a credit to the brand."

"Are you criticizing my beginnings?" bristled MacDowell.

"I don't criticize anybody."

"Well," growled High Wind, "see that you don't. And in reference to me, just remember this, young man . . . from the Sierras to the Pecos, they've never pried a settlement off me yet!"

34

It seemed to Tip Roddy that High Wind MacDowell, king of the Redregon, cattle baron, former gunfighter, long known as the toughest man to buck in the Southwest, was running a good deal to windiness in his old age. The old border raider — if such he had been — was sliding into the reminiscent stage without pulling in his horns by so much as an inch.

As the supper gong rang, they were joined by a lank mourner who was introduced as one Lem Wilkinson, High Wind's top foreman. This man shook hands with sorrowful suspicion, opined that it didn't look much like no rain, and relapsed into silence. Throughout the meal he divided a tragic gaze between Kit MacDowell and his plate, confining his conversational efforts to low affirmative moans upon being offered second and third helpings.

Tip Roddy sat through supper in an increasing daze. He could not look at Kit MacDowell without strangely stirring, upsetting sensations, and he could not keep from looking at her. She invariably caught him at it, which seemed to amuse her. Indeed, her eyes were no longer sober; her amusement had turned them sultry, and illuminated her glances with a new but not unfriendly light. Roddy was distinctly afoot in the sandhills by this time, with no common sense in sight.

Toward the end of the meal High Wind abandoned his stewed apricots long enough to go stumping out. Through the window Roddy saw High Wind out by the feed rack in the dusk, peering between the poles of the corral for a better look at Roddy's horse.

"If he's hinting around for me to give him that horse,"

Roddy confided to Kit, "he's just wasting his time. There's other horses . . . and he's got his share of 'em."

"I want to thank you for something," said Kit.

"Who, me?"

"I couldn't believe my eyes," Kit told him. "I've been here nearly two years, and you're the first man I ever saw stand up and shout back at this uncle of mine. It sure is a relief to see a man come in here and talk like one . . . and I, for one, want you to know I've enjoyed it."

Lem Wilkinson, whose existence had been forgotten, threw his spoon into his plate with a protesting clatter. The lank cow boss sat up straight for a moment to favor Kit with a stare of sorrowful rebuke, then rose without excuse, and tramped expressively out.

Roddy and Kit MacDowell grinned at each other. Left alone with this girl, Tip could think of nothing to say. He stared at her dazedly, until she flushed. "Do you like living here with your uncle?" he got out at last.

"It would be all right, if he didn't keep trying to marry me off."

"Try to! Who, him? Why, that old . . . say, I'll jump right down his throat."

"If he tries it on you?"

"Wait, now . . . that isn't what I meant. Say, is he trying to palm off this Wilkinson grief as a . . . ?"

"Oh, no. Lem Wilkinson is a volunteer. The other thing I don't like is seeing everybody back up for him.

'Yes, Mister MacDowell,' and 'Kindly, kick me again, please, sir,' until it's fair sickening."

"I betcha."

"Have some more apricots, Mister Roddy."

"Thank you kindly. Wait, though . . . I thought you said apricots. Them's the potatoes."

A silence fell — a silence that somehow became slowly palpitant. It was embarrassing, in a way. Yet Tip Roddy was sorry when High Wind MacDowell returned.

MacDowell dragged Roddy off to a smoky little cubbyhole of his own, the walls of which were racked with past-model rifles and feathered with an accumulation of trophies that ran from mountain lion hides to coup sticks, and back again. Here an effort was made to pursue business across vast arid plains of reminiscence having to do with the Life and Times of King MacDowell — His Exploits and His Deeds.

It was after midnight when Tip Roddy escaped from the pipe smoke — but Kit was there, to say good night at the door.

"You didn't need to wait up," said MacDowell. "You should have been in the soogans hours back."

"No trouble," said Kit.

The brief pressure of her hand was almost too much for Roddy, and he dropped his hat — but this time caught it again — as he took his leave.

"That's better," said Kit. "You've learned the ins and outs of that hat."

Tip Roddy rode off that night in exalted mood.

The next day Kit rode all day long with Tip Roddy and High Wind as they made a general pick and survey of the stock that Roddy wanted. High Wind was with them every minute, but there was a certain companionship about it that permitted them to get used to each other — better, in a way, than if they had needed to talk.

While High Wind was washing up that evening, Kit and Tip Roddy walked out to the corral to take a look at Tip's horse. He had ridden one of MacDowell's that day, to save his own for the long cattle drive ahead.

Two minutes after the feed rack had screened them from the house, Roddy swept Kit into his arms.

Kit brought a small fist up to his jaw with stinging accuracy, and took advantage of his surprise to fling free of him. "You're just like all the rest," she stormed, her voice low and intense. "I've got no earthly use for you."

He caught her wrist.

"That isn't so."

"Let me go!"

"I'm damned if I will," said Roddy. "Not now, nor ever. I'll tell you this flat . . . I'm not going back to the Moon Pan without you."

"Do you mean that?"

"I take that to be just a sort of form question," said Roddy. "Honey, come here."

This time she came into his arms as naturally as a pony puts its muzzle to fresh water.

38

Twice more in the course of the evening High Wind MacDowell excused himself to go out to the corral and take long stares at Roddy's horse. As Roddy saddled by the light of a lantern MacDowell had brought out, the old man struck his conclusion at last.

"I know him now! I knew I'd remember him!"

"Yes?"

"*That's Slade Tucker's horse!*"

"Is that so?"

"Yes, that's so! I never forgot an animal yet, and I'm right on this one now! You never bought that horse from no Indian! You're the man killed Slade Tucker!"

"Yes?" said Roddy.

"It's no use denying it!"

"I deny nothing."

"You killed Slade Tucker! I always wondered who done that. And you collected the reward, I suppose? No? But anyways stole his horse?"

"Stole, MacDowell?"

"Yes. And I say this, and I say it plain . . . when you shot Slade Tucker, you killed a better man than you are!"

"You knew this Slade Tucker?"

"No one," said High Wind, "knew him better than me. A fine, upstanding, straight-shooting, clean-living young squirt, Slade was, and the reward should never have been slapped on his head!"

"Now, just a minute, MacDowell . . ."

"Don't try to lie out of it with me! You killed Slade Tucker and took his horse, and I know that as sure as steers can't spit!"

Distinctly, High Wind's tone called for a smash in the nose. For a long moment Tip Roddy hesitated, trying to tell himself that this was an old man, and Kit's uncle at that. Then he mounted his horse. "Well, and what if I did?" he said from the saddle.

It sounded like cool insolence to MacDowell. Anger gagged in his throat, and, before he could find proper words of denunciation, Tip Roddy was gone.

High Wind had no intention of swallowing his wrath, however. He went stamping and breathing hoarsely into the house, and there poured himself a five-finger jolt of forty rod. When this was downed, his whiskey-laden bellow resounded through the house.

"Kit! Kit! Come here!"

"What on earth's the matter with you?" demanded Kit, presently appearing in nightgown and slippers.

"You know who we've been feeding in this house?"

"One mighty sweet young man," said Kit levelly.

"Oh, so that's the color of the wind?" High Wind was rocked back a little on his heels, and for a moment he hesitated; but he lashed himself and went on. "Well, if you don't know, I'll tell you . . . that's the man who killed Slade Tucker!"

"I don't believe it," said Kit, automatically defensive. "And who in the world is Slade Tucker?"

"Slade Tucker," roared High Wind, "was the best, straightest, squarest, whitest two-gun waddie that ever stood on his rights!"

"You're just tryin' to get yourself worked up," Kit told him. "I don't believe Tip Roddy shot anybody."

"Oh, I am, am I? And he didn't, did he? Well, he admitted it himself!"

"*Tip* did?"

"I put it straight up to him . . . 'You killed Slade Tucker,' says I. 'And what if I did?' says he, as cool as to hell!"

Kit hesitated. It set her back for a moment, hearing that the man she loved had admitted killing somebody, but she rallied loyally. "If Tip shot somebody," she said, "I guess he good and well needed shooting."

"He shot him for the reward," steamed High Wind, "and to get hold of Slade's horse!"

"I don't believe it! But I guess if there was a reward out . . ."

"Well, there shouldn't have been! That was just one of the fool things this country has done since it went sissy! Tucker was jumped four to one by a bunch that was poison mean, and he gunned 'em down, as any right-minded citizen would do, and then . . ."

"And then he ran into Tip Roddy," Kit improvised. "And that was something else again. I think more of this boy every minute, so I do!"

"And Roddy shot him in the back," said High Wind malignantly.

"That was whose story?"

"Don't you suppose there's such a thing as common knowledge?"

"I suppose Tip did no such a thing, that's what I suppose. And I'm going to ask him straight out, and let him say himself how it was."

"You'll not speak to him again," thundered High Wind. "No, and he'll not set foot on this place!"

"Who says he won't?"

"I told him to get off and stay off . . . and the same has stuck with more and better men than him!"

"You told him that?" blazed Kit.

"Well . . . I was about to tell him, but, when I turned around, he was gone."

"He'll be back," said Kit.

The next day was a long one for Kit. High Wind rose very late, red eyed and ominous. Kit was somewhat puffy eyed herself. Roddy, as she knew he had intended, was in another quarter of the range, looking over the offerings of a different brand, but he had promised to stop by the MacDowells' during the evening.

"Women folks bust up a man's business," High Wind grouched. "If he hadn't been rolling calf eyes at my niece, I wouldn't've had to run him off, and I could have sold him them stag bulls."

"You can tell him tonight," said Kit without interest.

"I won't have him on the place! I'll run no chances."

"Not much danger," said Kit, who had been doing a thinkover of her own.

"You give him up, do you?"

"What does it look like?"

"It looks like you're going to bawl. Women make me sick! Well, I can't sell him tonight, because he won't show."

The long day dragged away; and at last, as Kit had predicted, Tip Roddy came riding through the twilight. He was whistling "The Roving Gambler." He evidently, Kit thought, had set aside High Wind's objections to killers as a cranky whim, not to be taken seriously.

High Wind was out in the stables, and Kit had to receive Roddy in some fashion. She kept the screen door hooked between herself and Tip, until he could get the idea that all was not as he thought.

"My uncle will see you in a few minutes," she told him frostily.

"You're joking me," he grinned.

"Am I?" she said bitterly.

His face went black. "Why, Kit . . . what on earth . . . my name's Tip Roddy. You seem to have forgotten me . . . but last night . . ."

"I never knew you," she said. "I thought I did, for a little while, but it seems I was wrong."

"I don't know what this is about," said Tip, "but something seems to need talking over. Don't I get in any more, even?"

"Oh, come in if you want to."

When she had let him in, they stood looking at each other in the lamplight.

"Now, what's the matter, Kit?"

"I guess I took a lot for granted, Tip, that's all." Tears suddenly sprang to her eyes. "Oh, why couldn't you have told me yourself?"

"Told you what, honey?"

"Did you think I wasn't even interested in whom you killed, or where? Do you think it's just nothing . . . ?"

"I don't know what you mean. Unless . . . if you're talking about that Slade Tucker foolishness . . . ?"

"If you call killing a man . . . any man . . . just foolishness . . ."

He hesitated. For a moment Kit was swept by an impulse to tell him that it didn't matter, that whatever he had done was all right — he looked so lost, disillusioned, and uncomprehending, standing there with his hat in his hands. But that was before his mouth hardened.

He said slowly: "I thought . . . I *would* have thought that you'd know if I did something out of the way, why, I had a reason for it."

"Then you admit . . ."

"No . . . I never killed Slade Tucker, if that's of any interest to you."

She studied his face for a long moment; and she knew that she was wavering.

"But what's the use of that," he said wearily, "or anything else we say, if you're going to start off by doubting me, right from the beginning?"

"Tip, that isn't fair."

"I guess maybe I don't know what's fair and what isn't. I thought . . ."

The rear door of the room crashed open, and High Wind stood, solid and malignant, surveying them both. He was wearing his heavy gun belt, the holster sagging low on his right thigh.

High Wind looked Roddy up and down, deliberately. Then Kit cried out: "He never killed Slade Tucker . . . he says he didn't!"

"No, I reckon he never did," said High Wind. "And I reckon nobody else did, either. I got the dope on him now. I thought it was kind of funny, all along, nobody ever having collected the reward, and all. But I see through it, now. I've been talking to Lem Wilkinson. He recognizes him. Tip Roddy, huh? There's no such name, and never was!"

"What on earth are you talking about?"

"Kit, he didn't kill Slade Tucker, because he *is* Slade Tucker . . . Slade Tucker himself!"

There was a silence before Kit said: "But you told me you knew Slade Tucker, Uncle . . . that you were one of his best friends."

High Wind's face darkened above the bristly beard, but he did not answer.

"That part's simple enough, Kit," said Roddy, without shifting his eyes from High Wind's. "You've maybe met folks before that claimed to know people that never heard of 'em. He thought it sounded big, I guess, since everybody bragged up Slade Tucker as being so bad. So Lem Wilkinson identified me, did he?"

"Lem Wilkinson doesn't have the truth in him," said Kit contemptuously.

"Maybe I was fooled for a little while," said High Wind, beginning to raise steam, "maybe it's so that I only saw Slade Tucker once, and that time at a distance, and didn't remember him exact. But, by cat, I don't forget the horse! And the description of Tucker fits in . . . tall, sorrel hair, hazel eyes, salty way of doing business . . . it's him, all right!"

"Let him say for himself if he is," said Kit.

Tip Roddy smiled on one side of his face. "And what of it?" he said directly to High Wind, his voice hard.

"If you think," rumbled High Wind, "that a damned murdering outlaw with a price on his head can come here and make free with my niece . . ."

"Now just a minute," said Roddy. "Seems to me last night you had a whole lot to say about the name of Slade Tucker. He was a good man, according to you, then. Square shooting, you said, and white as they come, and a lot more apricot butter . . . right along the same lines . . . about this Slade Tucker that you knew so well. Seems to me you're kind of flighty, Mister MacDowell."

"I'll take no slack in my house!" roared High Wind. "Now you clear out! Git, and stay git, or by the great Almighty . . ."

"Yeah, I will," said Roddy, not moving. "But first I'll tell you this . . . you were a good man, once, to all accounts. But right now . . ."

"Shut your damned . . ."

"No, I won't. The waddies around here aren't men enough to tell you this, and maybe you'll never hear it again. But I'll tell you, by God, and you'll remember it. You're an old bag of wind, and a nuisance to the range, and not even fit to be hung as a cattle thief any more. Now you've got it . . . and you know it for the truth."

High Wind's face was purple. His hand whipped to the holster, where it fumbled once, for it was long since he had gone for the rod, but in another second the gun came up.

What happened then was confusing to the eye, and Tip Roddy did not understand the significance of it until a moment later, when the exploding gun had followed its own bullet to the floor. Roddy had turned to go out, but as the crash of the gun arrested him, he saw that High Wind was nursing his knuckles, and that Kit was holding a candlestick of Spanish brass.

That candlestick had come into Kit's hand as if of its own volition as High Wind went for his gun, and, as the gun had whipped upward, she had struck out blindly — but the blow had fallen true, and High Wind's broken hand let go.

Kit was weeping. "You might have killed him!"

"Why, Kit," — MacDowell's voice was queer, as if all the wind was out of him at last — "why, Kit . . . you turn on me, Kit . . ." It was the old tyrant of the Redregon that was the pathetic figure now, with all the iron tradition stripped off of him, leaving nothing but a humiliated old man.

"I'm ashamed of myself and ashamed of you," Kit stormed at him. "I don't care who he is, or what he did . . . he's the best man that ever stood up, and I had him, and I've lost him, and all on account of you . . . you old balloon!"

High Wind MacDowell rallied. His voice was low and gentle, as it had been once, when he had known how to clean out a tribe, or a range, but it was the gentleness of rattlers. "Get out," he said. "Both of you! Get out and stay out, and if ever you set foot . . ."

Roddy laughed. "Come on, Kit. We understand each other, I guess."

They rode slowly, their horses close together. Ahead winked the lights of Redregon.

"But you should have told me," said Kit.

"Told you what, honey?"

"That your name was Slade."

"Child, it never occurred to me."

"Never occurred to you? But didn't you suppose . . . ?"

"Of course, I've *heard* of Slade Tucker, but seeing that I've never actually been in the same county with him, so far as I know . . ."

"But the horse . . . ?"

"I bought him from the Indian, just as I said."

"But you let poor old Uncle think . . . Tip Roddy, you might at least have told him the facts."

"What would have been the use, honey, if he had his mind set to something else?"

"Tip, that's no reason."

"Well . . . you see . . . Kit, I figure it doesn't matter what a man did, for that might mean anything. What he is . . . is all that counts. I couldn't bring myself to lift a finger to defend myself to anyone, in a case like that . . . not even to you."

"Just the same," said Kit, "not that it makes any difference, but it is kind of nice to know what's my new name . . ."

The rumor about High Wind's statue of himself has been spiked at the source. "The trouble with this county," High Wind told Hep Blades, the concrete man, "is they ain't got any appreciation of art."

48

"Art? Art who? I thought this was going to be a likeness of your . . ."

"Go to hell," said MacDowell. "Anyway, I can't afford it. Didn't I have to drive off a thousand head of blooded stock, as a wedding present for my darned niece?"

Hell on Wheels

Sad Harry an' me was in the bunkhouse when we heard Bellerin' Bill tellin' it to Elmer. We could have heard him if we'd been in Jerusalem. I knew that Bill understood a few o' the finer p'ints of the art of cussin', but this time he dug clear down into the cellar for words that anyone ought to have forgot long before he learned 'em.

"Elmer," he bawled, an' he was jest a-boilin', "it ain't them wishy-washy blue eyes an' that 'Baa-baa, I want Mary' expression on yore ugly, freckled mug. Mebbe I could stand yuh if yuh could lay up that danged gun an' forget where yuh laid it. But when yuh shoot the heels off a man's best boots when he's standin' in 'em, knock the ashes off his cigarette when he's smoking it, make a sieve out of a water tank when he's under it, and then miss a wild skunk when a man is within six feet of it, I claims it's time to put in a few innercent remarks.

"Yuh put my saddle on Baldy with sandburs under the blanket," he howled on. "Disgraced me before a whole herd o' women, too, when I lit on my ear in the dirt. Yuh went out after mavericks an' put my brand on

50

a dozen Circle-Y calves, an' danged near got me strung up by the neck. Neighbors I'd known for thirty years, too. An' that's the end. Yuh can git off this ranch an' stay off!"

The ol' man stopped to spit and then started in again like the crack of a gun: "An' what's more, Helen's comin' home next week with a fine-lookin', refined, edicated chap from the East fer a husband, an' I don't want no sech lookin' animule as you around the place. A woman's first child is apt to take after anything unpleasant she sees, an', believe me, I don't want no wishy-eyed, freckled-faced, yaller-headed, simplookin' grandson. Not me!

"Now git goin'!" Bill bellered. "Yuh ornery, lazy, idiotic, simple-minded, good-fer-nothin' ignoramus. Yuh flop-eared, bandy-legged, mutton-headed, frog-footed son of a cross between a turkey-buzzard an' a fried mud-turtle. Git out of here an' don't yuh ever come back. 'Cause if yuh do, I might get mad an' say something mean."

I never said nothin' when Elmer come into the bunkhouse with tears runnin' down his nose. I knew it wasn't my ante, an' left it to Sad Harry to hand out the consolation, that bein' right in his line. Sad was the dolefullest creature that ever forked a broncho. He had only laughed once since he came to the Griddle Ranch eight years before, an' that was when Highpockets Hicks fell off the windmill tower an' busted his leg.

Elmer was near heart-broken as he packed up an' got ready to go. He had been on the Griddle ever since he was a little chap, an' he loved every inch of it. And as fer Helen, why ever' time he saw her, he got down an' groveled.

He almost cried when he was ready to leave. "I dunno what's got into the ol' man," he groaned. "I thought those calves were ourn, an' the posse really didn't hurt him very much when they started to hang him. Only stretched his neck a little an' that ain't very long, anyway. It wasn't anything to git mad about."

"Well, good bye, an' take care of yoreself, Elmer," says Sad Harry as they shook hands. "We sure miss yuh, an' mebbe some of the boys will be sorry to see yuh go."

"Don't you worry, Harry," Elmer flares up. "I'm comin' back some o' these days."

"Well, that's all right with me. We'll bury yuh over in that purty little glen where the wind sighs an' moans through the pine trees. An' we'll come and set there when we want to think about how awful the world is, and how downright ornery an' mean the people are. An' we'll put vi'lets on yore grave in the spring, an' roses in the summer and cockleburs in the fall, an' . . ."

"Oh, shet up!" Elmer growls as he climbs on his little pinto. "I'm comin' back to the ol' Griddle, an' I don't care what you half-wits say."

"By the way," called Harry as he put his hand in his pocket, "how are you fixed for money, Elmer?"

Elmer's face lit up like the sunshine comin' through the rain. "Well, that's mighty kind of yuh, Harry," he says, "an' to tell the truth, I ain't got but four dollars an' thirty-seven cents."

"Well, yuh want to take good care of it," Harry answers, "'cause that won't get yuh very far in a world full of wickedness like this. Don't spend it on licker an', above all, don't do much gamblin'."

"Thanks, Harry. I don't hardly ever drink anything stronger than sody-pop an' it's a cinch I ain't going to do much gamblin' on four dollars and thirty-seven cents."

He rode out a mile or so and then stuck around till evening, thinkin' the ol' man might change his mind. He stayed all night in Crow Butte an' then started out the next day for Dry Valley 'cause all the nearby ranches was full up with waddies. And, besides, the foremen all knew Elmer too well to hire him on.

Elmer was the beatin'est specimen that ever struck Dry Valley county. He was so kind of innercent-like, and yet he was all-fired with a six-gun. He could hit anything he could see, an' he always hit something whether he could see it or not. His idea of a joke was to shoot the cigarette out of a man's mouth, or to knock the heels off a new pair of boots.

He was always blundering and always having accidents, an' always doing the right thing at the wrong time. An' he always had an excuse for it that would drive a man crazy when he come out with it so innercent-like. When he missed ol' Sorg Baxter's cigarette and nicked the end of his nose, Elmer said it was a blessin' in disguise, an' if he could shoot off an inch or two more, it would make ol' Sorg look almost human.

The boys liked Elmer in spite of his loco ways, an' the Griddle Ranch was heaven to him, especially when Helen was there. It was after the Carson rodeo when Elmer mopped up in the shootin' and ridin' that Helen insisted on ridin' all the way home with him. It made the ol' man suspicious an' he packs Helen off to school. He always says she never would marry any good-for-nothin', forty-dollar cowpoke, but was going to have some fine-lookin', refined fellow that could take her into society.

It was about ten o'clock in the morning when Elmer started for Dry Valley. The sun was shinin', a cool breeze was blowin' from the west, and he begun to cheer up an' take an interest in life.

He rode past a prairie-dog town, shot the head off a rattle-snake what had got up too early, an' stirred up the dust under a ground owl what had stayed up too late. Then he began to sing. If he hadn't been makin' so much noise, he might have heard some shootin' just around the hill. As it was, he bumped into the nicest hold-up anyone ever seen.

The stagecoach was pulled up at the side of the road. The driver was slumped forward in his seat with his head hangin' down on his breast. The reins had fallen to the ground. A young woman was steppin' out of the coach where a masked man was givin' orders, and a fat drummer from K. C. was stuck halfway through a window where he had tried to get out head first.

One of the bandits was on top of the coach, unloading the express packages an' mail sacks. Another

54

was rippin' 'em open, and the fourth was standin' in front of the horses which was scared considerable.

Elmer took the most interest in the last one, 'cause he had a gun held plumb on the middle of Elmer's shirt front. "Git off-a that horse!" he yells.

Elmer did. He tumbled off on the far side an' come up shootin'. The feller kinda doubled up an' sat down with his hands over his stomach. Elmer banged away at the man on the coach, an' he come tumblin' to the ground head first. It all happened in a couple o' seconds, with Elmer shootin' from underneath his horse.

The stage horses had been rearin' and plungin' but couldn't get away as long as the man was in front of 'em. Now they went dashin' down the road, the reins strung out behind them, an' the fat drummer yellin' like a buck Sioux at the summer dog feast.

The two remainin' bandits began poppin' at Elmer, and one of them nicked him in the left hind leg.

Elmer had to stop shootin' in order to reload. He had a vague sort of notion about identifyin' the bandits, and noticed one of 'em was wearin' yeller chaps an' the other had on a big, gray Stetson.

Yeller Britches reached his horse an' then come chargin' up, leadin' the other cayuse, which Gray Hat climbs on.

Elmer began shootin' again, an' Gray Hat reeled in the saddle. Then he dashes in and scoops up the woman an' holds her in front of him for a shield, while the other man rides away. Elmer couldn't shoot at the man and was too danged chicken-hearted to shoot the horse. So all he could do was lay there an' cuss while the bandit backed away slow like with the woman yellin' and strugglin'.

Elmer stood up, and the girl must have seen him plain for the first time. "Elmer!" she screams. "Elmer, it's me . . . Helen! Help!"

Of course, that sent him clear off his noodle, an' he went running out with a beller like a locoed steer. Gray Hat took good aim and drops him in the dust, an' then went ridin' away, still carrying Helen who began to scream an' cry when she saw Elmer fall.

The two bandits had all they wanted of Elmer's fancy shootin', and didn't dare go back after the loot. Yeller Britches came ridin' back and said to bring Helen along and they'd hold her for ransom. She began to yell louder than ever at that, an' Gray Hat told her to shut up or he'd bust her over the head with his gun.

Elmer struggled up, fell down again, and then crawled to the pinto an' clumb into the saddle. His leg had kinda buckled under him. He had a bullet through the shoulder that he knew had touched a lung, 'cause he was spittin' red. Things was goin' around in a circle an' the ground seemed to be tipping up an' down like a big earthquake, but he yelled at the pinto an' started after the two men an' Helen.

That pinto of Elmer's wasn't much to look at, but it was made all of steel springs and India rubber, and it wasn't afraid of nothin'. At first, the bandits gained, but Elmer kept 'em in sight an' then drew up closer as his head cleared an' the ground stopped whirling an' tipping.

56

Finally they reached the foothills, an' the men disappeared around a bend as they dashed up a little cañon. Yeller Britches rode behind a big boulder an' waited while the other one rode on up the cañon with Helen.

Elmer never did have a lick of sense when it come to caution and, of course, wouldn't slack up to spy out what lay ahead. He came bustin' through the cañon with the pinto on a dead run. The horse must have smelled out something wrong, for it threw up its head just as a gun cracked behind the boulder.

Down went the pinto, and Elmer just had time to throw hisself out of the saddle. Both of 'em lay there, the pinto quiverin' all over, and Elmer gaspin' with the wind knocked clean out of him.

Yeller Britches was peekin' out from behind the rock. As Elmer lay perfectly still, he seemed to think all was over but the shoutin' and that he had winged a horse an' man with one shot. As a matter of fact, he had creased the pinto's head as slick as a whistle. Pretty soon it began to kick, an' next it struggled to its feet, an' stood there snortin'.

Yeller Britches stepped out from behind the boulder an' took a couple of steps forward. There was a crack from Elmer's gun, an' Yeller Britches tumbled over with a bullet square between the eyes. That was some more of Elmer's fancy rodeo shootin'.

Elmer struggled to his horse an' next moment was hittin' the trail up the cañon. He knew he'd catch up with Gray Hat an' Helen, 'cause no horse carryin' double could stand that pace long. Pretty quick he saw 'em up ahead, weavin' in and out along the trail.

Elmer's left arm wasn't much good. His leg was painin' like a thousand needles was stickin' into it, and he was bleedin' all down the left side. But he held onto the saddle horn an' kept shakin' his head to keep away the gray mist that seemed to be sweepin' down around everything.

"Helen!" he says over an' over. "Helen, yuh beautiful, wonderful little son-of-a-gun. I'm comin'."

A bullet sings past his head an' flattens out against a rock. Another whistles by somewhere, but Elmer didn't pay no attention to 'em. The way the pinto was climbin' over rocks, an' the way Elmer was swayin' in the saddle, the best shot in the world couldn't even a-dusted his feathers.

Then he heard Helen scream. The gray mist cleared away as he straightened up in the saddle. There they were, not more than fifty yards away, Helen strugglin' with the bandit. The road agent's hat was knocked off, an' he couldn't shoot again 'cause Helen was hangin' onto his gun hand. He began hittin' her, an' she socked her teeth into his wrist.

"Let go, yuh ugly little hellcat!" he yells.

"You're a liar!" Elmer shouts. "She's the sweetest, beautifulest, wonderfulest girl in the world."

Gray Hat got his gun hand free an' smashes down on Helen's head. She dropped to the ground an' sat down on a rock all groggy-like. The bandit shot twice at Elmer an' then dashed on up the cañon.

58

Elmer couldn't see nothin' but Helen, an' he jumps off his horse by her side. "Are yuh hurt, gal?" he asks.

"No I'm not. Get that fellow, Elmer! He hit me on the head, and before that he . . . he kissed me."

"*Yeow!*" Elmer yells. His gun roared three times, an' Gray Hat drops out of the saddle an' lay still.

"Golly!" Elmer says as he stood there, lookin' foolish-like at his gun. "Golly, everything is kinda smoky-like. Are yuh there, Helen?" Then he staggers a little an' plops face down in the trail.

Helen had been sitting without movin' while Elmer drops the bandit out o' the saddle, but now she jumped up and ran to his side. "Elmer, Elmer!" she cried. "What's the matter, Elmer?"

He looked up in a surprised sort of way an' then grinned. "Helen," he says, "I guess I brought yuh back fer that edicated, refined feller from the East." Then he coughed up some blood an' fainted dead away.

The pinto was standin' there chewin' up a soap-weed, an' Helen got the canteen from the saddle. She cut away Elmer's shirt which was covered with blood. The bullet had gone clean through his shoulder.

She was small an' slender an' graceful, but she sure knowed her oats when it come to bein' a nurse. All her life she had been patchin' up cowboys what had got shot or kicked or hooked, or had sat down on a hot brandin' iron.

She washed the holes in Elmer's shoulder an' tied 'em up with a part of her skirt. Then she sloshed water in his face till he opened his eyes. "Elmer," she says, "I've got to get you on the horse."

She did it, too, an' pretty quick she was up behind him, holdin' him with her arms an' steerin' the horse for old Sowbelly Williams's place two miles up the cañon.

Elmer kept faintin' an' then comin' to, and, by the time they reached the shack, he was clear off his head. Old Sowbelly wasn't home, but Helen got Elmer in bed an' did up his hurt again, 'cause it had started bleedin'.

She couldn't get a doctor or anybody to help her, but she buckled in to pull him through. She tied him down to the bed when he began to kick an' soused him with cold water when he began to rave.

Elmer talked about her an' about how heartbroken he was 'cause she was goin' to marry a feller from the East. Finally he let out a whole string o' love stuff that was so mushy she went down right by the bed an' begun to kiss him square on the mouth.

Sowbelly didn't come home till the next Friday, an' then he was so drunk he didn't know nothin' for two days. Elmer was better then but was still out o' his head. He come out all right a couple o' days later, an' the first thing he asked Helen was when she was goin' to get married.

"Oh, Elmer," she says, all red-like, "I'll marry you just as soon as you are able to go to town."

That wasn't what he was expectin' at all, an' he was so surprised an' tickled that he got kinda delirious again.

They rode into town a week later on the pinto an' a horse they borrowed from Sowbelly when he wasn't lookin'. There was still a lot of excitement in Crow

Butte over the hold-up. The stage had come in with the wounded driver an' the fat drummer still stickin' halfway out the window. But no one could find out who the girl an' the unknown hero was that the travelin' man told about after they sawed him out an' he got through cussin'.

They had all went back to where the stage was held up but couldn't find a trace of 'em. One of the gang was dead, an' the other was just enough alive to string up by the neck. They had to hang him quick, or it would have been too late. The mail sacks an' express was all there, so everything was lovely.

Elmer was kinda dubious about gettin' married. He only had four dollars an' thirty-seven cents, an' he knew that wasn't enough to set up housekeepin' on. Besides, he was kinda scared that Bellerin' Bill might say it with bullets.

"You leave it to me, Elmer," Helen told him as they rode into town.

"Well, all right, but I'm afraid he won't like it. Yuh know he run me off the place an' said never to come back."

"We will see. I'll call him up, and I am sure I can get his consent and his blessing."

"You're a wonder, all right, Helen," grins Elmer. "An' if yuh can do that, I'll let yuh be the boss for the next fifty years."

There was one of these here new-fangled telephone lines that the ranchers had strung across the fences, an' there was about fifty of 'em on it. You turned a crank so many times for each one, an' usually all the others listened in. Sixteen short rings an' eight longs was the Griddle Ranch.

Helen cranked away. She could hear receivers taken up all along the line an' finally Bill bellered: "What the hell do yuh want?"

"Pop," she cries, "it's Helen. I'm in Crow Butte."

"Fine!" howls Bill. "Get a horse at the livery barn an' come home as fast as the danged thing can run."

"I will. But I brought someone with me."

"Are yuh married?"

"Not yet, Pop. I was waiting for your consent and your blessing."

"Is he good lookin', Helen?"

"Oh, Pop, he's the handsomest man in the world."

"Is he re-fined?"

"Why, he's the most refined and considerate and gentle man I ever knew."

"Is he brave?"

"Brave! Why, Pop, he is so brave and wonderful that he shot up that whole gang of robbers that held up the stage, and he rescued me when they carried me away to hold for ransom, and he got wounded, an . . ."

"That's fine, Helen," shouted Bill. "He's jest the man I've been waitin' for. Get married right away an' come home as fast as them crowbaits can hit the trail. We'll be waitin' with the fatted calf ready for the meat axe."

"You're sure it will be all right, Pop?"

"Sure thing. Hurry up!"

Bill drops the receiver an' went shoutin' to the cowpokes that Helen was bringin' home that handsome, brave, refined chap from the East.

62

Elmer an' Helen got a license an' was married by the sky pilot in Crow Butte. It near busted both of 'em to pay the bill. Then Helen insisted on Elmer gettin' a new outfit of store clothes. "We'll charge it to Pop," she said. "He's so pleased that he'll stand for anything."

Pretty soon Elmer comes out of the store grinnin' like a Hallowe'en punkin. He looked just like the full moon in December. He had on a brown suit, a new purple shirt with red stripes, a green necktie, a high rubber collar an' one o' these round-topped bowler hats. He looked fine, except the hat was too large an' come down over his ears, an' the collar was so high it kinda made his chin stick up in the air like a deacon after church. The tie was one of these here patent contraptions, an' it kept gettin' unhooked. The sleeves of his coat was pretty short, an' his pants was so tight they raised him clear off the ground every time he took a step.

"Oh, Elmer!" cried Helen when she sees him. "You're marvelous. I know Pop will be pleased."

"But what if he ain't?" asked Elmer.

"Well," she says kinda thoughtful-like, "it will be all right, anyway, and I am sure he will come around when we give him a grand . . ."

She stopped an' turned red all of a sudden.

"Grand what?" asks Elmer, but she shook her head slow an' didn't answer. "Grand piano? Grand march?"

But she wouldn't say nothin', an' they started for the ranch.

The gang was all settin' on the corral fence, waitin' for 'em when they drove in. Bill come bustin' out o' the house an' grabbed Helen in a bear hug.

"Bully for you, gal!" he shouted. "An' so this is the new hero son-in-law."

He came forward with his hand out an' smilin' all over his face. Then he stopped, his hand dropped to his side, the grin faded away slow, an' he sat down on the well curb an' run his hand over his head like as though he was kinda drunk an' didn't know nothin'.

"My Gawd!" he said all thick-like. "My Gawd, it's Elmer!"

An' then we heard a shriek from behind that raised our hair an' sent the cold crinkles all up an' down our backs. We grabs our guns an' whirls around, but it was only Sad Harry, laughin' for the second time since he come to the Griddle Ranch.

Old Bill took it pretty hard, and we was afraid for his mind for a month or two. Then one evenin' Elmer comes to the bunkhouse grinnin' all over as though someone had tickled him.

"Bill will be all right now," he grins, "'cause Helen says there is goin' to be a grand . . ." Then he stops a while an' scratches his yeller head an' tries to think. "By glory!" he shouts all of a sudden. "Now I know what she meant over in Crow Butte when she was talkin' about grand somethin'. It's a good one on her that I found out. I guess I ain't so slow."

Old Bill sure has made up with Elmer now, an' he brags about his grandson so that yuh can hear him all over

Dry Valley County. You'd think that Glory Halleluyah hisself had come to stay at the Griddle Ranch. The most puzzlin' thing about it is that Bellerin' Bill, Junior, is a freckled-faced, yeller-headed little scamp an' looks exactly like Elmer.

Kindly Kick Out Bearer

Little seems to be known by Kettle country narrators of the history of Charley Busted Wing. He was an obscure and unconsidered Crow broncho rider when he rose to momentary prominence in the Wagon Bed water case — a case that is now history of the sort that cattlemen love to recount over and over again at roundup and rodeo. And he dropped back into total obscurity again when the Wagon Bed case was done. His part in the now famous water feud appears in the often-told story, of course, but of the previous history of Charley Busted Wing little is ever said. This is odd, for the extraordinary odyssey of Charley Busted Wing is perhaps the most curious part of the story of the fight over the Wagon Bed water.

At the time when it occurred to Charley Busted Wing to revisit the Redregon country of his youth, he had been a broncho rider in the Kettle country for almost fifteen of his thirty years. Since he was the only Indian in the Kettle country to make his living by broncho topping, he had managed to achieve not only toleration, but a certain reputation for being a good Indian. In this he was assisted, rather than hindered, by a popular opinion that he was short only one or two of his wheels. Not that he was mentally queer in any particular way; it was simply that no idea ever penetrated his thick skull without a furious struggle.

Perhaps Busted Wing's singular talent for improfundity was the reason for his believing that young Verne Harris, his last boss in Kettle country, was the greatest man he had ever known. Verne Harris was a smart and a shrewd business man, and he had extensive cattle-country holdings which he had inherited; but people who had done business with Harris could have told Busted Wing that, in spite of Verne's supremely plausible manner, he was not exactly the proper subject for a dumb Indian's admiring trust.

Nobody did so, however, and, when Busted Wing swung into the saddle for his return to the Redregon country which he had left so long ago, his proudest possession was a recommendation signed by Verne Harris of the Circle Bar. He would have been less sanguine, perhaps, if he had known what that recommendation contained — but Busted Wing could not read.

He arrived in the Redregon country in travel-worn condition. Somebody had got his horse away from him on the road, and he had tramped the last two hundred miles with his saddle on his back. Confidently, however, he offered his recommendation to the first range foreman he came upon in the Redregon, certain that the magic paper Verne Harris had signed would assure him of ready work, good pay, and all prosperity.

67

When he had handed the scribbled tally sheet to his first prospective employer in the Redregon, this is what the delighted rancher read:

To Whom It May Concern:
The bearer is Charley Busted Wing, run out of the Kettle country as the damnedest liar, thief, and drunkard out of the Crow Nation, which is going some. If he stops in your country, you will be missing calves, etc., and the truth is positively not in him. Kick him out.

V. Harris, Circle Bar.

Now the Redregon was more familiar with Indians of Busted Wing's general description than was the Kettle country. A considerable number of "first Americans" inhabited — *infested* was the word the ranchers used — the Redregon in a straggling and desultory sort of way, interesting themselves in sheep. This, in a new country, was bad enough. But, in addition, certain of Busted Wing's distant relatives seemed never to have grasped the law of property as well as they understood the white man's debt to the Indian; and many were the unfortunate misunderstandings which had come up from time to time.

The right or wrong of the matter — or the truth, either, so far as that goes — is less important here than the plain fact that Charley Busted Wing's race enjoyed but little popularity in the Redregon. Busted Wing was astonished to find himself classified as a nuisance on sight. On more than one occasion he found his efforts to secure employment diverted by the much more pressing necessity of making a sudden escape.

Anyone who knew the contents of Busted Wing's recommendation could have foreseen this much. What no one would have been likely to foresee — even one who knew Busted Wing's limitations well — was that Charley should continue to present that preposterous recommendation off and on for no less than four long years. Four years of tramping up and down the long reaches of the Redregon, his saddle on his back; four years of mysterious explosions on the part of the white man, including fourteen kinds of unpredictable assault; four years of continuous demonstration that all the world had gone crazy except himself!

Sometimes he was able to sponge for a time upon relatives, but the Indian families of the Redregon were in no position to feed him long. For the most part he was reduced to ignominious pilfering, a practice that did nothing toward promoting love and respect for the red man in that locality. Four years! That is the incredible thing — that Busted Wing's outrageous odyssey should have lasted for so long.

Toward the end of the fourth year a suspicion began to dawn upon Busted Wing that something might be wrong. He began to doubt whether, after all, he was really wanted in the Redregon. So, at last, he pointed his saddle — it was still on his own back — southwestward toward the far Kettle country, which he had so unadvisedly left with his recommendation in his hand.

69

It took him more than a month to walk back over the mountains, but it was almost as if the fates had called him at an appointed time, for as he arrived at the edge of the Kettle country, the fight over the Wagon Bed water, in which Busted Wing was to play so important — though unconscious — a part, was already begun.

And there at the edge of the Kettle country he came upon Verne Harris himself, heatedly changing the tire of his long yellow roadster. Busted Wing completed the job for him, recounting as he did so his experiences among the crazy people of the Redregon, and, when this story and the tire change were complete, Verne Harris, weak with laughter, thanked Busted Wing very decently, refused his application for a job, and drove on.

A short distance down the road, however, Harris stopped, turned his car, and drove back.

"I've changed my mind, Charley," he said, studying the travel-worn Indian with a speculative eye. "Report at my ranch. I've got a short job that I think you can handle probably better than anybody I know." Busted Wing almost broke into tears as he promised to obey, and Verne Harris once more turned and drove on.

He did not offer the foot-weary Indian a lift, and that was why Busted Wing was still footing his weary way to the Circle Bar when he came in sight of Hugh Douglas's ranch house early next day. Charley hesitated, then made furtive approach. He was hoping to steal a breakfast — or at least to beg a little something, even if Douglas was so lucky as to see him first.

70

Six o'clock on the morning of June 5th — the hour that Charley Busted Wing chose for his appearance at the Two Box — found Hugh Douglas in a mood of singular bafflement. This was unusual. At twenty-six Douglas had already brought back to some semblance of prosperity the herd-dotted miles of over-grazed land that his father had left him. Horses he had topped, as well as men he had hit, might have testified that there was no indecision about Hugh Douglas at all. But this, he told himself, was different.

Early as it was, the morning had already brought word that rumor, for once, was correct. Verne Harris of the Circle Bar had actually begun his long-threatened fence on what Douglas had good reasons to believe was Douglas land. Now, as Hugh Douglas stood looking out across the long sage-broken reaches of the Kettle valley floor, several plans for the frustration of the encroaching Circle Bar were in his mind — all of them, it seemed to him, very poor.

Still debating with himself, Douglas turned and walked back through the cool, dark hall of his adobe to the kitchen, where Steve Garrett was warming beans and bacon for breakfast. Steve was one of those chronic mumblers found wherever bust-ups force free American citizens to lay the saddle aside and pick the skillet up. He was mumbling now — something that sounded like: "Aw, nuts! That's what I say . . . nuts!"

"I didn't quite catch that," said Hugh, his mind elsewhere.

"I thought," said Steve, thundering an armload of wood into the box, "I thought I had a broncho topper out here for you. Old Charley Busted Wing is out here, and I thought . . ."

"Is that the Crow that was riding twisters around here four, five years ago?"

"The same."

"He'll do. Have him . . ."

"He says he told Verne Harris he'd show up at the Circle Bar."

Hugh Douglas exploded: "Harris! Harris! All I ever hear is Harris this, Harris that. All my damn' life," he added in a muffled growl.

"Uhn-huh," agreed Steve. "He's fencing off your land, and he's stole your best water, and he's beat your time with your girl, and now he's done you out of a twist rider. Some say he's stole your cattle, too. I perdict that some day . . ."

Douglas pretended not to hear him. "If you mean that wreck on the woodpile, Steve, that isn't Busted Wing."

"The old buck is looking kind of hard wintered," Steve admitted. "But it's him. Bet you five dollars it's him."

"All right."

Steve, afterward, claimed that right there, in that exact moment, Kettle country history was made.

Douglas was stalling himself, holding back his decision on what he meant to do about that fence. For once he was reduced to concealing his own indecision from himself — pretending to be interested in a broken-down Crow, making petty bets with his cook. He approached the woodpile, and a certain gleam in his

72

eyes caused the Indian to take one look and shoulder his saddle for flight.

"What's the idea, boy, claiming to be Charley Busted Wing?" he said. "You don't look like Busted Wing to me."

"I can prove it," the itinerant suggested. He eyed Hugh speculatively before rummaging from his pocket a flat tin-covered box that had once contained snuff. He stood looking at this object, half reverently, half suspiciously, for so long that Douglas thought the man was turning over some ancient tribal fetish, one in which he had somehow begun to disbelieve.

Out of the tin the Crow finally took a yellowed bit of paper, worn through at the creases by long handling. As he handed it to Douglas, Hugh saw that it was a sheet torn from a tally book, and bore a penciled scrawl:

To Whom It May Concern:
The bearer is Charley Busted Wing, run out of Kettle country as the damnedest liar, thief, and drunkard out of the Crow Nation, which is going some. If he stops in your country you will be missing calves, etc., and the truth is positively not in him. Kick him out.

V. Harris, Circle Bar.

Steve Garrett, spelling out the words over Hugh's shoulder, let out a great guffaw. "That's good! That's hot! Boy, that's a whizzer!"

"Yes," said Douglas deliberately, "that is a very comical joke, in its way." He turned to the Indian. "We'd better tear this up, Charley," he said. "You realize this paper makes you out a liar and a thief?"

"You lie!" the old Indian snarled at him. "Give it here! I need!"

Never, thought Douglas, *had Harris's plausibility obtained a greater tribute than that.* He wasn't used to being called a liar, but he handed the paper back. "You going to work for the Circle Bar?"

"Short job."

Even in his anger it occurred to Douglas that Harris might be planning one joke more on a victim who had had enough. "If you find the short job is used up," he told Busted Wing, "come here . . . I'll give you a job any time."

Douglas hunched his shoulders and went into his adobe house with deliberate long strides. He turned aside to lift his gun belt from a hook in the wall, and strapped it on, then went out the front of the house to his battered touring car.

Steve followed him. "What you aim to do?"

Hugh appeared not to hear. But now Steve noticed the gun belt, and for the first time seemed to perceive the quality of Hugh's crazy eyes. "Holy smoke, kid! Wait a minute! I'll be with you right off!"

"The hell you will!" said Douglas.

His engine bellowed, dust spurted from his rear wheels, and the old car swung into the downcountry road.

74

If it had taken a Crow twist rider to get Hugh started, it now required a girl — a particular girl — to swerve him from his immediate purpose. A yellow roadster was coming to meet him, ripping up the downcountry road into a mountainous, trailing phantom of dust. Just at the fork where the uptrail parts from the valley track to writhe twistily up the mountain way to Loper, the yellow car whirled on locked tires, coming to rest squarely across the road, and there waited for him. That yellow roadster belonged to Verne Harris, but, as he brought his own car to a grinding stop, Hugh saw that it was not Harris, but Dee Daniels herself who was at the wheel.

Hugh had gone to school with Dee Daniels years ago and never noticed her, and he had forgotten her altogether when he went away to study law. Recently, however, he had rediscovered her and wondered amazingly why this remarkable person had escaped his attention for so long. She had loose, curly chestnut hair and humorous eyes that squinted into the Kettle country sun, and she was in several other ways the most interesting thing included in his range-limited world.

He had fallen in love abruptly and completely. Yet he had made but little headway — and Verne Harris, of course, was the stumbling block, as he always was, as he always had been, for Hugh Douglas.

Just now, however, as he dismounted and walked over to the other car, he was staring straight through her. Beyond her, beyond the rolling horizon of the sage, he was seeing the figure of Verne Harris on a classy horse, watching the building of a fence. And he knew well enough why she was there. The whole Kettle country knew about the approaching fight over the Wagon Bed water, and nobody knew more about it than Dee Daniels, who, of course, had heard both sides. Dee Daniels liked both Hugh Douglas and Verne Harris. She dreaded, and had tried before now to postpone, the open outbreak of hostilities that was bound to come. There was an attempt at lightness in her voice but a determined set to her lips as she spoke to him now.

"Where you going with the artillery, boy?"

"Thought I might jump a coyote. I've got something to see about, down here, Dee." He started back to his car. He couldn't talk to her, today.

"Hugh!" That was an order, and he stopped. "I bet you're going down to the Wagon Bed fence!"

Seeing Dee at the wheel of Verne's car brought the blood into Hugh's head again. "I've been meaning to have a war talk with Harris," he admitted.

"Hugh, you're not going down there."

"No? Why?"

Dee hesitated, studying him. "I suppose you know his foreman is standing over that job with a sawed-off shotgun?"

"That's good."

"Verne says . . ."

"Damn Verne!" he exploded.

They looked at each other in silence, their eyes strange to each other with an unaccustomed hostility. Twice before she had dissuaded him from action in just such a situation. He was determined that she should not dissuade him now.

"Well, there's no use going down there and rowing with him, anyway," said Dee stubbornly.

"I'm not going to row with him. I'm just going to put him off my land, that's all, and his outfit with him."

"You think you can?" she asked curiously.

He smiled twistily and shrugged. "I suppose you think I ought to file suit, and run into a . . ."

"No," she said. "For heaven's sake, Hugh, don't try going into court against Verne! I know you're supposed to be a member of the bar, but you've never practiced a day, and, if you get in there against the smart counsel he'll dig up . . . I don't want it. He makes fools out of enough people. It isn't good for him."

Then abruptly wheels spun in the sand as she backed the roadster, and in a moment more he was watching the recession of the dust geyser that Dee's style of driving always tore up from the rutted Kettle country roads.

Hugh went and sat behind the wheel of his stopped car. A terrific impulse swept him to descend like a thunderbolt upon Harris at the Wagon Bed. Instead, he unbelted his gun and shoved it into a door pocket. Then, jerking his hat over his eyes, he wheeled his car into the Loper road.

As Hugh Douglas stood up, the drone of conversation in the courtroom subsided to a buzzing undertone, then a rustle of whispers. Judge Wes Randolph, seeing Hugh hesitate, kindly shifted his bleak gray gaze from

Douglas long enough to rap for better order. After that, the courtroom was still with that heavy, thick stillness of crowded air.

"This," began Douglas — and found that his voice tangled in his throat. It was his first appearance at any bar. Not yet, however, did he regret that he had stubbornly rejected all assistance himself. "This," he said again, "is just one of those cases, Judge, that grows out of the burning down of the old courthouse. If the fire hadn't burned out the records, there wouldn't be any need for bringing this suit. But now I aim to quiet title and get hold of an injunction stopping the defendant from using Wagon Bed Springs the same as if it was his own. I'll open by calling Bill Freeman."

In the momentary pause, Hugh let his mild blue eyes wander over the courtroom. Clear at the back he could see the crinkly brown head of Dee Daniels beside that of old Noah Daniels, her father.

"Bill," he began his examination, "what were you doing in Eighteen Ninety-One?"

Freeman, white mustached and with age-bleary eyes, pulled himself together to state that he had been a government surveyor.

"Did you get to Wagon Bed Springs that year?"

"Yes . . . once. On the fifth of July."

"How do you remember so close, Mister Freeman?"

"Because," said the witness, "at the Wagon Bed camp I was hit by a skunk."

"I got a mind to clear the court," said Judge Randolph, pounding.

Freeman now identified the Wagon Bed Springs property by surveyors' description, and Windemer, for Harris, waived cross-examination.

"Call Henry Martin," said Hugh.

Martin's aged face was hairless as his gleaming head. When he was seated, Hugh, remembering that the old man was deaf, raised his voice: "Mister Martin, were you county recorder in Eighteen Ninety-Nine?"

"I don't care if I do," came the answer.

Randolph tapped for order, and Hugh went nearer. Under close-range questioning Martin admitted his past recordership, remembered Pete Douglas, Hugh's father, well, and declared that he recollected perfectly most of the titles he had recorded in the year mentioned. Conveniently for Hugh, Martin had a great reputation for memory in the vicinity of Loper.

"Who recorded title to Wagon Bed Springs?" Hugh shouted.

"Dutch Bill," came the prompt reply.

Hugh was rocked back on his heels. "You mean to tell me that Dutch Bill took title to Wagon Bed Springs?"

"I remember distinctly," Martin answered. "It was a corking-hot day in the latter part of June, and a Tuesday. Bill . . ."

"Try to collect yourself," Hugh bellowed. "Don't you remember perfectly well that in September of that year my father, Peter Douglas, recorded title on the basis of script that . . ."

"Here, whoa up," Windemer protested. "We can't have this. He's literally leading the witness all over the range."

"Sustained," said Randolph. "You can't put that, I think."

"As to Dutch Bill," shouted Hugh, shifting his ground, "do you mean to tell me that, after all these years, you even remember the weather . . . ?"

"I object to that, too," Windemer interrupted. "Learned counsel is trying to impeach his own witness!"

"You've got a foot through the wire, Hugh," said Randolph gently. "You put him a definite question, and he answered it, and you can't turn around and try to discredit him now."

"I'll call Tom Casey," said Hugh hotly. "Call Tom Casey, Martin's assistant recorder!"

"If I can get a word in edgeways," Windemer chuckled, "I'd be pleased to cross-examine first. I'd like a crack at the local memory wizard myself."

"Take him," snapped Douglas.

Walt Windemer rose. There were pockets under his warily confiding blue eyes, and his face was pink instead of tanned, but the bristle of his short white hair was a war cry. Today the folds of the old jury advocate's long-used face wore an apologetic look, in addition to his customary expression of absolute surety. He was crushing a mere gnat, a nice boy who had been to law school, but who could hardly expect to stand against the best trial lawyer the Kettle country had ever known.

"I'll show the witness," he said, "a description of this property exactly as set out in the petition of the plaintiff. Is this," he bellowed at old Martin, "the land recorded by Dutch Bill?"

80

Martin mumbled over the description for a space of moments. "No!" he said vehemently. "This is the Wagon Bed Springs lands that was recorded by Peter Douglas!"

All Windemer's practical psychology had blown up in his face, and all over the courtroom was felt the shock of that explosion. Yet he did not flinch, and his hesitation was a matter of a second only.

"But," he roared, "you said a minute ago it was Dutch Bill!"

"Oh, I thought he said Hackenschmitt Springs!"

A slow rustle ran over the audience, gradually becoming a rumble, and then a roar, as the significance of the cross-examination dawned. For once Windemer's headlong attack had landed him in the barbed wire. Yet, in the face of misfortune, he made the most of the moment. Windemer turned, and stood with drooping shoulders, facing the audience with an expression of such utter pathetic woe that the laughter rose anew.

"Let's try to be a little quiet," said Randolph. "Go ahead, Hugh."

Douglas, pushing his case through sharply, now called three cattlemen who testified that the Wagon Bed was commonly known as Douglas land. They brought out plainly that, although the Wagon Bed had, from time to time, been overrun by many brands, a small sum per head of stock had often been paid Peter Douglas by those who used the Wagon Bed land. Three cowboys next bore witness to the fence-building of Verne Harris upon Wagon Bed, and there, esteeming that he had established a case of title and trespass, Hugh wound up his case and sat down.

"I move the case be dismissed," said Windemer.

"Why?" asked Randolph. "It seems to me he's established a perfectly good *prima facie* case of title, Walt."

"Oh, was all that to establish original title?" said Windemer. "Why, my client was prepared to concede that!"

"Why didn't you say so before?"

"I really couldn't make out what he was getting at," Windemer apologized. "Well, well, well. Call Newt Magnusson."

Windemer now called three witnesses who testified consecutively that the elder Harris had expressed an intention to buy the Wagon Bed, that he had said definitely he was on his way to buy it, and that subsequently he had referred to the Wagon Bed as if it was his own.

"This is hearsay," Hugh Douglas objected.

"*Res gestœ*, strictly," said Windemer sagely.

"A slight weakness in the knees does not make testimony hearsay," Randolph decided. "Proceed."

A slow, dark doubt was stretching its shadow over Hugh Douglas. It was plain enough, by this time, what line Harris had instructed Windemer to take. Hugh could guess, too, just about what evidence existed in support of that defense. At the same time he knew Windemer for a daring, often a reckless, strategist, and Verne Harris, of course, could be depended upon for no scruples at all. How far this pair would dare go before Judge Randolph, with no recourse to a befuddled jury, and what would be the result, he had not the experience to judge.

Of the first four witnesses, Hugh cross-examined but one — a cowman who testified that Rack Harris, Verne's father, had "generally kept his accounts in his pants pocket."

"What kind of records did Peter Douglas keep?" he asked.

"Rotten," said the witness. "Worse than Rack Harris."

"A fine way of doing business," Randolph allowed himself to comment. "And now with the county records burnt . . ."

George Calender, accountant, testified next that he knew the veritable signature of Peter Douglas, that there had been given into his keeping, for auditing, a mass of receipts, and that among them were fourteen receipts which acknowledged that the elder Harris had paid the elder Douglas sums amounting to nearly seven thousand dollars. Only one of these contained any notation of what the payment was for, but this one, sufficiently damning, seemed indicatory of the significance of the rest: "Received from Robert Harris on Wagon Springs account" — the witness read aloud — "the sum of eight hundred dollars. Signed . . . Peter Douglas."

"These receipts," Windemer asked, "obviously represent a purchase of that land?"

"They might," conceded the witness.

The assembled cowmen stirred, recognizing the force of Windemer's latest wallop. Nor could Douglas break the witness.

"As a matter of fact," he put, "you know very well that these receipts represent a lease, and not a sale?"

"No!"

Again the restive air.

"I was going," said Windemer, "to call a lot of witnesses to show that my client is in possession of this land. I think, however, that the plaintiff's own witnesses have already cleared this up very nicely. Now I'll call the coroner ... unless Mister Douglas concedes that Charley Phillips, county recorder in Nineteen Ten, is now deceased."

"I'll admit he's dead," said Hugh.

"And his assistant?"

"Yes."

"Is that your case, Walt?" Randolph asked.

"You may well ask," said Windemer. "Certainly it looks like case enough. I agree, we have not only established the transaction circumstantially, but we have exhibited receipts covering the payments. Possession has kindly been established for us by Mister Douglas, and we have nicely covered the absence of further records. I'm going to call the tax assessor."

The latest witness, hardly less damaging than the one before, now testified that Harris had been paying taxes on the Wagon Bed range for at least three years and probably, by implication, for a long time before that. Stroke by stroke, the Harris-Windemer combination was literally cutting the ground from under Douglas's feet.

A crazy anger was on Hugh Douglas. He saw now that in his inexperience he had bungled his case, and he knew that he could never wipe out the defeat that he already read in Judge Randolph's kindly eyes, nor the faint, derisive grin from the face of Rack Harris's son.

"Just as a finishing touch," Windemer's ululating voice was saying, "we will call one witness more. In fact, we have sent downstairs for him. Call Charley Busted Wing."

Having been sworn, the Crow agreed that he was of the name given, and a cowboy. A snicker from some place greeted this description, and Busted Wing looked about him with surprise. For the first time he seemed to become aware that he was conspicuous before any number of people. He made a move to leave, but a bailiff urged him back.

"You've been away from the Kettle country some time?" said Windemer with that unctuousness that passed with him for gentle handling.

"Four year," said Charley promptly.

"What is this Wagon Bed fence dispute, Charley?"

"Never heard of it."

The counsel for Harris peeled off his coat. He was getting ready for one of his deliberate, nicely timed, dramatic moments.

"You just got back? And have you found employment?"

"Huh?"

"Who do you work for?"

"Hugh Douglas."

"Who, me?" said Hugh.

A faintly pleased gleam of recognition shone for a moment in Busted Wing's apprehensive dark face. "Uhn-huh. You said . . ."

A sharp riffle stirred the crowd. A Two-Box cowboy — roughly speaking — was about to turn in the final evidence against his boss!

"What were you doing," Windemer asked the witness, "in the summer of Nineteen Ten?"

Marveling, Hugh Douglas checked his poker face. A new urge of battle was pounding into him as he listened to the most extraordinary testimony he had yet confronted. In the short sentences that examination worked out of him Busted Wing testified that in 1910 he had been cook at the Two-Box, that Rack Harris had stopped by and asked the price of the Wagon Bed, that, after a long argument, a price was agreed upon. Money passed, and papers were written. Charley could not read, but he was certain that the Wagon Bed land had been bought and paid for that hot day in 1910.

It was true, Hugh recalled, that Charley had once cooked, for a short time, at the Two-Box. What deal the Indian thought he remembered, Hugh had no notion. He could imagine, however, how Harris, arrogant in his long run of luck, might have been tempted to a bold and unscrupulous stroke, and he could picture well enough the plausible Verne, deftly wheedling the Indian back to a memory of fictitious events. And he was pretty sure that once scared — and Busted Wing was worried — the Crow would stick to his recital through whatever verbal storm.

"How do you know it was Nineteen Ten?" Windemer was concluding.

"That year, I just come," said Charley. "I know some times, huh?"

"You sure do, Charley," chuckled Windemer. "And I may as well say now," he added, turning to the bench, "that when this witness has been cross-examined and washed up, that is going to be our case."

"Quite a case," commented Hugh.

"My boy, it's a screamer," Windemer agreed. "Take the witness."

Hugh Douglas got to his feet. "You say you can't read, Charley?"

"No."

"No can, or no can't?"

"Can't read."

"Then why," Hugh said, "did Verne Harris give you written instructions about what you were to say here?"

Windemer shot to his feet. "Now, honestly, if Your Honor please! I certainly don't want to make it any harder for the plaintiff than it already is, but I really have to object to that!"

"I think you don't realize, Hugh," said Randolph, "that question, leading or not, comes pretty close to an open charge."

"Judge, I aim to impeach this witness," said Douglas. "This is going to be about the worst impeached witness ever seen in this court."

"Are we trying the witness?" asked Windemer.

"What it amounts to . . . ," began Judge Randolph.

"Excuse me," said Windemer. "Don't say it yet! Will you please reserve decision for just a moment?"

Verne Harris, an evil glimmer in his eye, had pulled his attorney's arm and was whispering instructions.

"On second thought," said Windemer, "we withdraw our objection. After all, as my client puts it, a show is a show. By all means, let Mister Wing answer."

"Let's not twitter out and in," said Judge Randolph. "Is that final on this point, Walt?"

"Yes. When it comes to proving written instructions to a witness that can't read . . ."

"Please let Douglas proceed," said Randolph wearily. "I've set at this bench on and off for fifteen years, and I've about given up trying to break this county to legal procedure. Go ahead with Busted, Hugh."

"Charley," said Hugh Douglas, "hand the judge that paper you've got in your pocket . . . the one that starts out by telling who you are."

Once more a gleam of independent intelligence showed in Busted Wing's unbright face. From his pocket he drew the flat tin-covered box that had once contained snuff. Carefully he took out of it the yellowed tally sheet.

At this point the vague, restive suspicion that had begun to tinge Verne Harris's face was seen to give way to something else. He clutched Windemer's arm and was whispering furiously as the paper passed to Judge Randolph's hand.

"Object!" barked Windemer. "Incompetent, irrelevant, and immaterial!"

"We had that up a minute ago," said Randolph peevishly. "You withdrew your objection."

"There is such a thing as carrying nonsense too far," Windemer blustered. "In all seriousness, I object on perfectly sound grounds of procedure."

"The Court," said Hugh Douglas, "has already admitted the exhibit."

"I made no ruling whatsoever," said Randolph. "The objection to this line of cross-examination was withdrawn. I'm getting tired of this gee-haw in what is already a drawn-out case. For once I am going to make a perfectly strict ruling around here. The . . ."

"Gimme that back!" yelped Charlie Busted Wing.

With a perfunctory gesture, the exasperated Randolph extended the tally sheet to the witness. "The objection is . . ." His hand and voice stopped abruptly in mid-passage. His eye had caught upon the tally sheet like a wasp lancing against fly paper. "Just a minute," he said.

"Now, if Your Honor please," shouted Windemer. "I don't know what that paper contains, but . . ."

"Order!" snapped the judge. His face was as implacable as living rock as he smoothed the worn tally sheet before him. The courtroom was utterly still, now, as Randolph's slow hand adjusted unnecessary nose glasses.

"There are times," the bench declared at last, "when an exhibit needs not only to be admitted, but to be made known throughout an entire jurisdiction. This is one of those times."

"Good Lord, he's got no sense of humor!" sounded Verne Harris's agonized whisper.

To let that whispered remark be heard was possibly the worst thing he could have done. Randolph, who had opened his mouth, now closed it and slowly impaled Harris upon an iron stare. "Are you interrupting me, sir?" he demanded.

"No, sir!"

"If Your Honor please . . . ," Windemer tried again.

"How would you like a contempt of court?" Randolph said savagely. Slowly, bearing down on every word, he intoned to the Kettle country the message of Busted Wing's worn recommendation: "'To Whom It May Concern. The bearer is Charley Busted Wing, run out of the Kettle country as the damnedest liar, thief, and drunkard out of the Crow Nation, which is going some. If he stops in your county, you will be missing calves, *etcetera*, and the truth is positively not in him. Kick him out.'"

He took off his glasses and looked over the assembled cowmen. "'Signed,'" he finished, "'V. Harris, Circle Bar.' That, gentlemen, is the defendant's conception of his witness."

There was a short, incredulous pause, then an enormous volcano of laughter went up from the crowd with the rumble of a distant dynamite blast. Through the uproar the gale was seen to rise and fall repeatedly, but its crash of wood on wood was lost in the storm.

"I've run this court for fifteen years with an easy and liberal hand," Judge Randolph exploded, when at last he could be heard again, "and I suppose this is what I

90

get for it. I'm free to state that never in all my experience have I seen such a bald-faced damn' insult to an American court of law!"

Once more laughter rocked the building, while Randolph polished his glasses and put them away.

"Is that your case, Windemer?" he said at last, his voice cold in the disturbed air.

"Not by a whole lot," said Windemer. "I'll put Verne Harris on the stand!"

"Put him on!" snapped Randolph. "Put him right on! But I'll tell you now if Verne Harris goes on that stand, I'm going to question him myself!"

"You can't do that! Procedure . . ."

"Damn procedure! Put him on, and we'll see if I can!"

Verne Harris, his face blank, met the harsh gaze of Randolph briefly, but his own eyes wilted away. He hesitated, while all the courtroom waited. Hugh Douglas watched intently. He was praying with all his heart that, if it was in Verne Harris to turn tail, he should turn now. And Harris had reason enough to dread the witness chair. Once thoroughly aroused, Randolph had wit enough, and more than experience enough, to trap better men than Verne. Nobody could say what incriminating facts, what humiliating details, would be tricked out of Harris if once he subjected himself to Randolph's raking fire. It was an ordeal no man could look forward to with confidence, and Harris least of all.

"Well, well, Harris," Randolph pressed, "will you give evidence or not?"

Harris's one word came out low and thick under the silence.

"No!"

It seemed enough, yet, when Hugh Douglas had freed himself from the enthusiasm of the crowd, the day still held for him one unexpected revelation more.

Dee Daniels was waiting for him in his dusty old car. "Are you going to give me a lift? Dad's busted down, and . . ."

"Bet your life." He wondered a little as he watched Harris's long yellow roadster slide out of Loper ahead of them, and that wondering made him feel tired and sad. It took some of the thrust out of victory to find out that Dee was another who rallied around the victor, the same as everybody else.

Charley Busted Wing, tagging along behind Hugh, climbed apologetically into the back seat, carrying his saddle. He was oblivious, apparently, to the significance of anything that had happened. Some thought it was the pounding of the bronchos that had made him that way. They took the road, tooling down the ruts of the Loper switchback in the dust of the general exodus.

"I want to tell you something, Hugh," said Dee at last.

"Yes?"

"I'm a fool. You know the idea I got, watching the trial today? Most people are cheap and small, and that goes for myself."

"Why?"

"And I'm sorry for the way it went, and I think it wasn't fair or right," she finished, hurrying out the words. "And now you can let me out."

"You mean . . . ? What wasn't fair, Dee?"

"You should have won," she surprised him.

"But . . . wait a minute, here. I thought I did win!"

"Hugh . . . is that true?"

"Didn't you hear Randolph give me the decision?"

"No! It made me so mad to see the case going against you that I walked out on the whole business. Why, Hugh . . ."

"Dee . . . say, you wouldn't fool me, would you?"

"Oh, glory, Hugh! *No*."

A slow grin altered the face of Hugh Douglas almost past recognition. He pulled the car up, turned, and opened a door of the back seat. "Mister Wing," he said firmly, "I'll see you next week. Indian, you're afoot!"

Minus its third passenger, the battered car roared down-grade full throttle, at its heels a mounting tower of dust.

The Biscuit Shooter

Just as I was about to blow out the lamp, the dogs all started hurrahing again, and I pulled my boots back on. After you have been hunting cow-country lions for bounty for about twenty years, you hardly ever mistake what hound talk means, and this time I knew for sure that somebody was coming up the road.

We had lost us a lion that day, and I was dead beat and disgusted, so at first it made me mad to think that here come some darn' saddle bum, no doubt all set for a good square meal, 'specially cooked up on late request by yours truly, Old Man Coffee. But I set the coffee pot forward, and, when the pony finally eased up outside, I opened the door in time to see Lynda Clayton swing down.

She was certainly the last party I was expecting to see, way up here, practically in the dead of night, and it sort of took me off balance, so that I didn't say anything for a minute, but just stood gawking. She didn't say anything, either, but just gave me one slow look, and walked past me into the cabin.

"Come in and set, Lyn," I said, some late.

"I have," she said.

I set out a cup of coffee, and took one myself. "The last of that bear meat has just freshly spoiled on me," I told her, "but I can fix you up with chili beans and sow flooring."

"Nothing, thanks."

I set down and filled my pipe. Lynda Clayton was a biscuit shooter at Old Man Hepmeyer's eating house, down in McTarnahan. Let me tell you something. Ninety per cent of the girls who wait on table out in this neck of the woods are real people — good, game girls, not afraid to strike out on their own, nor afraid of their luck. This is more than can be said for a lot that stay home.

Even so, Lynda Clayton was considerably out of the common run. She was not as tall as most cowboys, but taller than most girls, and she was thin as a wintered pony, but with good bone, and strong. But the special thing about her was that something had put hate into that girl, and she was strong enough to carry it calm and quiet. She had sulky, rebellious, scornful eyes, and she looked at you with her chin dropped, kind of as if you didn't count for much except as a likely unpleasantness, while, meantime, she was just biding her time, without much hope, but waiting for the breaks.

But underneath all that she was maybe the prettiest girl I ever saw. Especially now. There was a kind of a live, fighting look in her eyes tonight, like a spark, that I had never seen there before. And her hair was down to her shoulders in waves and tangles like a sand-colored mane — maybe on account of no hat, but anyway the effect of that was like something you might see a picture of sometime, but wouldn't ever expect to run across yourself.

"Are your dogs any good?" she asked by and by.

"It's owing to what standpoint you take," I told her. "Why?"

"Tommy Beckwith has killed Lije Evers."

There you had it! I knew something had bust. "Well," I told her, "it was a sightly choice. Lije ain't been much good."

Lyn Clayton went ahead with her story. Lije Evers and Salt River Smith were partners in a pretty good thing called the Blackcap Stope, up near the head of the Little Vermilion. Beckwith had got hold of a string of ten, eleven mules and had put in the fall packing the Blackcap high-grade down to the McTarnahan stamp.

Just lately, a fine top-fire quarrel had busted out between Lije and Beckwith, the main event coming off in Hepmeyer's eating house. Salt River was there. Lije had been pretty drunk, but Tommy Beckwith knocked him down anyway, at the same time mentioning that he reckoned he'd kill Lije if ever he caught him sober.

"Tommy said Lije short carded him in a two-handed poker game," Lyn explained it.

"He's lying," I came out flat. "You can't any more have a two-handed poker game in McTarnahan than you can have a two-fly molasses barrel."

"I know," she admitted. "Next day, or maybe the day following, Tommy went up to the Blackcap Stope to bring down his mules. The Blackcap was fixing to close down for the winter, and Lije and Salt River tried to get

96

Tommy to make just one more pack. But Beckwith said to hell with them, and set off down the trail.

"He got down as far as Soldier Gorge, and come dark he off saddled in a little side cañon called the Fourth Recess. Then, while he was cooking, he heard a horse coming, and he sat listening while it came on downtrail and turned into the cut where he was.

"About a hundred yards off the horse pulled up behind the brush, and all of a sudden a gun opened up from where the rider sat. *Wham!* and Beckwith's cook fire exploded where the bullet hit. The rider fired twice more, and Beckwith threw himself flat, jerked his gun, and fired once in answer.

"As soon as Beckwith fired, the horse lit out and went crashing back across the Little Vermilion. Then Tommy walked out to see if by any chance he had shot himself anything. There lay Lije Evers, shot through the head."

Lyn stopped, having become kind of shaky in the voice.

"I can't see anything irregular about that," I told her. "Lije come for it, and he got it, that's all there is to that."

"It isn't all," said Lyn, her voice lower yet.

Beckwith moved on down to McTarnahan, getting in about daylight, and turned himself in to the sheriff. Some later in the day Salt River pulled in, leading Lije Evers's horse. He give out that he had gone fishing after Beckwith left, and, when he got back from fishing, Lije was gone. Later Lije's horse had come back to the Blackcap corral, and Salt River figured something might have happened to Lije. And that was all *he* knew about it.

So far, so good, nobody yet having questioned but what Tom Beckwith done rightly. But now Sheriff Pete Crabtree took a couple deputies and went up to the Fourth Recess.

"I borrowed a pony," Lyn said, "and I went along."

"*You* went along?" I sat up. "What did you want to go up *there* for?"

"Want to? Good God!" It was the first time I ever heard her cuss like ordinary folks, and it give me a turn. Then I saw she had turned white as a boiled shirt. "I had a hunch," she said. "Pete Crabtree hates Tom Beckwith."

Ace that one, will you? Many a time I had seen Tom Beckwith sit drinking coffee he didn't want till he was like to bust, and all the time following Lyn Clayton with his eyes, but she was waiting on him as casual as you would feed stock, hardly ever answering him when he spoke. And now she just casually tells me that she let herself in for a twelve-hour ride, just on a lame hunch in his favor! Well, none of us can foresee everything.

What Sheriff Crabtree found out at the Fourth Recess didn't check in with Tom Beckwith's story, no, not any. Lije Evers had been gunned in the back of the head, just below the hat line, from so close that there were powder burns in his hair. And his gun was in his holster, clean and unfired.

"Panic," I said, mournful. "I would have thought better of Beckwith. He should have told the truth in the first place."

"He did!" She seemed sure of that.

"But Lije Evers' gun . . . ?" I began.

"Somebody cleaned that gun, and reloaded it."

"And the powder burns . . . ?"

"Faked," she declared, "with a blank cartridge!"

I sat back, feeling sad. Why, I could see what had happened in the Fourth Recess just as well as if I had been there — Beckwith walking out to meet Lije; Tommy's temper coming up till he jerked his gun, probably grabbing Lije's gun arm with his other hand; Lije, in the saddle, trying to duck out of the way, so he caught it pointblank in the back of the head. Common murder, was what it come to.

"So you come for Old Man Coffee," I said.

"Mister Coffee, I want you to take your dogs up there."

"Dogs? Which, these lion hounds? Take 'em where?"

"I want you to take them to the Fourth Recess," she said. "What I'm hoping is that Pete Crabtree reloaded that gun right there on the spot. I didn't see him do it, but it could have been done. Maybe your dogs can find the empty shells."

After all, it was kind of touching. I suppose I never heard as silly a suggestion as that one was, nor one so far off from what lion hounds can and can't do, even was it useful to begin with. And the plumb foolishness of it somehow kind of went to show how awful serious and kind of desperate she was in her mind.

"All right," I said, "I'll go."

"Thanks," she said quietly.

Of course, all that was open for me to do was to make a lot of false motions, just to satisfy the girl. So I went back to McTarnahan with her, and next morning I looked over Lije Evers's gun and saddle and one thing and another that they had got together. And I rode on up to the Fourth Recess with fourteen hound dogs cruising in front, and pretty near a dozen kid cowboys, out of work since the fall roundup, trailing along behind to see what I was up to.

There had been a fall of rain up in the Soldier Gorge country, and the man don't live that could have trailed a chuck wagon through the Fourth Recess, all trampled up and rained out like it was. But seeing that the cowboys was along, I looked wise, and set the hounds to milling, and I went over the place foot by foot.

A hound pup by the name of Gumboots set up a bawl, and I went and looked at what he found, which was a porcupine track, and said: "Uh-huh." And I cut a short stick out of some innocent bystanding buck brush, and saved it, and said — "Aha." — and I measured off the distance between a stale cow track and a sugar pine and said — "Oho." And finally I took two pebbles out of the Little Vermilion and wrapped them up careful, and said: "Well, I'll be damned!" The cowboys didn't have a real tracker among them, and it was pretty near worth the ride up there to see their faces. I don't know when anything has done me so much good.

After that, I went on up to the Blackcap Stope. Naturally there wasn't anything to be found out up there, either, but I went over it careful just the same.

About all I done up there was cut a six-inch piece of board out of a pine table while the cowboys was out gorging their horses on Salt River's oats. That last, coming on top of the rest of the hocus-pocus, was too much for them, and they owned up they was beat.

When I got back to McTarnahan next day, I looked over Lije Evers's stuff again, and no one was more surprised than me when all of a sudden a kind of funny idea come to me. I went and hunted up Pete Crabtree.

"Pete," said I, "how come you let yourself in for this fix?"

"What fix?" he asked.

"Getting yourself elected sheriff," I said.

"You voted for me, didn't you?" he said, real salty.

"It was right mean," I admitted. "Howsoever, I apologize, because now I want to ask you something. Where," I asked, "is Lije Evers's hat?"

Pete kind of shifted on his feet, and looked disgusted, and bothered, too. "Hat?" he said finally. "There ain't no hat."

It lifted me right off the heels of my boots. "No hat?" I yelped at him. "Hey, you! You can't just lightly say . . . 'There ain't no hat.' There's *got* to be a hat!"

"Well, anyway, there ain't," he said, kind of sulky.

"You're sure you didn't lose it on the way down?"

He riled up again. "Don't never ask me . . . 'am I sure' . . . unless you're joking," he told me.

"This thing has gone beyond a joke," I said. "You and me better talk to the prisoner, Pete."

Tommy Beckwith looked almighty competent and well put together, sitting there with his head down in the little one-room jail. Only, when he looked up at us, he looked like a young kid.

"Son," I said, "where is Lije Evers's hat?"

"Don't you . . . 'son' . . . me, you old Gila lizard!" he jumped me. "Just because I'm in the jug don't mean I'm free to be insulted."

"Nevertheless and notwithstanding," said Pete, "it ain't going to hurt you none to answer his question. It may seem like a fool question, but Old Man Coffee sets store by it, and I . . ."

"I never seen any hat," said Tommy Beckwith. "What would I want with his damn' hat?"

I went off and sat on the top rail of the Bonanza corral and give myself over to thought, and the more I thought, the more I was dead certain I had jumped an almighty well-concealed truth. Maybe you think that made me feel smart, and successful — but it didn't. Instead, it give me a real humble, sickly sort of feeling, for I already had a hunch that all hell was going to have a hard time roping Tommy out of the hole he was bogged down in. I went and found Pete Crabtree again, and hauled him off where we could talk it over.

"Pete," I said, "it's too bad we can't find that hat. Because if we could find it, that hat would hang a man."

He looked at me very squint eyed and thoughtful.

"That hat," I said, "is lost in the rapids of the Little Vermilion, somewhere between the Blackcap and the Fourth Recess."

Pete Crabtree sat quiet. "What then?" he said at last.

"Lije Evers wore his hat jammed down so hard on his head that sometimes he pretty near had to take a bootjack to it. That hat never went sailing off his head as he was just riding along. Pete, you look here . . . the night Lije Evers was killed, he traveled to the Fourth Recess, hanging head down . . . crosswise over a saddle horn."

Pete sat looking out across the flats for a little while, and I knew that he had thought the same as I did, all along.

"Seems like to me, Coffee," he said at last, "you aren't going to prove nothing just on the strength of no missing hat."

"If you found just one good bear track," I asked him, "would you say there had been a bear?"

He looked at me sort of ugly. "Name your bear," he said, "if you're so sure."

"I will," I said. "Salt River Smith killed Lije Evers."

He didn't say anything, nor look surprised.

"After that," I went on, "he took Lije across the saddle horn of Lije's horse and rode down to the Fourth Recess, where he knew darn' well Tommy was camped. There he fired out of the dark, and, when Tommy's gun answered, Salt River dropped Lije and rode back to the Blackcap Stope."

"All that," said Pete, scornful, "just built up on one lost hat! You ain't even got a motive for Salt River."

"Yet, right now as you sit there," I told him, "you know Salt River done it."

He didn't deny it. "There's been a sight too many unsolved killings around here since I've been sheriff," he said. "I can get a conviction on Tommy Beckwith in a minute. Salt River . . . I'll never hang anything on him."

"But, good God, man . . . you wouldn't hang an innocent man just to get a notch in your stick?"

"It ain't up to me to say who's guilty and who's innocent," Pete said, kind of vague and stubborn. "That's up to the court."

I'd known Pete a long time, and he wasn't a bad sort of feller, either. It just went to show up the human race, the way he could switch right and wrong, and then find a way to let himself out.

"You haven't got any real motive on Tom Beckwith," I told him. "That fool story about a two-handed poker game . . ."

"There wasn't any poker game."

"What was it, then?" So long as I was horning in, I figured I'd better at least know as much about it as the rest.

Pete come out with it, easy enough. It seems that this Lije Evers had been another *hombre* that was gone on Lyn Clayton, even worse gone than the rest of them. The more she stood him off, the crazier he got on the subject, until Lije wasn't really in his right mind where Lyn Clayton was concerned.

Finally one night he came into Hepmeyer's eating house tighter than a New Yorker, and threw it in her teeth that she wasn't any good, anyway, and that, when he had first known her, she was living in Steamboat Springs with a man that was no kin to her, by marriage or otherwise.

104

That last hadn't any more than got out of his mouth than Tommy Beckwith caught Lije with a full swing alongside the head, laying him flat. Salt River was going to swear that Beckwith threatened to kill Lije when he caught him sober. Probably Old Man Hepmeyer would swear to it, too, he having been listening from the kitchen.

This time it was me that got mad. "In the first place," I told him, "I'm ready to say flat that Lije Evers lied. The least hair on Lyn Clayton's head is worth forty carload of such skunks as Lije Evers."

Pete Crabtree began to look ugly again. "In the first place," he said, "it appears you don't know nothing about law, because under the law a murder is a murder. And in the second place, you don't know nothing about women, and when it comes to putting the petty annoyances of some knock-about biscuit shooter ahead of a man's life . . ."

I shouted him down. "Maybe I don't know women, or men, either! But, by God, I've handled enough dogs to know about guts. And I'll say to your face, of all the jug-headed, brass-bound guts I ever see . . ."

"I've got a good mind to take a poke at you," he said.

"Who's holding you down?" I asked him. And I walked out.

The preliminary hearing was the next day, before Judge Rumbaugh. It's been a good many years since Rumbaugh last hesitated to stretch a point of law in order to get justice, and I judged that, if there was any bright spot in this darn' business, he was it.

I gathered four, five old billy goats like myself around me, and explained the situation. Some of them had brains and others had less, but none of them could see an out this time. Rollie Marshall took a bunch of riders up the Little Vermilion and all but sieved the waters fishing for the lost hat, but they come back without it, and in the end I hadn't accomplished a dog-gone thing.

Lyn Clayton come to me just before the court was opened up for the hearing.

"Mister Coffee," she said, "is there any hope at all?"

I started to tell her — "No." — but I wasn't equal to it. So I hauled off and lied, one time more. "They haven't got any case against Tom Beckwith," I told her.

After she had moved off, I stood cussing myself. And then, all of a sudden, a kind of an idea come to me at last, and I called her back.

"What time did the questioning attorney get into town?" I asked. This prosecutor we had, he had to come over from Lordstown to try these district court cases on circuit, and on a preliminary hearing like this he very often didn't get here in time to work up his case so very much.

"He didn't come," she told me. "He's tied up with a federal water case in Phoenix."

I broke and run, and loped upstairs over the store to where Judge Rumbaugh was holding court. It was in a small room, plenty jammed with people, and with more filling the hall, but I managed to get them four, five friends of mine outside where we could talk.

Old Rollie Marshall was cussing a blue streak. "He should have got him a lawyer to begin with," he stated, "but he was so darn stubborn and so darn sure he was right . . ."

It was some minutes before I could get them quieted down to where I could start hammering in on them what I wanted. Even after that it took some little time to make them see the wherefores, so that, by the time I judged they were all primed, we had to hurry to get back into court before it was over.

We jammed our way back into the courtroom by main strength. Salt River Smith was almost finished telling about his angle of it.

"How is it going?" I asked Jack Doyle.

"Take your elbow out of my gizzard," he said. "They've got Tom Beckwith sewed up, is how it's going. You missed it. They had to hold Tommy down when they brought out what reason he had for killing Lije."

I saw that Judge Rumbaugh was looking kind of sorrowful, as if he already knew he was going to have to bind Tommy over.

"Judge," said Pete Crabtree, "I guess that's about all there is to this case."

I gave Rollie Marshall a poke in the ribs, and he swung his hat above the heads of the crowd. "Wait a minute," he said. "I've got a little dope that I'd like to throw in the pot."

"Come on up, Rollie," said Rumbaugh, and Marshall went up.

"Judge," said Rollie, "I just want to make sure there's no possible suspicion going to be left on anybody that hasn't got it coming. Now, Salt River Smith, here, has already explained where he was at. I just want to put in to back up his alibi."

Salt River looked kind of surprised. "It don't look like I need any . . . ," he began.

"Shut up, Smith," said Judge Rumbaugh.

"Well, Judge," said Rollie, "the day that Lije Evers was going to be killed that night, I was up beyond the head of the Little Vermilion looking for some lost stock. And along about nightfall I come up to the Blackcap Stope, and Salt River Smith was there cleaning some fish. And he said Lije Evers had rid on down to town, and would I light and squat for a bite. And after supper I rode on down to McTarnahan, getting in right late."

"That backs up Salt River," said Judge Rumbaugh, "if there'd ever been any question concerning him in the first place. Salt River, how come you didn't mention that Rollie Marshall was up there?"

Salt River Smith hesitated for just a second. He had a lean, bony, kind of dried-up face, very hard to read. "This ain't my hearing," he said. "I haven't seen any call to drag nobody else in."

"Is this all?" asked Judge Rumbaugh.

"Wait a minute," said Barney Donovan. "Leave me dab in my rope." He come shoving up, and they swore him in.

"And what do you know about this?" said Rumbaugh.

"I'm like Rollie Marshall," said Barney. "I come up here to say that I was with Marshall, and back up what he says."

"Rollie," said Judge Rumbaugh, "you never said Barney Donovan was with you."

"I'm like Salt River," said Marshall. "I didn't see no sense in dragging no extra people in."

"Well, if this is all the testimony . . . ," Judge Rumbaugh began.

"I'd just like to say one word, Judge," Happy Dixon sung out, and *he* come pushing forward. There was a general stir and buzz in the pack of people.

"I wasn't exactly with these other two," Happy Dixon told Judge Rumbaugh. "Me, I was prospecting up the other side, and come evening I dropped down to the Blackcap in hopes of something to eat. I et with Salt River, too, and then rode on down to McTarnahan with Marshall and Donovan. And I back up everything they said."

Judge Rumbaugh began to look kind of funny. "What was this," he said, "Old Home Week at the Blackcap?"

"We just happened to be up that way, Judge," Barney put in.

"And you all just decided to spend practically the whole night riding spent horses," Judge Rumbaugh said, looking at him square.

Just then Bill Eads butted in. "Judge," he said, "I suppose it's none of my business, but something is haywire around here. I just happen to know that two of these fellers that just testified have lied . . . because I was with them two the night they're speaking of, and they wasn't no such a place!"

A big rumble of surprise went up from the crowd, and Judge Rumbaugh began to get mad. "Now you people look here," he said. "Just because I don't hoist you with all the technical procedure I have in stock doesn't mean that this court isn't handling serious business. You four fellers come up here and stand in front of me," he said.

The four of them stood up there, Bill Eads looking kind of stubborn and dogged, and the other three sheepish and resentful.

"If two of you have perjured yourselves in this court," said Rumbaugh, "you may just as well own up to it. Because, by God! . . . I mean to hook you for it in the end."

The four of them just stood there.

"Judge Rumbaugh," I said, "I guess right here I ought to put in a say myself, bearing on this same point."

"Come on with it, then," he said.

I went up, and I took out of my back pocket that six-inch square of board that I had sawed off of Salt River's pine table up at the Blackcap Stope. And I told them what it was, and when I got it.

"I'll read you what's written on this board," I said. Of course, you understand I hadn't found anything written on that board. "It says here on this board," I said, " 'I owe Salt River Smith for one meal, together with oats for horse, et here in this cabin Thursday night, October Twenty-Seventh.' " That was the night Lije Evers was killed. "And it's signed," I said, "by one man . . . the one of these three that really did stop by at the Blackcap Stope that night."

"And whose name is signed?" said Judge Rumbaugh.

110

I turned to him slow, and I laid the piece of pine board on his desk, face up, so that he could read what was wrote. All that was on it was just six words I had marked on it:

Make Salt River name the man.

I waited, and I knew that a turning point had come in Tommy Beckwith's life, and in Lyn Clayton's, too, and Salt River's — and maybe, for all I knew, in mine. And quite a little minute passed.

Then Judge Rumbaugh turned the pine board over, face down, quiet and slow, so that those that was craning their necks forward couldn't see what was really wrote. And I knew then that he was going to play out the hand.

"This writing on the board," he said, "ain't hardly needed, I guess. Two of these three men, in testifying that they were at Salt River's cabin, have sworn to a lie. The other was really there. But . . . all we need to do to find out which is which is to ask Salt River Smith. Salt River, which of these men was at your cabin that night?"

I looked at Salt River Smith. His dried-up old face was as hard to read as ever, and he didn't answer right away.

"Salt River," said Judge Rumbaugh, quiet and slow, "you have done your part toward swearing away a man's life. Part of your testimony is that you were at your cabin at the time we know Lije Evers was killed. Now we discover that one other man was at your cabin

that night. I'm asking you, and you'll have to answer
. . . *which of these men was there?*"

It was so quiet in there that you could hear people
breathe, and still for a minute Salt River Smith didn't
speak. You see, he didn't know! For he hadn't been
there himself. He'd been riding down the trail that
night, Lije Evers across his saddle horn. At first, when
Rollie Marshall come forward, Smith had thought it
was just a friendly lie, to help out. But now . . .

He could name any one of the three, in hopes that he
would guess it right. Or, if he should happen to see
through it that it was all a put-up job, he could just say
— "They've all lied. There was no one there." And that
was his only out, to save his alibi.

Almost he made it through. Almost. But just at the
very last second it was too much for him, and he broke.
Salt River Smith's voice just naturally exploded in that
quiet courtroom. "I don't believe a damn' one of them
was there!" he said.

There was silence for a little minute more. "You
don't *believe*," Judge Rumbaugh repeated after him
finally, his voice quiet, but fit to take the hide off a
mule. "You have sworn you were there, and that Lije
Evers was not, and now you don't *believe* that anyone
else stopped by the cabin that night. But, Smith," he
finished, "you . . . don't . . . know!"

The rumble of voices that rose in the courtroom then
came pretty near up to a roar, and here and there in the
crowd was fellers that was looking mighty black.

Judge Rumbaugh just sat looking at Salt River
Smith, as bitter hard as if Smith was something he had

never seen in this world before, so that for two or three minutes there the old judge didn't seem to notice all that noise that had rose up around him.

Finally, though, he begun pounding with his little wooden maul.

"Judge Rumbaugh," I said when he got it quiet, "me and these four boys want to apologize for messing around somewhat with the facts. But I guess you can see where some free-hand lying has helped bring the truth out, after all. And now I'd like to lay all joking aside, and make a few serious statements about Lije Evers's hat."

"Go ahead, Coffee," said Judge Rumbaugh, "and speak your piece."

Pete Crabtree was awful put out about that case. Pete put in to have the case continued over for a week, to rake up some more evidence, or at least to leave Judge Rumbaugh cool off; and the old judge continued it like he asked.

Right there the thing begun to unravel some, like these things sometimes do when you pass the turn. First thing, it come out that the Blackcap partnership didn't have any money in the McTarnahan bank, Salt River Smith having transferred it all over to somewheres else. No doubt Salt River could have explained that some way — but Salt River had high-tailed it right shortly after court adjourned.

A hunter that had a cabin over the other side of Little Dutchman Pass come in to say that Salt River had been boarding a good horse there since a week before the murder, and that he had just now come and swapped a ridden-out pony for the good one and pushed right on. And another fellow brought in about the same story from fifty miles farther down. And they found out now where Salt River had transferred all that Blackcap money to, which was at Riverton, and that he had just now drawn all of it out, and a garage at Riverton put in that Salt River had bought a fair-sized car a little while before, and left it there until just now — he had come and got it and headed south. After that, it wasn't any trouble to find out where Salt River had got over the border into old Mexico, considerable widespread interest having been roused up in Salt River Smith by then.

Pete Crabtree was smoking mad. He jumped me about it one day.

"Why, you old fool," he said, "you'll never convict Salt River! Even if we lay hands on him again, which I doubt."

"I wasn't trying to convict him. What do I want with a conviction? I got Beckwith loose, didn't I?"

"Oh, of course," he said, real bitter, "if you figure *that* was anything worth doing . . ."

Fact is, I hadn't much, not to set any real store by it. But about a week later something came up that made me see the whole business in a new light.

It was after nine o'clock, and I was turning in mighty tired, owing to running a lion. But now the dogs started a fresh whoop hurrah, and their sarcastic tone told me somebody was coming up the trail.

114

Sure enough, it was Lyn Clayton again, only, this time Tommy Beckwith was with her. They was riding out of the Frying Pan country, as quiet as they could, and they aimed to get married when they got across the pass. I put them up for the night. And it was all kind of awkward and funny, none of us wanting to talk about that killing case much.

But the next morning, when they were leaving, Lyn Clayton stuck out her hand. "Mister Coffee," she said, "if it hadn't been for you and your dogs, I don't know what would have become of us."

I started to pass it off. "Tommy sure is lucky," I said, "that Salt River lost Lije Evers's hat. If it hadn't been for that one thing, no question about Salt Rivers's part in it would ever have come up."

Lyn Clayton looked at me very queer. "It *was* funny about that hat," she said.

Something in the way she said that gave me a kind of a turn. "Just what," I asked her, "do you know about Lije Evers's hat?"

She held back a minute. Then: "Mister Coffee," she said, "I knew all the time that, if I could get you and your dogs onto the case, the truth would show up in the end. All I was afraid of was that you would jump to the wrong idea, like the rest, and never set your mind to it. So that was how it was about the hat."

"So *what* was how it was about the hat?"

"I kicked that hat under a rock in the Little Vermilion," she said, "when I rode up there with Pete Crabtree and his bunch."

115

There was a girl, I can tell you! At first, of course, I felt kind of like a fool. But as I watched them ride off up the trail, I wasn't so much thinking about being took in as I was noticing the sure, easy way that Lyn Clayton rode, and the way she turned to look up at Tom Beckwith with a new look in her face, and all the old chin-down, what-do-I-care look gone out of it altogether.

Guns Flame in Peaceful Valley

Sheriff Lon Stevens swung down from his saddle before the neat, vine-covered back porch of the Tinplate ranch house. With a sigh he looked down over Peaceful Valley that stretched below him like a flower-strewn green lawn in the faint haze of afternoon. Then he cat-footed toward the door. A very unsheriff-like grin creased his boyish face.

He inched the door open, and the grin was wiped from his lips as he gazed in consternation at the girl who looked up from the floor.

"'Lo, Lenny," she greeted with a smile. "You would come just when I'm in such a terrible mess."

"Joan," he protested, "I jest can't stand seein' you scrubbin' floors that way."

"Scrubbing doesn't hurt people," she retorted. "I don't mind it, and how else can a body keep a house clean when two lazy cowpunchers come right in with muddy boots? I'm getting everything spick and span for the new boss. He's coming today."

"The . . . the new boss?" Lon's heart sank. He had held a vague hope of getting together the money to make a first payment on the Tinplate ever since old

Hank Tucker decided to sell. Hank had gone to a sanitarium in Denver. He didn't need much cash paid down, and he would trust Lon.

"Yes," Joan went on happily. "I got the letter yesterday. Old Hank sold out to a man who is going to come here and start a dude ranch. His name is John Stoneham. Isn't that thrilling, Lon?"

She sat at the edge of a river of soap suds and looked up at him. He noticed the dimple in one cheek and the mischievous twinkle in her large eyes.

"Just think, Lon. Perhaps John Stoneham is some handsome, young millionaire who will take me for long rides in the moonlight, and perhaps he will . . ."

"Yeah?"

The dimple in her cheek deepened at Lon's frown. Then the young sheriff grinned. It was not the first time Joan had tried to tease him.

"Yeah, that's right, Joan. An' mebbe some o' these here beautiful millionairesses that come to the dude ranch will want a big, strong sheriff to protect 'em when they ride over the range. Of course, to be protected properly they'll have to hold the sheriff's hand an' . . ."

"I'd just like to see them try it!" the girl flared.

They both laughed, and Joan sprang gracefully to her feet.

"But, Joan!" Lon was serious again. "I can't have you here cookin' for folks that you don't know."

"I like to cook," she reminded him. "My school won't start for almost two months, Lonny. I have to do something till then."

118

He looked at her with a deep hunger in his steel-gray eyes. "Honey, if you'd only say the word . . ."

"Lon, you know what I think about that. I will never marry you while . . . that is, I mean I will never marry a sheriff. Ever since I can remember, I have been haunted with fear for my father. Never can I forget the awful worry mother went through. I . . . I believe she might be alive now if it hadn't been for that. And I'll never forget the night they carried Dad home."

"Yeah, honey, I know," he soothed. "But it won't be for long. I got a couple o' thousand saved up, an' someday I'll corral a big reward, an' then we can get our own little spread."

"Oh, Lonny, that's what Dad was always saying, too. And it never happened."

The thud of hoofs sounded outside the house, and someone drew up with creaking saddle leather. Joan opened the door. Lon peered over her head.

Three men had ridden up on blowing horses. Lon instinctively loosened his gun as he looked at them. Tough and hard these men were. He had seen their kind before. *Born with a noose around their necks*, he thought. He didn't know them.

The tall one, who appeared to be the leader, swung down and confronted Joan. Lon looked closely at the craggy face, tanned to the color of old leather, the close-set eyes, and high cheekbones. The man spoke between thin, bloodless lips.

"My name is John Stoneham." He paused and eyed them as though to let the fact sink in. "A cowboy directed us here. We are lookin' for the Tinplate. I bought it from a man named Tucker."

"Ye-es," Joan answered doubtfully. "He . . . he wrote me about it."

Stoneham turned to the others with an imperious gesture. "Get down an' put up the crowbaits. We're home."

Lon hid a grin. So this was the gentleman who was starting a dude ranch and would take Joan for long rides in the moonlight. He glanced at the girl. There was a frown on her face. She stood aside as Stoneham shoved his way into the room.

"I . . . I am Joan Carter," she told him. "I have been working here for Mister Tucker since . . . since my father died, but now . . ."

"Shore," he interrupted with a leer that disclosed his tobacco-stained teeth, "that's all right. Yuh can stay on. We need a cook."

A cook! Lon gritted his teeth and stifled a hot retort as Joan introduced him.

"Mister Stevens is sheriff of this county," she said, "and is an old friend."

Stoneham looked at the badge coldly, and then his eyes raised to Lon's face. He did not offer to shake hands.

"The two boys are out fixing fence," Joan went on. "Mister Tucker said you would keep them . . ."

"Changed my mind," Stoneham interrupted tersely. "I brought my own men with me."

He turned and strode into the adjoining room, leaving muddy tracks on the wet floor.

120

"Joan, you can't stay here," Lon breathed. "I'm taking you away with me right now."

"You are not! I can take care of myself, thank you."

Lon suddenly realized he had been too assertive. He knew Joan was very near to tears, and he knew how bitterly she had been disappointed.

"But, Joan, you can't stay here. I think . . ."

She drew herself up to her full height of five feet three. "It doesn't matter in the least what you think, Lon Stevens. This is my job, and I'm staying. At least," she added, "until I have some cause to leave."

He didn't know what to say. He knew Joan had no money, for she had paid her father's funeral expenses with her small savings. He shrugged his shoulders helplessly, for the girl's independence would not permit her to accept help from him.

Suddenly Joan smiled, and the flint went out of her soft, brown eyes. "I'll be all right, Lonny. Don't worry about me. I know how to take care of myself."

He swung into the saddle a moment later and rode past the cavvy where the men were unsaddling the horses. He heard a coarse laugh, and caught a few words of conversation.

"Some little spread the boss has picked up."

"Yeah, I reckon he'll start right out with sellin' off the stuff."

There was another laugh. Lon rode on, a deep frown clouding his brow. He knew hard men when he saw them, for he had served as deputy under Cass Carter before the old sheriff was downed from ambush as he rode homeward in the night. These men were hard.

They were typical gunnies of the range who earned a precarious living, and died with their boots on. Lon couldn't savvy a man like Stoneham starting a dude ranch. Something was wrong somewhere.

He rode slowly back toward town, and his heart sank as he thought of Joan alone with these men. So absorbed was he in his gloomy thoughts that he scarcely noticed a rider approaching till the fellow drew up and spoke to him. Lon's eye glanced at the horse first, from force of habit, and his frown deepened. The animal was gaunt and covered with dried lather. It stood with flanks heaving and head down as though it had been ridden to the point of exhaustion. The brand was a T in a box, which did not belong in Lon's county.

Lon looked at the man. He was a pale-faced individual in a dirty blue serge suit. No chaps, boots, or spurs.

"I beg your pardon, sir," the man spoke nervously. "But can you direct me to the ranch that is known as Tinplate? I believe that is merely a colloquial term. The place has a Circle B brand to distinguish its horses and cattle from those of other ranches."

Lon wanted to laugh.

"Straight ahead," he gestured over his shoulder. "Turn to the left when the trail forks, an' yuh can't miss it."

"Thank you, sir. I appreciate your kindness."

Lon looked back at the receding form as the man urged the exhausted horse down the trail toward Peaceful Valley. Then he shrugged his shoulders and rode on.

The stage had come in when Lon reached town, and he stopped at the post office for his mail. A letter from the sheriff from an adjoining county told of the escape of a killer, Drag Vincent. There was a five thousand dollar reward, dead or alive.

Lon's eyes widened as he read the description:

Medium height, pale-faced, talks like a book. Doesn't look like a Westerner, but has killed six men in Texas and one in Colorado. When he escaped from the Sherman County jail was wearing a blue suit. Has a slight squint to the left eye.

It was an exact description of the man Lon had met on the trail, and who had asked the way to the Tinplate. So that innocent-looking chap was the famous Drag Vincent.

Ten minutes later Lon hit the trail back with a fresh horse. He had heard much of this bandit killer who had built up a huge reputation as rustler and road agent. He was even suspected of robbing the local bank the night Sheriff Cass Carter was killed from ambush. No one had ever seen Vincent's face, at least not till he had been captured and put in the Sherman County jail.

Five thousand dollars' reward, dead or alive! Lon whistled. It was a big sum. Few men were worth that to any state, but this was a combination reward that had grown steadily larger as Drag Vincent's flaming gun had added to his toll of victims.

Dust was mantling its soft hand down over the prairie as Lon approached the Tinplate. He heard the soft lowing of cattle that is soothing to the heart of a cowboy, for it tells him all is well. A hundred or more prime four-year-olds were near the corral. Evidently Stoneham had lost no time in rounding up a herd to sell.

Again Lon felt a pang of regret that the Tinplate had passed into such hands. Like every cowboy, it was the kind of a spread he had held in his dreams. It was the place he wanted for Joan. There was the pretty, vine-covered porch, overlooking Peaceful Valley that lay like a flowered carpet below, the bunkhouse for the two men, the corrals and cavvy, the windmill tower and steel tanks, the . . . He shook his head. It was too late. The Tinplate was gone, sold to a hard *hombre* who was going to get rid of most of the stuff and turn it into a dude ranch.

Just now the place seemed to be slumbering in the deep twilight. No one was visible. The bunkhouse was dark. Lon knew that Stoneham must have fired the cowboys who had worked so long for Hank Tucker, and that they had pulled out for one of the other ranches.

What did Drag Vincent want at the Tinplate? Was he here now? Lon asked himself these questions as he swung to the ground and stood listening. It occurred to him that Stoneham and the other men might be part of Vincent's gang. If so, it would go hard with Lon when he tried to arrest the killer.

He touched the cedar handle of the .45 that swung low against his thigh. Then he strode straight for the house. He determined to go in through the front door, ready for whatever should come.

A burst of laughter came from within, and he paused. A voice rang out, the voice of Stoneham: "Come on, sweetheart, an' give us a kiss. I'm the boss, yuh know."

There was a cry as though from someone in pain. It was the voice of Joan. It tore every shred of caution from Lon. He darted forward, whipping out his gun as he ran.

A spear of orange flame seared out from the corner of the house, and a bullet fanned his face. He dropped to the ground just as a second shot snarled overhead.

He squeezed the trigger, and his gun roared. He had fired low, as he knew that he was apt to overshoot in the dark. There was a shout from inside the house, and the light went out. Lon sprang to his feet, determined to take a bullet if necessary. He charged straight for the door.

He expected another shot from the corner, but none came. Again sounded that stifled cry. It was to Lon as a red rag to a bull. Shouting an answer, he smashed into the door. It flew open, and he lurched into the pitch-black room.

Spang!

Red flame stabbed the darkness. The roar of the gun was almost deafening in the small room. Lon fired once at the flame, surged forward a pace, and stopped. He did not dare shoot again for fear of hitting Joan.

The stillness of death! He could hear no sound except the beating of his own heart. He wondered if the other men were there, or if they had slipped through an inner door, taking the girl with them.

"Joan," he whispered.

There was a stifled gasp nearby. He groped toward it as a gun thundered within six feet of him. Again Lon paused and listened, wondering at the fact that he had not been hit.

A voice called from the outside: "It's that tin-badge sheriff. He's in the house." The voice seemed to choke, and Lon was not surprised when it continued weakly: "He got me in the laig. I can't do nothin', Drag."

Drag! So the killer was here. Stoneham and the two other men were his tools.

Lon cursed himself for a fool. Instead of bringing a dozen straight-shooting cowboys with him, he had blundered into this den of outlaws alone. How differently old Cass Carter would have handled it!

Silently he inched his way forward, gun before him, ready to crack down at the slightest sound. He heard a stealthy step and paused. Someone bumped into him from the side. He swung. Then two powerful arms pinioned his own to his body.

"I got him!" roared a voice close to his ear.

Lon jerked backward with a terrific wrench. The arms held. He tried to use his knee, but the man tripped him, and he nearly went down. He stamped hard with his boot that met something soft. The voice bellowed a curse.

A light flared up. Lon caught a glimpse of a match, with the craggy face of John Stoneham leering above it. He set his teeth and put forth every ounce of his

126

strength as he tried to pull out of the grip of those terrible arms.

He saw Joan in the corner, her eyes wide with terror, her arms bound to her sides, and a gag twisted around her mouth.

A shadow trembled above him. Then a flash of red fire seemed to tear the earth apart. He went down — down! It seemed to him that he was sinking into the deep blackness of eternal night.

A voice brought him back to consciousness, the growling voice of John Stoneham. He opened his eyes. He was lying across a door that led into the darkened room adjoining. His hands were lashed behind him.

Stoneham stood there on unsteady feet, glass in hand. His face lit up in a devilish leer as he contemplated Joan.

Lon wondered if he were dreaming. Then he realized that Stoneham really was there before him. The man was drunk, and was bragging of his crimes.

"Yeah, I killed the sheriff the night we robbed the bank. It always pays to rub out the lawmen first. Yuh say he was yore dad, sweetheart. Too bad." He laughed shortly, then drew back his head and gulped down a fiery draught from the glass.

"I don't think yuh ought to blab about them things," snarled a low-browed giant who was standing against the wall. "Somethin' might go wrong. Yuh can't tell, Drag."

Drag again! Lon realized the man had called the leader Drag. Were there two Drags, then?

The leader laughed and drank again. "We ain't takin' no chances," he leered. "We'll rub out the sheriff an' take the gal with us when we go. I want her. What's the use of bein' called king o' the outlaws unless yuh got a queen?"

"When are we goin' to leave?" asked a weak voice.

Lon could see the third man propped against a chair, a bandage around his thigh. He must have been the one hiding at the corner of the house.

"As soon as we sell the stuff."

Stoneham turned and looked at Lon. His eyes narrowed.

"I should 'a' shot him," he snarled viciously, "but I couldn't do it 'cause I was scared o' hittin' Dave. What'll we do? Shoot him now or hang him?"

Joan gasped, and her head sank forward on her breast. She was sobbing softly, and she knew there was no use appealing to the better natures of these men.

"Mister Stoneham," she said behind the gag. Her voice was muffled, but her words could be understood. "You say you want me to go with you. I . . . I will go willingly if you . . . you will let . . . Lon go free."

"Joan!"

Lon gnashed his teeth and tugged at his bonds till the blood spurted from his wrists. He saw the three men through a red mist. He would die willingly to save Joan from them.

The bandit leader threw back his head and roared out his drunken laugh.

"Yuh're comin' whether yuh want to or not, sweetheart," he informed the girl. "As for yore boy friend, here, we're havin' a nice little necktie party for him, same as he'd give us if he had a chance. We don't like sheriffs."

Almost insane as he was, it seemed to Lon that he heard a stealthy step behind him in the darkened room. He tried to listen calmly as the three men continued their conversation and passed around the bottle.

Then he felt something soft against his wrists, the touch of fingers groping. Suddenly the bonds loosened. A gun was thrust into his hand. What miracle was this?

He clutched the smooth handle of the gun with his numb fingers. He wondered if he could shoot straight enough to kill the bandit leader. He felt that with Stoneham dead Joan would be comparatively safe from the others.

"I don't think we ought to bother with hangin' him." It was the low-browed giant who had grappled with Lon. "I move we shoot him right now an' bury the body in case someone comes."

"Hangin' ain't so good," agreed the wounded bandit. "We'd have to go a couple o' miles to find a tree."

"All right!" The leader threw up a coin and caught it. "Who'll shoot him . . . Dave or me? Sloe-gin is out of it 'cause he's hurt. Heads or tails, Dave?"

"Tails," growled the giant.

The leader spun the coin.

"Tails," he announced in a disappointed tone.

With a grin Dave drew his gun. "Yuh got the last one, Drag, so it's my turn, anyway."

He took a step forward. Lon grasped the handle of the gun that had been thrust into his hand. Some of the tingling sensation had gone from his fingers, and he shoved the first one into the trigger guard.

Slowly Dave brought down his arm, a wild light in his eyes.

Then Lon whipped out the weapon that he had held behind him. A streak of flame pierced out from the end of the gun. A black hole appeared squarely between the eyes of the leader. He turned partly around, crumpled, and sank to the floor. Lon got the man he wanted, regardless of consequences to himself.

There came a terrific blast from the adjoining room. Dave cried out. His knees buckled, and he went down. A load of slugs had been poured into his body.

Lon's gun had cracked down toward the remaining wounded man. The fellow stared wide eyed a moment and then put up his hands. Lon sprang to his feet, disarmed the outlaw, and leaped to Joan's side. He tore the bonds and gag from her, and then gathered her, half fainting, into his arms.

A man stepped in from the adjoining room. Lon stared. It was the white-faced stranger, the man described in the letter as Drag Vincent. He was carrying a double-barrel shotgun.

"My name is John Stoneham," he announced. "I was held up and robbed by these three men four days ago. They took my horse and papers, among which was a deed to this ranch. They left me with a horse and saddle that I learned had been stolen by an outlaw named Drag Vincent. I was arrested. *Arrested!* Imagine it, sir.

130

"They called me this Drag Vincent, and there was nothing I could say to the idiots that would disclose to them their error. I was imprisoned, but managed to put a sleeping powder I had with me in the drink of the guard. I escaped. Not knowing where else to go, I came to this ranch, thinking I could remain here till my baggage arrived and I could prove my identity. My horse gave out, and I just got here a few minutes ago.

"Peeping through the curtain, I found this Drag Vincent and his men were here before me, bent on mischief as usual. I made my way in through the back door and found a revolver and shotgun hanging on the kitchen wall. You know the rest."

He paused and looked at Lon inquiringly.

The sheriff held out his hand. "You came jest in time, partner. I'll never be able to repay what you did for me an' Joan. I shore wish you success with the Tinplate."

"Success! You insult me, sir. I shall sell the place immediately. The . . . the . . . I beg your pardon, sir . . . the people are entirely too primitive and violent for the purpose I had in mind. If you know of a buyer for this ranch, I will sell very cheap."

A week later Lon stood with his arms about the girl he loved. They looked down over smiling Peaceful Valley.

"In spite of all, dear," Joan whispered as she looked up with shining eyes, "I love this beautiful place."

"Yeah," he answered happily, "especially now that I have you, an' we both call it *home*."

And Him Long Gone

Cantrell turned his head to look at the girl who rode beside him in the raw dusk. Her profile under the brim of her broad hat did not show its usual lively color, and the black scarf tied to frame her face made her look pale and curiously fragile. A background of raw rock and stunted juniper somehow makes a woman seem a strange and infinitely precious thing, as much a center of her setting as if she were a source of light. Having turned his eyes to Marjory Andrews's face, Cantrell found it almost impossible to turn away.

Cantrell didn't know what Marjory was doing here in the wet, raw wind of the twilight. She had met him, as if by chance, at the fork of the trail. She was always on a horse, always appearing where you would expect only men and horses to be, and these reluctantly, by the laws of work and circumstance. He did not question; the presence of Marjory Andrews any place was a gift of fortune, and to be accepted as such in unquestioning gratitude.

"Yesterday," the girl said slowly, "was my birthday."

The cowboy turned sleet-blue eyes straight ahead, and slapped his romal against his chaps, but he said nothing.

After a moment she went on: "Last night we had a party for my birthday. You knew about that. And you weren't there."

There was a reason why he had not been there. But he considered, as a cold gust of rain whipped across their faces, that he could not very well tell her that it angered him to see her with Jim Grover. Jim Grover was young, strong, square set, and could work like the devil. He already had his own cow outfit. He was striking his roots deep into the range upon which he had been born. Tom Cantrell, ne'er-do-well, wandering cowpuncher, saddle bum, had no call to criticize the likes of him. But if Marjory were going to dance half the night with this Jim Grover, Cantrell did not want to be around.

"I wanted to see how the stock wintered up in the Standing Horse," he said. "It's too far to take a good look in one day. I spread my bedroll there."

"And, of course," she said, "no other time would do."

Cantrell sat tall and straight up in his saddle, rigidly facing the trail. He made his voice an expressionless drawl: "I'm just a cowhand. I don't hardly have a right to be thinking about birthdays, not with any work to be done." It sounded thin, and it was thin; but he supposed she couldn't go around it.

Yet she chose to go around it. She looked sidewise at him, and it seemed to him that he could feel the vital gray warmth of her eyes as definitely as a physical touch. "But you did think about my birthday. These are lovely reins you made me, the nicest I ever saw. Where did you learn to work rawhide like that?"

"Oh, an old Indian showed me the weave, once, in the Sierra Madres, and the knots I got from another Indian, once, in the Cœur d'Alêne." He was moved to an unexpected confession. "I reckon I would have been gone from here three weeks back, only I wanted to finish those bridle reins."

"Gone? Why?" Marjory seemed startled, which was odd. She must have known before now that he would be moving on. "Don't you like our outfit? Isn't your job good enough?"

He hesitated. This girl had always lived in this one valley. There wasn't a chance in the world that he could explain to her how, when the geese began going over, his blankets fretted him at night so that he could not sleep, and the trail pull became an irresistible hunger, jerking the heart out of him until he turned shaky and almost physically sick. He had been on the trail since he was fourteen years old.

"I think some of drifting north," he said. "I want to see how spring looks, north of Oregon."

Unexpectedly she said — softly, moodily, without looking at him — "I'll be sorry when you go."

Cantrell stirred uneasily in his saddle, but his clean-carved face, weather stamped beyond his years, remained without expression, almost sleepy. He noticed now that he had to hold his horse to a slower and slower gait to keep pace with hers. And he suddenly realized that this was perhaps the last time he would ever be with her alone. He pulled his pony to a stop, and they sat looking out across the great valley through the dusk.

"I've worked here three months," he said. "I don't suppose I've hardly ever worked in one place so long as that. I've been on the loose nearly twelve years, and I've worked cattle from Sonora to Saskatchewan, but never found a place that could hold me yet."

Marjory said slowly: "Don't you like Fifty-Mile Valley?"

Even in the bright sunlight of a spring morning, with the trail pull fairly roaring in his ears, he would not have known how to explain to her that the Fifty-Mile seemed to him an imprisoning little cup in the hills, in which rooted people lived rooted and unendurable lives. And now the sun was gone, and a raw cold wind was moaning down from the northern peaks with a whip of sleet in it. His pony shifted on tired feet, blowing out a long, complaining breath, and the rider fell victim to a queer, lonely, gone sensation. He hummed a line or two of his own particular song:

Long gone, sweetheart, long gone;
For I know a better place where we can go . . .

The song lacked conviction. Far scattered over the valley floor, some little pin-point lights marked places where people were getting somewhere, and making themselves comfortable — giving themselves a break. And suddenly it seemed to Cantrell that all he had seen in his driftings was cheap and meaningless compared to the worth of one lighted window somewhere in the dusk, with warmth behind it, and a girl waiting for him — this girl.

135

Tom Cantrell was built all in one piece, and hardly any man could outdo him in the handling of a horse. His sleet-blue eyes — they seemed lighter now by contrast to the dark bristle on his jaws — saw photographically, without effort or apparent attention, and he understood what he saw. He knew how to take care of himself in a hundred situations these rooted people had never seen. But he could not compete with Jim Grover, or any of them, on their own ground. Among them he stood discredited, so that now he sat cold and broke on a tired horse, a saddle bum whose time had come to move on. His temper rose in a kind of fury, and on a rebellious impulse he did what he had long ago decided he would not do.

"Listen," he said. "I'd just as leave be dead somewhere, horse and all under a rock slide, as to ride out of this valley and leave you behind."

He thought her breath drew in, but she did not speak.

"I don't amount to shucks in this valley," he said. "But I know cattle and horses, and I know this country. I can take you where it's never winter and the desert blossoms out in flowers as big as my hat, such as you wouldn't believe. I can show you spring coming into the Black Giants, where the snow brooks make waterfalls in the big timber. I can show you a thousand things that nobody in the Fifty-Mile has ever seen."

She had pressed her gloved knuckles against her mouth and was sitting very still. She did not look at him, even yet. Her voice came to him hardly more than

136

a whisper, very near in the dusk. "What are you saying? You . . . you don't know . . ."

"I love you," he said, his voice a low, slow drawl. He leaned toward her, looking into her face, trying to compel her eyes. "I loved you the first moment I saw you, and I'll love you the last day of my life. You say the word, and I'll work for you as I never worked for anything in this world before."

She sat silent for so long that he thought she wasn't going to answer him at all. "Do you think that's fair?" she asked him at last.

He was mystified. "I don't get you."

"There aren't many things," she said, "that a ranch-born girl can do to make her own way. Cook a little? Wait on table? Maybe. People rush into things like that. It kind of hurts to say this, Tom, but it seems to me a life like that must get kind of tiresome in the course of the years."

"You mean," he said without belief, "you don't think I could take care of you?"

"Tom," she said, "I . . . I'd rather bite out my tongue than say this. But you asked for it. You know cows and horses . . . maybe better than anyone who ever rode for the Circle Three. For that" — her voice contracted as if she had to force the words out — "for that you get sixty dollars a month. And by your own account, you never held a steady job in your life."

He sat perfectly still for a long minute. A crazy black temper came up into him as swiftly as if somebody had taken a bite out of him with a rope end. Against that slash he was defenseless, for he knew that she happened to be right. He waited until the anger died out, and, when he spoke, it was entirely without expression.

"All right," he said at last. "I'll ride on, and you'll stay here. By and by you'll marry Jim Grover, a good, solid, young man, with a coming ranch. You'll marry him as a matter of course, in the regular run of events."

"Yes," she repeated, "I expect I will . . . in the regular run of events."

The quick vitality had gone back from the surface of his face again, and his cool eyes were sleepy on the far fade of the trail. He let his horse shift its feet, in silent suggestion that she move on ahead. Yet, for a moment she paused there, waiting as quietly as he. Somehow, in that moment Cantrell knew that, job or not, money or not, hope of a future or not, she would still go with him if ever he asked her again. He sat motionless and silent, and at the end of a minute she let her horse drift downward into the thin dark.

Cantrell did not move on that week, or even that month, though why he stayed he had no idea. He saw now, for the first time in his life, that his wandering career had brought him into a blind cañon. Not only had the long trails given him nothing to offer Marjory Andrews; they had also disarmed him of any means to a remedy. Jim Grover had six years' start on him. Grover had worked hard and stubbornly, and apparently with luck. He had a few hundred head of cattle, a few dozen horses, and, though he had mortgages and debts, he had credit, too. Jim Grover had accomplished more than anybody had a right to expect of a man at Jim's age. In comparison, Tom Cantrell was as good as afoot.

Certainly he could not ask Marjory to stick around half a dozen years to see if he could overcome Grover's start.

Too, now that he thought of it, his effort to get Marjory to run off with him was not such a hot proposition as he had wanted it to look. Many a time Cantrell had slept hungry in the rain, dog dirty and living like a wolf. For the trail of a saddle bum is a whimsical trail, beset with many a good slam on the nose.

Yet Cantrell stayed on, often asking himself what he was waiting for. In a general way he was studying the valley — working along in it, familiarizing himself with its possibilities and people. At bottom, of course, what he wanted was a miracle that would enable him to go to war against Jim Grover. But he kept this hope down and simply stayed on.

And this situation, he found, was one that could quickly grow worse. Spring came over the hills with a rush, and it was time for branding. Cantrell had learned roping in Sonora; his sixty-foot rawhide reata had almost the dexterity of an elephant's trunk. He always looked forward to the brandings. But now, because he had not expected Cantrell to stay on, Old Man Andrews had made other arrangements, and Cantrell was not needed in the brandings. The best the Circle Three could do for him was a job behind a scraper and a span of mules, along with an itinerant muleskinner named Happy Withers.

Walking behind the scraper and the mules, Tom Cantrell marveled at himself.

"I never thought I'd sink so low," he told Happy Withers frankly, but without bitterness. "If you had told me I was ever going to be found afoot, playing a tune on the back end of a mule, why, I'd have laughed at you."

Happy Withers was a weary and washed-out little party who, through many vicissitudes, still thought of himself as a buckaroo. "Me, too," he agreed. "But me, I sunk even lower once. I once milked some cows."

For three days Happy and Tom Cantrell grubbed ineffectually in the weed-grown bottom of an irrigation ditch. There had been little snow, and the stored waters of the Wagon Box River were so far short of expected levels that water stood even lower than the big concrete sluice that was supposed to carry it to Circle Three cultivation, and east winds had already dried out the hay fields beyond. The ditches had to be deepened to carry it to the lower land back from the river, and the sluice gate rebuilt, when Andrews got around to it. Happy and Tom Cantrell were not supposed to accomplish much, merely to muddle along in the crumbling mud until further notice.

Cantrell stuck to this program for better than two whole days. Mid-morning of the third day he pulled up his mules, and sat gloomily on the back of one of them, his sleet-blue eyes on the broken horizon.

"I don't know but what I'll quit, too," said Happy Withers.

"The Oregon country is great stuff in spring," Cantrell said. But he was thinking of something else. There should have been some other way of getting this work done. There was a broken-down tractor on the place, but it lacked parts, and the company which had made it was extinct. There should have been some way of siphoning the water, instead of the massive labor of building a new sluice, but the levels were all wrong, and there were no materials. There was one power pump in the valley, but someone else was using that.

Cantrell unhooked his team. "I'll be back by sundown."

"You figure to draw your time?"

"Not yet."

The black anger was on him again, driving him into unsparing effort. For five days the fit held on.

On the sixth day Cantrell showed up on Bitter Flats, where Andrews was branding. He was equipped for rope work.

"Well, the water's running on the hay."

Old Man Andrews was tall and stooped, with sun-weary eyes that had lost their color, and a bony bald head. When emergency roused other men to a fury of action, old Andrews was accustomed to spit ironically and hold his own pace. But now genuine terror whipped across his craggy features.

"If you've cracked those dikes . . ."

"We wouldn't fool with dikes or gates. We rigged a siphon."

"Siphon? There's no pipe for a siphon. And there's no . . ."

"We found some tile," Cantrell told him, "and faked us a siphon."

"Tile won't siphon! The water seeps . . ."

"Bunk," said Cantrell.

"But you didn't have any pump to start the siphon."

"We plugged the ends and dipped up water with pails."

"But that main ditch wouldn't carry. The levels . . ."

"We deepened the ditch."

"You mean to tell me two men with mules . . . ?"

"Happy and me was anxious to get through. We worked in shifts and run the tractor all night. After that it went faster."

"The tractor? What tractor?"

"One day I went to town and bought a wrecked car on credit. That night I patched up that old tractor with pieces of the car."

"But, man alive, even with the tractor . . ."

"Well, it did go kind of slow, until we rigged the drag line."

"Drag line?"

"We found a way to rig a drag line out of that big hay stacker."

This was too much for Andrews. He had to see it for himself. When he had seen, he stared a long time, his weather-beaten façade expressing disbelief. "Where the hell did you fall into all this loose-running savvy?" he demanded at last.

"I helped move dirt in the Imperial, and Montana, and Gila Bend," Cantrell told him. "I never was much of a hand to stay put."

"I'm damned," said Andrews. He turned his horse and started back to his branding. He hardly ever referred to the irrigation stunt again. When he did refer to it, it was in tones of incredulity and disbelief.

After the trick irrigation job was done, the work of the range proceeded. The spring was gone, and the summer wore on, and still Cantrell worked for the Circle Three. Now that he saw for sure that he had nothing to offer Marjory Andrews, he realized that she was the only wholly desirable thing he had ever seen. And he cussed himself, but he stayed.

Three evenings a week, as regularly as clockwork, Jim Grover rode with Marjory Andrews. To live near Marjory and see her every day of the world was a supreme privilege, but to catch and saddle her horse and then see her ride off with Jim Grover was a bitterness almost impossible to take.

Cantrell at one time or another had fought eighteen bouts in the professional ring, and he could have taken Grover apart. Cantrell had broken horses in eight states, and he could have outridden Jim Grover in any style Grover cared to name. Yet it was Grover who would presently marry Marjory Andrews. Everything Cantrell had done, everything he could do, summed up in a grand total of helplessness in the face of a destiny that he had not foreseen. In the light of these things, it was a welcome relief when old Paul Andrews transferred Tom Cantrell from the labors of the range to the feeding corrals at Bluestone.

Bluestone, at the foot of the valley, was a little dump that was trying to make itself into the beginnings of a town. As everywhere in the Fifty-Mile, the hand of Old Man Andrews showed prominently, for he owned the big feeding pens that justified Bluestone. Here a nearly senile old man named Ollie Macpherson was boss for the Circle Three. By pure force of habit this old-timer directed the feeding of cottonseed cake to the market cattle, the idea being to put such covering of meat onto them as would force a yell of enthusiasm from the cattle buyers. It was a very bad year for enthusiastic yells, or even whispers. Meantime, the actual work was done by a handful of antedated cow hands — *mestizo* breeds mostly — and by Tom Cantrell.

Cantrell saw less of Marjory Andrews here. Once a week — sometimes oftener — Marjory Andrews came down to Bluestone. On these occasions she often sat for a quarter hour with Tom Cantrell on a corral fence, a slim, bright-faced figure, as out of place as a flower pinned on a steer. Cantrell inhaled smoke and tried not to look at her too much. Sometimes after he had talked with Marjory the mood of fury with which he had licked the irrigation project came back to him, so that he swore he would lick the Fifty-Mile if it took a hundred years.

After a mood like that he would take a spurt of working like three men at whatever project he could dig up. He doubled the capacity of the loading chutes, and set up a new quarantine pen beyond the tick dip. He got the tractor from the Circle Three, rebuilt it again, and graded half the feeding pens, so that in another spring the cattle would not stand hock deep in mire, as they usually did. Gradually he took over from old Macpherson the cutting and rationing of the beeves,

144

introducing ideas he had picked up on feed lots from Brawley to the Buckeye Valley.

He even argued three weeks persuading Andrews to trim out his barren cows and feed them for beef. This was the reason that the Circle Three alone, in all the Fifty-Mile, fed cows that year, their raw-hipped she cattle were a laughing-stock among the overflowing pens of smooth, straight-built baby beeves.

Then presently he remembered he was just a sixty-dollar cow hand, after all, and the trail pull returned, jerking at him unendurably. Sometimes he would think of the sultry, sweet-aired nights of Mazatlán, where little adobes clustered close in the light of stars hardly farther than the palm tops, and endless Mexican songs wailed softly to the beat of murmuring guitars. Or on hot days he would get to thinking about the icy little streams of the Cascades, and he would almost smell the trout frying, and hear an elk whistling beyond timber where hardly anybody realized an elk would be any more. Or he would think of the branding fiestas of California, where all the neighbors get together and make a joke of the work, the girls roping and riding with the men. And he'd know for sure that a cowhand shoveling cottonseed cake at Bluestone might just as well be dead.

But still he stayed on, because he knew that, once he rode out of the Fifty-Mile, he would never see Marjory Andrews again. He stuck the summer out, and on through the fall works. Away from the feeding pens, riding hard in the roundup, he was able to get a perspective on the year he had spent. Head down at his work, he had been unable to see the herd for the cows. But in the saddle again, he was able to see what he should have seen before. He knew now that he had failed — that his failure had been certain from the beginning. He had stifled the trail pull and stuck to his job; he had done the work of three men. And he was right where he might have expected to be. No place. He saw this all clearly by the time the fall work was done. He went to Old Man Andrews.

"I've got four months' pay coming, I think," he told the boss of the Circle Three. "It's time to be moving on."

He said the words almost reluctantly. The trail pull was on him very strong, like the nagging beat of a toothache, but more than ever it was difficult for him to imagine a life in which Marjory Andrews did not exist. He knew every glint in the high-country light in her fine hair, every shift of color in the moving depths of her restless eyes, and he could not leave these things behind him forever without an insuperable sense of loss.

To himself he said: *Here goes nothing . . . that much is done with . . . and it's time.*

Long gone, honey child, long gone,
And he ain't coming back no mo' . . .

But now Old Man Andrews was studying Tom Cantrell with a hard, fixed eye. Cantrell had changed somewhat. He looked thinner and harder, and perhaps a little older, as if holding down in one place had let time catch up with him.

"No," Andrews said with a heavy and utter finality.

For a minute Cantrell could not think what the man was talking about.

"You aren't going to quit on me," Andrews told Cantrell. "Men that can get something done come too far between."

Cantrell began: "It's time I . . ."

"It's time you laid off this jumping from job to job, and set out to make something for yourself," Andrews said. He looked more weather beaten and more tired than ever; it had been a bad, tough year. "I've been figuring Macpherson is old, and about done. I'm old, too. I got too much on my hands to run everything at once. You take over the feeding pens. When you get them organized to suit you, take the crop lands and the irrigation, and run that, too. I don't know where you soaked up the savvy on all such stuff. But you proved out you know what you're up to. You showed a less cost per pound of beef than we've ever had at Bluestone. And you know cattle. You were right about feeding those cows."

"Those cows," said Cantrell, "lost out in the market."

"All beef lost out," Andrews amended. "Fat baby beeves are being kicked back onto the range, full to the eyes with cottonseed that will never put money in any man's pants. The only profit in all the Fifty-Mile come in on those eight hundred cows."

The young man and the old man looked at each other in silence for a minute. "The valley has taken a terrible shellacking," Andrews said. "Jim Grover, and lots of others, have their backs to the wall. A hundred and fifty is the best I can give you. But you take hold, and we'll dope out a scheme whereby you'll be cut in on the profits, if any. The Fifty-Mile has a future. You can just as well grow up with the valley, if you want to stick."

Just as Cantrell could have given no good reason for having stuck the year in Fifty-Mile Valley, he could think of no reason now for not jumping at an offer like that. He had worked hard, fighting the times as he would have fought a bucking horse, and he had seen himself as helpless and disarmed in the end as in the beginning. And now, suddenly, it seemed the whole victory was being handed to him on a plate, with Grover as good as licked. It was the offer of a cut-in that was the big thing. From that start there was no doubt that Cantrell could build to a full partnership in the end, and become a power, of a kind, in that valley.

He knew that he should feel elated, but he did not. He only felt dazed. He rode off into the hills and spent the day by himself, and taught himself to realize that this thing was true — that he had won. But still he felt no sense of triumph. It was as if he had put too much into the winning, and had nothing left with which to enjoy the unexpected victory. Or perhaps something else was wrong.

148

His trail back to the Circle Three led him past Jim Grover's home ranch, and now he remembered that early in the day someone had told him Grover was looking for him, wanted to see him. On an impulse — perhaps because he was obscurely reluctant to go back to the Circle Three — he turned into Grover's layout.

Grover had built his layout himself, and he had a big, fine barn with a corrugated roof; but the house in which he was baching it was an adobe of three small rooms, only two of which had wood floors. Not so much, but often, in riding by this place, Cantrell had speculated morosely on what a pretty place Marjory Andrews would make of this when she came to live here — a place worthy of all a man's life.

He went around to the back where a light showed that Jim Grover, alone now that he had fired his extra fall help, was cooking himself a belated supper. Tom Cantrell glanced once at the room, littered and dimly lit by the smoky kerosene lamp, then leaned in the doorway, easy and balanced, light on his boot heels, as he always stood. Grover swung from the stove to face him, stoop shouldered and head down, like a crowded steer. He was big and square built, but with a weariness in his young features that foretold the dark doggedness in toil toward which this man's destiny was set.

"I heard you were looking for me," Tom Cantrell said.

"Maybe I am," said Grover. The wall of studied politeness they had always kept between them fell away. "Hardly figured you'd come for it, though. Come in here."

149

Cantrell took two steps into the room, grit crackling under his high heels, for Grover's layout caught the blow of the sand from the range. Jim Grover picked up the lamp and set it on a high shelf. Cantrell knew what Grover wanted with him, when he did that. Then Grover crossed, kicked the door shut, and leaned his back against it. He began to make a cigarette, studying Cantrell as he did so, with eyes gone as expressionless as the eyes of a pike.

"You're shot with luck, aren't you?" he said at last.

"Some say I am."

"I understand," Grover said again, "you've been drifting up and down the country since you were fourteen years old."

Cantrell nodded.

"I ran off from home about the same age," Grover went on. "I figured to do like you've done . . . get out of this valley, drift up and down the world. Only, I turned back."

"You used your head," said Cantrell.

Grover disregarded him. "For the last ten years I've worked like hell. Even as a kid I was trying to figure out ways to amount to something, to get ahead. After ten years a man can't change. A way of going at things builds into you, and you can't get loose. I could be standing in your shoes now. But I turned back. That was my mistake. One mistake . . . and one to last me all my life. But you were shot with luck, and you stayed out."

"And that," Cantrell said, "was my mistake."

150

"Mistake, hell!" Grover roared with anomalous fury. "How was it you could swing that irrigation stunt that knocked everybody cock-eyed? How did you get ahead on things like grading feeder steers? How was it you knew that baby beef was going to choke the market, but could show old Andrews how to clean up with his no-good cows? Because you're better than the valley men? Like hell! You built up that dope drifting up and down the West, all that time I was sweating to grow a few cows in this dusty hole in the hills!"

"Something wrong there," Cantrell said. His sleet-blue eyes were dreamy, off in the distance beyond the close walls, beyond the far-cupped ranges. "I can tell you this . . . trail dusting doesn't fit any man for anything, except moving on."

"The devil it doesn't," Grover snarled at him. Cantrell was amazed at the black bitterness of the man. Perhaps working everlastingly in one place built up a man's capacity for hate. "You're the smart boy, aren't you? You're the boy knows it all. You took one summer, and you built yourself into a partnership with the biggest cowman in the Fifty-Mile. One summer . . . and you set yourself up for life! That's what you learned to do, huh, giving yourself a break? And you learned to turn the head of a girl, and gather her in, just easy, with one hand behind your back!"

"What is it you want with me?" Cantrell demanded. His eyes came out of the distance beyond the walls with a snap, and met Grover's gaze with still points of steel.

"I'll tell you what I want with you. I'm through, and I'm beat, and I know it. But I don't like you. I don't like your looks, or your ways, or the shape of your hat. And right now I'm going to whip you."

Cantrell drew a deep breath of the kerosene-smoked air. "Well," he said, "I'm ready."

Jim Grover came with a rush, releasing all the furious energy of a defeated man, of a man who had worked ten years and seen his winnings tricked away in a moment by a Johnny-come-lately who had spent his life having a good time. Jim Grover weighed two hundred and four pounds, and what of that was not bone was muscle hardened by the labors of the saddle. He came fast and he came hard, charging like a cross between a longhorn and a silvertip. And Tom Cantrell swayed away without even raising his hands, and let Grover bring up against the wall with a crash that shook the solid adobe.

What chance has a good saddle-toughened boy against a man who has gone eighteen battles in the professional ring? Jim Grover turned, gathered himself, and came again, and Cantrell stabbed out with a reaching left, his balanced weight leaning behind it. That was the beginning. They were not going to come to the end for a long time.

Unless Grover could close in upon Cantrell in the cramped quarters, and make use of his sheer power, there could be only one kind of end. But he could not close in. It must have seemed to Grover, as his eyes closed and the wind went out of him, that he could not even find Cantrell. Cantrell went down once from a wild, high blow on the side of his head, and his arms and shoulders turned hot and lame from heavy battering, but when Grover finally did close in, weary and windbroke, Cantrell ripped his right hand four times to the heart, and the fight was done.

Done as far as any doubt of outcome was concerned, yet not done. It was not until Grover was whipped and definitely through that he showed the stuff he was made of. He showed it by getting up and coming on, over and over again, when everything he had was gone, and all hope was gone, and what power he had left would not have broken a paper bag. He was still trying to fight, staggering stone blind, groping for his enemy, when Cantrell pushed him to the floor in a corner and held him there with one hand.

Grover struggled to sit up, his back braced against the wall, but swayed crazily even then. "Come on and fight," he said dimly.

"It's the end of round one, fella," Cantrell told him. The sweat was running down his face, and, with his hair clawed into his eyes, he appeared as if he were looking through the mane of a horse. "Sit quiet until you hear the gong."

He got water and poured it over Grover's head. After a while Grover peered out of his swollen eyes and seemed able to see Cantrell. "I suppose," said Grover at last, "you learned this stuff at Fish Creek, or Madre de Dios, or some place."

"Mostly at San Berdoo."

"Uh-huh," said Grover. "If she's given me one sample of what you did in outlandish places, she's given me a million. Don't go away. I'll whip . . ."

153

"As for me," said Cantrell, "I wish to hell I'd killed you. That crack on the head must have waked my brain up, and I'll never forgive you for that."

"I don't know what you're talking about," Jim Grover said.

"I never heard such infernal blather as you talk," said Cantrell. "All day long I've known something was wrong. I knew things couldn't have worked out so good. Not on the level. But I didn't realize what a lot of baloney it all was until I heard you spiel it out in one long parade of bunk."

"When was this?" Grover mumbled.

"All this stuff about how come I got ahead of you . . . I never heard such hooey," Cantrell said. "Hitting the trail never taught any man how to settle down to a success with cattle or anything else. For more than a little while."

Grover lifted his head, fighting ugly yet. "The hell it didn't," he said. "It taught you cattle, but leave that out. If you didn't get anything else out of it, you anyway learned how to gather in a girl."

"And turn to living off her father," Cantrell said, his low tones fit to skin a mule. "A fine end for a man who's rode the country I've rode!"

"You turned her head," Grover insisted doggedly.

"When you've made love to a hundred girls, I reckon it should be no great trick to make some sort of showing with one more."

The other got to his hands and knees, and tried to climb up the wall to his feet. "As soon as I get up," he said, "I aim to break your back!"

154

"I wish you had," said Cantrell.

Grover half rose, but his knees buckled under him again, and he went down. "You mean that now you've won her over, you don't want her any more?"

"I want her," said Cantrell, "worse than I ever wanted anything in my life."

He found his hat, trampled under the broken table, and left Jim Grover still sitting on the floor in the yellow light of kerosene.

He knew now what had been wrong all day long. If Grover had seen the truth and had told him outright that the trail fitted a man for nothing but the trail, if he had told Cantrell that he was a fluke and a fraud, and was lined up to sponge a living from the father of the girl he loved, Cantrell would have bucked, and thrown it off. But when Grover had voiced the very phrases that Cantrell himself had tried to think, the unsoundness of the whole thing came out, clear and plain and ugly, so that he could not evade it or put it down.

The bag of tricks the trail had given him were trivial tricks — impressive to a valley-bound man and a girl. But Grover had said one true thing — that after ten years a man can't change. If one thing in the world was certain, it was that the everlasting, unconquerable pull of the trail would sooner or later twist the heart out of him, and make him worse than useless to Marjory Andrews in the end. Cantrell turned his horse toward the Circle Three with a reluctance that was almost dread.

* ★ *

It was coldly raw and starless as he put his pony up the back trail that had first brought him into the Fifty-Mile. When he had told Andrews that he was on his way, he had not been able to bring himself to stay under a Circle Three roof another night. He pushed upward, seeking the southward track.

At the fork of the trail he pulled up his blowing horse and sat for a little while, looking back. Far out on the valley floor he could make out the tiny yellow lights of the Circle Three, marking a place of friendliness and warmth in the vast, cold dark. Farther yet, winking behind distance, he could make out two or three more, where people of other ranches were getting somewhere and building up families around them. More than ever in his life, he felt that nothing in the world had any meaning compared to the worth of one lighted window, somewhere far off in the dusk, with warmth behind it, and a girl waiting.

And he knew that down in this valley there was a girl who would have waited for him — perhaps forever, if he had asked it. Tonight, for all he knew, her pillow would be wet with tears.

He tried to hum his favorite song:

Long gone, sweetheart, long gone,
He eased off into them hills . . .

But the picture that had come to him of a gray-eyed girl in tears took the song out of him, along with nearly everything else. He tried to spit through his teeth, and

156

found that for some reason he could not. Then he spoke out loud. Yes, they had him talking to himself. "Better tonight," he said, his voice thin and unfamiliar against the wind — "better tonight than all through the years." He turned his horse downwind and drifted south.

Saddle Bum

Everybody saw the change in Bob Porter when he came back to his father's ranch — the Diamond Dot — in the Sunrise River country. Some change, of course, was noticeable at sight, for he was considerably filled out and more mature (he had left at the age of nineteen); but it wasn't until he had been around for a few weeks that they began to realize what a punk effect four years of wandering had really had upon him.

To old Raff Porter, Bob's father, it seemed that his son had had the heart taken out of him, somewhere in those four years. He tried to draw the boy out about where he had been, and what had happened to him. Bob Porter had been a lot of places — as far north and east as Oklahoma, as far south as southern Sonora — and he had wandered a crooked round-about trail between. He spoke readily, though without enthusiasm, about any part of his travels that anybody seemed interested in, but his father was unable to discover any clue to the change in his son.

Sometimes Raff Porter, letting his memory drop back ten years, thought that Bob was acting a whole lot like some of the boys he had seen return from the A. E.

F. This did nothing to modify his bafflement. Bob Porter had not been to any war, for there had been no war. That he had not been uniformly unsuccessful in his wandering was attested by the fact that he still had eight or nine thousand dollars left from a clean-up he had made in some oil-well shenanigan in Oklahoma. Yet, the unmistakable symptoms of something wrong were there: a lack of interest in anything whatsoever which an evident effort to dissimulate was not able to cover up and a general silent wordlessness, as if the effort involved in speech was out of proportion to the possible accomplishment thereof.

Raff Porter was not the only one who noticed the change. Neighboring cattlemen, some of whom had known Bob all his life, noticed it too; and Madge Alexander noticed it, and she was, perhaps, the most puzzled of all.

For four years Madge Alexander had hung onto her mental picture of the reckless, hard-riding kid that Bob Porter had been when last seen in the Sunrise River country. Physically, at first glance, she found that he more than lived up to that picture, but something not physical was very obviously and literally gone. Men might have called that missing element by the homely name of guts. Madge, recognizing the change perhaps more keenly than anyone else, did not know what to call it, even in her own mind.

But what Madge Alexander noticed was that Bob Porter hardly ever came to see her now that he was back. He had been home two months and a half before he rode over to the Alexander place for the third time, and even then there was nothing satisfactory about it to a girl who had carried Bob Porter's image in her mind all the time he had been gone.

It was only shortly after midday, but Lee Heston had stopped by in passing, as he frequently did, and his presence made it even worse. Lee was the outstandingly eligible young man who is always among those present wherever a man is trying to raise an attractive girl. Heston already had his own average-size outfit that he had inherited from an uncle. And he had been after Madge Alexander ever since she was nineteen years old — which is to say, ever since Bob Porter had been away. Everybody assumed that Madge would ultimately drift into marrying him, if ever she got Bob out of her head.

And it looked as if Bob Porter were in a fair way to count himself out. Madge was much too wide awake, to say nothing of short tempered, to dedicate herself to a washout.

Now, as they sat on the broad gallery of the Circle Slash ranch house, watching the mouse-colored shadows of the Volunteer Peaks eclipse the mesas, it appeared that Madge found herself unable to watch the slow death of an hallucination any longer.

"What are you going to do, Bob?" Her voice was casual, yet all three must have recognized that a direct challenge had come to the surface at last.

"Do? Do about what?"

"Are you going to stay in the Sunrise River country?"

Bob Porter had sat as motionless as a resting dog for the better part of an hour, but now he stirred with an uneasy restlessness. "Why, I might," he said vaguely. "But maybe I'll push on up Saskatchewan way."

"Are you right sure you'll find it much different from where you've already been?"

"No," he admitted; "I expect not. I suppose that's the reason I can't hardly make up my mind to go. I kind of don't dare go to Saskatchewan, I guess."

"Don't dare? What do you mean?"

"Seems like I'd kind of like to save out one place, in this cow belt, that I haven't actually gone and sifted out myself."

"Sifted? For what?"

There was another of those dopey silences Bob Porter made a specialty of nowadays. "I'm not right sure I know for what," he finally brought out.

Nobody said anything for a little bit. Then Madge asked in a curious voice: "What's her name?"

"Name? Whose name?"

"Let it go," Madge said.

Lee Heston allowed that he had heard that Saskatchewan was a mighty pretty country, and that they paid good wages, too.

"Yeah?" said Bob. He hitched himself to his feet slowly, straightening up his long length. "Well, I'll be drifting along." He idled his way toward his horse. "Take care of yourselves."

"Hurry back," Lee Heston called after him with an imitation heartiness.

"O K," said Porter, and rode shuffling away.

When he was gone, the thickness of the dusk gave Madge hope that she could snap herself out of the dark

161

mood that had come upon her in time to conceal it from Lee Heston. With her boots as silent as moccasins she danced a slow solo step the length of the gallery and back, snapping her fingers to the time of a low-chanted song. It was a new song that the radio had brought in only a few days before:

Try another song,
Try another tune,
Try a different man . . .

Lee Heston had leisurely got up to dance with her, but Madge suddenly turned away from him to burst into tears that could not be hid.

Old Man Porter and Roddy Morton, who had ridden over with Bob to talk feed with Jess Alexander, were waiting for Bob out by one of the corrals. The three rode back a different way than they had come, Old Man Porter wishing to estimate certain possibilities of the winter graze.

"A feller over at Phoenix," said Roddy with irony, "was telling me that the old open range is gone. "The cow country is all fenced up," says he, 'and privately controlled.'"

"I'd like to lay hands on a feller like that," said Old Man Porter vindictively. "Lord knows, I wish he was right! But seeing that only about one-sixth of Arizona was private-owned by the Nineteen Twenty-Five report . . . I guess a few thousand of us will have to keep right on blundering ahead on the delusion that we're still up against open-range conditions."

162

He drew up his horse on the edge of the mesa they rode and waved a buckskin-gloved hand at a broken twenty-mile expanse. "Open range!" he repeated bitterly. "I can remember when we was strong for it." He ran a disillusioned eye over the very visible results of too long a usage without control.

"Look at it now!" Porter urged them. "*That's* what you might call over-grazed! Sometimes it seems like it's time to move on."

Bob Porter laughed, a harsh sound, unexpected in the quiet of limitless space. "Move on, huh? That's a hot one!" The embittered, derisive note in his voice was unfamiliar, but his father did not take affront.

"Maybe down in old Mex' . . . ," the old man's voice trailed off.

"I've just come from old Mex'," Bob Porter reminded him. "You're as good as looking at it now. Or maybe you think you'd like to push north. I can tell you you're looking at Nevada, too, just while you're looking at this basin."

His father glanced at him curiously, then wheeled his pony and led the way northward along the shoulder of the mesa. "I'll show you something that looks some better, pretty quick, now, Bob," he promised. "I reckon it'll do us all good to take a look at the stretch we're coming to now."

"You mean this reserve range up here?"

"It's the first reserve winter feed we've been able to hold out for years. It was plenty hard for the Sunrise outfits to get together to save this out, and we took an awful chance on some outsider coming in on it. But

163

when we come to the end of this shoulder, you'll be looking down at something the Sunrise country hasn't seen for many a long year . . . near ninety sections of winter feed, untouched by the summer graze."

"It sure should look almighty good," Bob admitted.

Then, as they reached the northern shoulder of the mesa, there came to them a familiar odor and a familiar sound, and they reached the crest of the pitch to find themselves looking upon a broad, long-reaching scatter of grazing sheep.

The elder two looked at each other, and Roddy Morton's leather face twisted in a wry, dusty grin.

Raff Porter had a peculiar genius for counting any amount of stock at a glance. "Eight hundred and eighty-odd," he said wearily, "not counting lambs hid behind ewes."

He set spur to his pony and went loping down the break, the others trailing after. An Indian whose rank hair almost reached his shoulders sat on the hillside, overlooking his flock. Beside him lay a silver-sprinkled old dog, like a wolf. A couple of dusky striplings squatted on their heels off to one side on the plain below, and there were four more dogs of that peculiar smoky-blue desert breed that has so long worked Southwestern sheep. Porter rode directly to the man on the slope, who watched his approach dourly, without salute.

Raff Porter demanded: "You on herd contract or payroll?"

"Contract, for the Double O."

164

The man spoke as good Western English as Porter, and that in itself seemed to anger the old man. "What do you think you're doing here?"

"Why not?" he said. "This range is free. You ain't using it."

"Nor you either," Raff Porter snapped at him. "All that's been threshed out ten thousand times. No sheep come this side of Mike's Wash, and you know that as well as me. Already you've cut a half-mile-wide belt through ninety sections we was holding for winter feed. Now you get them sheep back beyond Mike's Wash!"

"Abe Atwood is back of these sheep," the herder warned him. "The law says . . ."

"To hell with Abe Atwood! If you and Atwood want law, I'll give you law!"

The herder appeared to consider. Curiously, he showed no resentment — perhaps because he felt no surprise. "All right," he said at last, his eyes contemplative upon the sheep. "It'll take maybe three, four days to get them moved."

Bob Porter suddenly rose in his stirrups. "Three, four days, hell! You'll put those sheep over the line tonight!"

"We can't . . ."

"You can't move 'em, huh? By God, I'll show you how to move 'em!" He struck steel to his horse, and the cow pony exploded into a thundering streak of dust. The hazing yell that is yet heard in old Mexico rang out: "Aye, *che-wah-wah!* Pick 'em up! *che-wah-wah-wah!* Get gone!"

165

The sheep at the margin of the herd blundered into a stupid bunch. Those nearest the horse put their heads down and cannoned into the others, fighting to get into the middle. One half-moon sweep threw the woollies into some semblance of a driven herd, another put them on the move. "Aye, *che-wah-wah!* Whoppee!" The shuffle of hoofs changed to a ground-shaking rumble, then a continuous, muffled roar.

Young Porter rode back. "You keep them on the prod . . . and if you know what's good for you, you'll never stop until you're across Mike's Wash! I aim to ride this range tonight . . . and Lord knows I'm hoping I'll find you here!"

Bob Porter held to his intention. He went back to the home ranch with the others, for supper and a fresh horse, but rode out again, and breakfast was half finished before he reappeared, saddle worn and dusty, but not apparently tired.

"Come onto any sheep?" his father asked him.

Bob answered: "There's no sheep in Powder Basin."

That was all that was said then, but late in the day a rider from the Bar Five stopped by, bursting with news peculiarly disturbing to old Raff Porter.

"Did you hear about the sheep run?" was almost the first thing the Bar Five cowboy said. "Somebody jumped down on one of the big Double O herds, over in the Soapweed Flats, and scattered near two thousand head from hell to Tuesday!"

Raff Porter turned a slow eye upon his son, but Bob Porter's face was expressionless.

166

"Abe Atwood is swearing he'll have somebody's scalp if it costs him his last cent. Seems like somebody caught a herd of wool over on the Powder Basin land, and they figure the row must have started there, but Abe Atwood claims that herd was only moving down to the desert for the winter lambing and pushing along as fast as it could. The sheepmen are in an almighty boil!"

That night Jess Alexander and Lee Heston, representing the Seven B and the Circle Slash, rode over to the Porters' to talk of what might well prove the beginning of another expensive war.

"Look here," said Lee Heston, speaking slightly out of turn, but with great reasonableness. "Old Abe Atwood's the toughest sheepman in the Sunrise. First thing we know there's going to be reprisals, and what kind of shape are we in for that?"

"Better let the thing rest," Raff Porter recommended. "Sheepmen have to be put in their place every so often, anyway. For all we know this will turn out to have done more good than harm."

"The Sunrise won't be cow country again until somebody buys out Atwood. He's the root of sheep trouble here," Heston fretted. "He was near ready to sell when this broke, but now he'll stick like a fever tick. Still, if you want to let this drift . . ."

This they decided to do. There the matter rested for all of three days.

On the third day Bob Porter elected himself to ride night herd on a bunch of long yearlings that were being held in one corner of the Diamond Dot range, pending a disposition not yet decided.

That night a red glow upon the sky told the length and breadth of the Sunrise valley a story which the swift news of next day confirmed. A brush corral in which Double O herders had bedded nearly fifteen hundred head had gone up in flames.

By the testimony of the herders the fire was no accidental blaze started by a cook-fire spark. The sheepmen had heard at least one ridden horse, shots had been exchanged, and the herders had been driven back.

They added to this the details of a scene which, to sheepmen at least, appealed as one of devastation and horror. As the dry brush had roared up in sky-reaching flame, more than two hundred head of sheep had died, trapped and trampled in the smoke. Fifty-eight head died in a straight-sided wash into which a part of the herd avalanched in the dark, and all along the long course of that merciless drive the weaker of the lambs and ewes were left wind broken on their knees, many of them never to rise.

The herders had recognized no one, except that they could swear to the one long yell that the hazing rider had used as he drove down upon the stampeding sheep: "Aye, *che-wah-wah!* Get gone!" Nobody in the Sunrise valley used that yell except just one man.

In less than a day the news had spread. That night, as the coyotes gathered from afar to the scent of the scorched wool and mutton, the cowmen of six brands gathered at the home ranch of Porter's Diamond Dot. Among them also appeared Tom Frazier, Sunrise sheriff, who arrived alone.

"Look here, Raff," Jim Earle, owner of the Bar Five, put it up to the boss of the Diamond Dot, "this thing's going to cause trouble . . . what your kid did to them sheep last night."

"Who said it was my boy?"

"Why, it's all over the range that them sheep herders said it was him . . . or as good as said so."

"Some sheep herders as good as said," Raff Porter repeated ironically. "You've got crust, Jim, offering me that!"

"What does *he* say," Lee Heston demanded sharply, "about where he was last night?"

Raff Porter looked him over with a cool eye. "In the first place," he said, "I wouldn't have the nerve to ask Bob where he spent his night, no, not me! In the second place, it happens he did mention where he was going to be. I suppose I might ask him now if he ran a sneak, under cover of a lie, to go trample under a lot of stock that was minding its own business on its own range. But if you think I'm going to, you don't know me!"

Restless glances turned to Bob Porter. He did not look at all perturbed.

"Ain't you got anything to say, Bob?" Jess Alexander asked.

Bob Porter smiled faintly and shook his head.

The cattlemen, upset by the Porters' reticent stand, were momentarily at a loss. By ones and twos they went their way, uneasy and uncertain. These were men quick enough in action, once they saw their way, but very slow to make decisions that would alter old ties.

169

Tom Frazier stayed after the others. The Sunrise sheriff was a lank, loose-knit man with a friendly eye and huge, competent hands.

"People," he said, "this here is a real serious thing. I'm asking you, is this the right way to do?"

"Let's not begin to yell before we're bit," Raff suggested.

"I'll smooth over whatever of this I can," Frazier assured him. "But hell's going to pop before we hear the last of this." He rode off, looking serious.

Now three days passed in that utter quiet which the untrusting human mind invariably associates with coming storm. In this time nothing was heard from Abe Atwood or his faction. The sheep stayed on their own side of Mike's Wash. Yet the air was full of electricity. No one doubted for a moment that reprisals would come. The cowmen waited, restless and dark tempered.

At the Diamond Dot, Raff Porter remained as good as his word: he had never asked his son for an explanation of his whereabouts upon the night of the raid, and Bob offered none.

On the fourth day Bob Porter saddled a good, tough circle pony, and guessed that he would go to town. "Don't look for me until tomorrow," he told Raff Porter. "I don't know but what I'll be coming back in a kind of roundabout way."

The elderly, wistful look that came into Raff Porter's face swiftly turned to something pretty dark and grim. He opened his mouth, but he closed it again. Afterward, he blamed himself for that, for that night saw history made on the Sunrise range.

170

Shortly after midnight a red flare once more painted the sky, and the rattle of gunfire perforated the desert night. Far downwind the coyotes pricked up their ears to the bleat of lambs lost from a stampeded herd and their noses to the suggestive odor of burnt wool. It was the ultimate injury-upon-insult, the final turn of the screw.

Bob Porter and his ridden-out pony did not get in until the middle of the next afternoon.

His father faced him with bleak eyes, his face hard. "Bob, boy, what the hell am I supposed to think?"

Bob Porter threw his hat at a nail, and skidded the frying pan onto the stove. "Dad, the fact is, I haven't been right sure what you'd think. But my mind was set. I figured to go about my own business my own way."

Raff Porter exploded. "You infernal young squirt!" he bellowed. "If you've gone to work and . . ."

"Take your time!" Bob Porter checked him. "We've got a visitor here."

Sheriff Tom Frazier was with them again. He stepped in uninvited, and shot an angry glance from father to son.

"By God," he said, "this thing has got to stop! If you think you're going to send this country up in a cloud of yells and dust, you can think two times again!"

"Now just a minute," Bob said. "You want a stop put to this messing with sheep, do you? I'll put a stop to it for you."

"You're damn' tootin' you'll stop it. And that ain't all . . ."

Bob Porter turned so hard an eye upon Frazier that he was given time to speak. "Let me ask you one thing," Bob said. "Were you ever taken for a fool?"

"Maybe I was," said Frazier belligerently.

"So I have been," said Bob. "Not only by you, but by everybody on the Sunrise range, and even by my own dad."

"Who? Me?" said Porter.

"Yes, you," said Bob. "If I was going out to burn out a passel of sheep under cover of dark, you think I wouldn't have any more sense than to go at them yelling . . . Aye, *che-wah-wah!* . . . the one yell that nobody uses but me? I'm sick and tired of this, and I don't aim to stand for it any more!" He started pulling on his chaps.

"Where you going?" Frazier demanded.

"I'm going to put a stop to these here night raids," Bob told him, "and don't you worry but what I know where to go!"

"If you're starting more trouble," said Frazier, "I'm coming along."

"You'll stay back," Bob told him. "There isn't going to be any trouble, not any trouble at all!"

It was sundown by the time Bob Porter, arriving by the saddle cut-off, pulled up at the Circle Slash.

Lee Heston was there. It had taken no great application of brains for Bob Porter to figure out where to start looking for him. Just now he was sitting with Madge Alexander on the top rail of the corral.

Bob Porter swung down without being invited, and tied his horse to the fence.

172

"Howdy, Bob," Madge said.

"Heston," said Porter, "I'll talk to you."

Lee Heston stiffened. "Go ahead and talk," he said.

"Heston," said Porter, "there's going to be an end to this hazing of Double O sheep."

Lee Heston regarded him ironically. "You should know best!"

"I'll make it my business to know. And one reason for that is, the Double O sheep are my sheep!"

"They're what?" Heston was jolted out of his studied calm.

"I took over the Double O yesterday. The losses from last night's stampede are my losses."

Heston looked blank. "It's an outright lie," he decided. "You haven't got enough cash to buy half interest in a thrown mule shoe!"

"You'll find that Abe Atwood and the Sunrise bank figured I had enough."

"Then," Lee Heston hazarded, "you ran those first two stampedes to break Atwood's price, and you ran another last night on a corral of your own . . . willing to take a loss to cover up your tracks!"

"There isn't going to be any loss," Porter told him. "In the first place, I bought the Double O for the same price I offered before the first stampede. In the second place, Heston, you're going to pay damages for every sheep you've run to death. You're up against a cowman now."

"You mean to say I . . . ?"

"I mean to say it's you that tried to start this sheep war, and put it off on me. It's been almighty thin. I know exactly how you found out each of those three times that I was going to be away from home. I know what your idea was . . . which was to break Abe Atwood's price to where you could swing it yourself. I even know what horses you rode."

"You'll never prove a nickel's worth of it," Heston lathered. "If you think you can come back here and high lord me . . . why, you worthless saddle bum, I'll . . ."

"I'll high lord you all right! I'm ready to prove what I said, but that will come later. Just a minute ago you gave me the lie. Heston, my lad, you're about to have that remark jammed right back down your throat."

"Wait a minute," Heston snapped. He turned and ran for his saddled horse at the far end of the corral. As he turned toward them again, they saw that he was buckling on his gun belt. "Now come on with it," he raged. "You talk big, standing there with your gun on, to an unarmed man. Come on with your . . ."

"You make me sick," said Porter. He strode forward, his gun swinging idle against his thigh, and with his right hand slapped Lee Heston's face with such a swinging crack that Heston reeled backward against the fence.

It must be said for Heston that he was neither a coward nor a fool. He shot one glance at Porter's still idle gun, then let his own alone, put his hands in front of him, and came on.

Between those two was not enough ring science to fill a glove. They swung long, full-armed blows, pouring in punishment with the fury of fighting dogs. Under

174

their trampling boots a fine haze of hoof-ground corral dust rose, thickening the obscurity of the twilight. Jess Alexander and two Circle Slash cowboys came up on the run to offer unheeded cries of advice.

Abruptly, without forecast to the watchers, Lee Heston's rushing attack was brought up as sharply as if he had run into a braced timber, and his whimpered curses were checked in mid-word. He was thrown reeling backward, and brought up against the pole corral.

Madge Alexander screamed: "Bob, look out!" She had not moved from her seat upon the top rail, or uttered any sound, but now she was the only one of them who saw Lee Heston's right hand grope and find his displaced gun. Porter, who had turned away, whirled and once more drove in upon his man. He wrenched the bright .45 from Heston's grip as it came from its leather, and threw the gun into the horse corral. Then as Heston's hands came up once more, Porter brought his right to the jaw in one last knee-lifting jolt. Heston's head snapped back, and his whole weight seemed to lift. He swayed dizzily for an instant, then went down in the dust like a dropped saddle.

"Throw some water over him," said Bob Porter thickly, "and stick him on his horse."

"That was a right interesting brawl," said Jess Alexander. The cowboys were untangling Lee Heston, who was out sufficiently cold.

Porter hunted around for his hat. When he had found it, he stood for a moment before Madge

Alexander, holding the battered Stetson in his two hands. "I'm sorry to bust loose this way," he said, "but it was needful, I guess. And I couldn't seem to get hold of him any place but here."

"That's all right," Madge said.

"I'll be drifting along now," he told her. "I'll just say this. Everything I said to him was true." He turned away.

Madge Alexander caught her father's eye, and they held each other's gaze in a long, sidelong interchange, without words. "I don't know," Madge said, "but what the boy has got his gumption back."

"I don't know," Jess Alexander agreed conservatively, "but what he does seem more like himself."

Madge slid down from the fence. "Wait a minute! I believe I'll be riding your way, a little piece."

They were silent on their idling horses for a mile, two miles. The afterglow was draining away, leaving behind it a starlit desert night.

"I've got something I want to talk to you about," Bob Porter said.

"I thought maybe you did."

"I arrived back here from my general tour of the cow belt kind of out of guts," he confessed.

"I noticed that," she agreed.

"I was looking for a place where I could set up my own stand. After I found it, I meant to come back and get you to throw in with me. I don't know as I ever mentioned that in so many words."

"I don't know as you did," Madge said. "Still, you did kind of leave me with that general impression."

176

"There isn't any such place as I was looking for," he declared. "For a while after I found that out, it seemed to me there wasn't any room for a fellow to go ahead with anything any more, and that was the way I was feeling when I got back here."

"Anybody can see that things have changed," Madge said. "Anybody that wants to bet that they haven't, or that they won't . . . he's sunk, that's all."

"It's just lately come to me," Bob said, "that there's one more bet open, yet I'm willing to bet now that times will change again."

"What way, Bob?"

"Madge, bad as conditions are, we've got our hooks in an almighty power of land here. It won't always be Public Domain. Some day those of us that stick it out will make these ranges our own. And by that time something else will have happened, too . . . a cow on the hoof is going to be worth some money then!"

"I thought you were going in for sheep."

"Sheep? I'm going to strip this range of sheep. I've put up all I had, and everything I could borrow at the bank, to make first payments on the Double O, and I'll put that range in cows. I don't know how we're ever going to see it through. But somehow we're going to have to hang on, and keep on hanging on, till that day comes."

"We?"

"You and me," he told her.

Delayed Action

That was the time Pete Crabtree, the Frying Pan country sheriff, got backed down into his hole and recommended to pull the hole in after him, which he done. And what made it so bad, this here was on a late Saturday afternoon in the hot, slack season, so that pretty near everybody was in McTarnahan to see it. Even yours truly, Old Man Coffee, was there, which was unusual, because lion hunting for bounty leaves me very little time to fool away in towns.

But the thing that made it the toughest for Pete Crabtree, sheriff of the Frying Pan country, was that Edith Prescott was there, too, and saw it all.

A buckaroo name of Homer Chamberlain had rode in from over by Lordstown on a zebra dun that was easy the best horse there that day, and it kind of looked like to me, when the rider got off this horse, that maybe he figured he had some extra rights, too, by reason of being the best man. I saw him two, three times in the course of the afternoon, and he was drunker every time. And it was an ugly drunk, the kind where a man goes quiet and kind of stiff, but means to stand on his rights against man, mule, or automobile.

178

And then I seen him the fourth time, and that was the time he brung himself to the attention of all of McTarnahan and all those fellers gathered there, and most especial to the attention of Pete Crabtree.

I was standing in front of Crosby's store, talking to Art Dwyer and Doc Garrett. Art Dwyer was a little bowlegged feller with a kind of a hatchety face, and an eye to politics. So far, he was only deputy sheriff, but he was always trying to soap somebody up, with a view to laying aside a vote, and that's how come he was talking to me. Doc Garrett was more of a refined, sad-looking sort of feller, with a long horse face — one of the few fellers called "Doc" because he *was* a doctor.

As we was standing there, old Johnny Hall come rack-wheeling up to the hitch rack on a slattery buckboard and shoved in next to Homer Chamberlain's horse, and one of those wobbling wheels tipped the dun on the hock. The dun pony whirled and let fly both heels at old Johnny's horse, and Johnny let go with a rope and that made fur fly on the dun, taking most of the gunpowder out of him thereby.

Then, as Johnny climbed down over the wheel, Homer Chamberlain had him by the scruff of the shirt. "You son-of-a-bitch," Chamberlain said, "I seen that. Who give you leave to run down my horse? You get your buckboard out of here, and you keep it out!" With that he heaved old Johnny aboard.

"Now get gone," Chamberlain says, and old Johnny, who hasn't worn a gun in fifteen years, just backed out and drove away, looking a whole lot like a turkey in the rain.

I looked at Art Dwyer. He was watching Chamberlain so green-eyed that it come to me that maybe Art had tangled with Chamberlain himself, some place. Doc Garrett was looking pretty ugly, too, about the ugliest I had seen him look, which was plenty ugly, he being a sour cuss. Still, nobody did anything; and after a minute Art Dwyer kind of growled and drifted off through the crowd.

But now Pete Crabtree come forward through the ring of folks that had gathered 'round. Pete's real job was that of sheriff, but old Tim Wiley, the regular town marshal, had busted a leg, and Pete was filling in for him. He was looking uneasy and red in the face, like he always did whenever he tackled somebody.

"I don't know," he said, "but what you're going to cause trouble, acting thataway around here. Come to think of it, I don't know but what you better let me take that gun, and check it aside where you can get it when you leave."

Hardly anybody ever wears any guns any more, unless they just happen to be riding along with one in hopes of shooting a coyote or a snake. But every once in a while the law officers was accustomed to take a gun off a drunk.

Chamberlain turned slowly, and he looked Pete up and down with an eye like a cold-fried egg. Pete Crabtree was a good big strapping boy with very quick-working hands and a straight eye, but this Homer Chamberlain was not impressed. "God bless my soul," he said at last, and the way he said it, it was the most insulting darn' thing I ever heard.

"I'll take that gun," said Pete again, very stubborn.

Chamberlain kind of showed the edge of his teeth in a little smile, like a stallion that's fixing to reach for you, and there was quiet a little minute more.

"Go ahead and open it up," said Chamberlain at last. "Do you want to fight or not?"

"No," said Pete. "All I . . ."

"Then reach up your hands," Chamberlain said.

I don't think Pete Crabtree was scared. He was no more than a youngster, a big rope-and-saddle type of kid, but already he had made something of a reputation for himself. Especially when he went out and took the two Gormson brothers, the time they killed the three men breaking jail; and again when he walked two hundred yards across the open floor of Blanket Cut, with Walt Hanrahan shooting at him all the way, and buffaloed Walt with the barrel of his gun when he got to the other side. Only, for all that, Pete was none too fast in the head, and in Chamberlain's case it may be Pete first figured it wasn't right to kill a man just because that man was drunk.

"Reach, I said," Chamberlain told him again, and Pete Crabtree's hands come up, real slow.

Pete's gun was in his waistband, and now Chamberlain jerked it out and stuck it in his own. "Now stick your tail between your legs and get out of here," Chamberlain said.

Pete turned and went, walking slow through all that half-drunk crowd that had gathered 'round. He was looking dazed and flabbergasted. I believe it was only then that he was beginning to see what he had done and how tough it was going to be for him to recover the ground he had lost with the people of McTarnahan. The crowd yelled and cheered and whooped, taking the side of the top man, like they'll always do if the underdog turns tail. And when I looked around, there was Edith Prescott standing in the doorway of Crosby's store.

Edith Prescott was a kind of a tall slender girl, with a lot of black hair, and eyes as blue as ever I see. The first time I ever saw her she was a mighty scared, lost-looking youngster who had landed in McTarnahan, God knows how, except that something seems to keep pushing these Irish-looking people all over the world, whether they like it or not. To look at her then, you wouldn't have thought that she could take hold of things and run them like a man. Old Mrs. Hepmeyer gave her a job washing dishes, out of sympathy. And the next thing I heard, Edith Prescott was up at the Crown King, contracting the feeding of more than eighty men and making a pile of dough!

She had also made a lot of changes in Pete's life, such as causing him to sweep out his office, and wear a necktie on week days, though I hadn't heard whether he had made any special impression upon her thereby. But now as I looked at Edith Prescott's face, I saw that maybe he had, for she looked as if she had just seen one of her main landmarks come down, one that she had counted on and marked her trail by.

I walked over to her. "Things don't always mean what they look like they mean," I told her.

After a minute or two she glanced at me as if she hadn't heard what I said, and didn't give a hoot, either. "Mister Coffee," she said, "I can't hardly believe my own eyes." There was a quiver in her mouth, and you could hardly hear her voice at all.

"There's times when it's a mistake to believe your own eyes," I said. And then suddenly she pushed past me and got away.

It was getting dusk by this time, and I went and had supper, meaning to find Pete afterward and point out to him the ways of the righteous. Near as I could see, the one thing left for him to do was to get another gun and then go and get Homer Chamberlain, dead or alive, drunk or sober. But after supper I met Art Dwyer, Pete's deputy, and found out that advice from me wasn't going to be any use.

It seems, while I was eating supper, Pete Crabtree had set out to get Chamberlain, all right. Only, he had met Edith Prescott on the way. Art Dwyer didn't know what was said. He didn't know even if Edith had spoke to him at all. But anyway, all Pete Crabtree's good intentions had flopped like a calf hitting the end of the rope, so that he just let Chamberlain slide. Having seen Edith with all the life and color gone out of her face, but still the loveliest thing in the Frying Pan country, I could understand what had folded Pete up. It must have been an awful thing for Pete when it finally soaked through his head how bad his play had looked to everybody. And when he found out that not even Edith believed in him, I guess it took the starch out of him

183

altogether, so that he wasn't the same man at all as when he had taken Walt Hanrahan.

I didn't know at the time where Pete Crabtree spent the next two hours. Afterward, I found out that he'd just been skulking around, drinking fairly steady, and keeping out of people's way.

But at about ten o'clock a gun spoke somewhere in McTarnahan, and most of the town stopped to listen, and, as they listened, the gun spoke three times more, fast as a man could pull. And it wasn't fifteen minutes before the whole town had word of what had happened. Homer Chamberlain was dead.

I walked up the street toward Old Man Hepmeyer's rooming house, where Homer Chamberlain had been killed. There was a considerable crowd out in front by the time I got there. This house was a one-story affair, and people was tramping all around it and trying to look in the windows, and the room where Homer Chamberlain had been killed was all lighted up and full of men. And some was saying that any officer of the law who would shoot a man in the back through a window deserved to be strung up, and that, if McTarnahan had any men in it any more, by God, he *would* be strung up, and before sunup at that.

"Pete? Why pick on Pete?"

"Why, nobody could have done it but . . ."

"But just one of three men," I said.

"Three . . . ?"

"After all," I said, "this has turned out to be a pretty simple case. It shouldn't be any trouble at all to figure out which one of the three it was."

184

"Where do you get this three?" Art Dwyer demanded to know. "It looks to me like . . ."

I didn't hear what it looked to him like. I had opened the door and was looking up and down the street, and I didn't like what I seen there at all. Down in front of the sheriff's office a big crowd had gathered.

Art came to the door.

"Damn the day that made me deputy," he said real low, at last. "I don't mind going out to take a man the law wants, but this darn' thing . . ."

His voice trailed off. I never realized what a kid Art Dwyer was till I seen him looking so gray and scared.

"Come on," I said. He came trotting at my heels as I went down toward the sheriff's office at a running walk.

Doc Garrett stepped out in front of me, looking mighty serious. "Coffee," he said, "something terrible is going to happen here. I just want to say that if you and Art think of any way to keep order here, you can count on me."

"Good," I said, snapping him up quick. "If it comes to a fight, that adobe-walled house of yours is as good a stand-to as we could want. You and Art go on up there, and I'll bring Pete Crabtree. Hump, now!"

They hesitated a little bit, but after a minute or two they went.

I went on down to the sheriff's office, and wormed through the crowd. And I tell you, for a man that was not a part of it, that crowd was enough to make your blood run cold. They was set on getting Pete Crabtree.

I went straight into the sheriff's office. Crabtree was there, and he had Old Man Hepmeyer backed up in a chair, trying to pry out of him stuff that wasn't in him to start with. Pete was looking mighty anxious.

As I came in, he turned on me, savage. "Get out of here," he said, very barb wire, and I turned and got out.

Maybe I would have tried to reason with him, but it just then come to me that I'd started wrong end to. The one person who had been able to make all those free-hand changes in Pete Crabtree's life was the only one who had a chance of handling him now. So I broke into a dead run and set out to look for her.

I didn't have far to look. I had set out to see if she wasn't with old Mrs. Hepmeyer, but on the way I run into her hurrying along the walk.

"You got to do what I ask you, and do it quick," I told her. "If you don't, it's all up, that's all."

"What is it you want?" Edith said.

"Write a note to Pete," I said. "Tell him you're at Doc Garrett's house. Tell him to come there and come quick." She stood and looked at me for a minute. Then she took the pencil I gave her and did as I said.

"Now," I told her, "go there and be where you said you'd be. Wait! If and when Pete and I get there, you tell him to listen to me." She nodded, turned, and was gone.

The crowd had drawn in closer in front of the sheriff's office, and that droning, buzzing noise that a mob makes was louder now. I elbowed through, and pushed up to the sheriff's office again. Pete had the door locked this time, but I showed him Edith's note through the window, and he let me in.

"What's this now?" he snarled at me.

I let him read it for himself.

"All right," he said, "I'll go."

To get away from there we had to walk out through that mob. So we walked straight out, and it worked, partly because a mob is the slowest-thinking thing on earth. They didn't even follow us, right then. Yet, as I looked them over, it seemed to me it couldn't be more than a matter of minutes until hell would bust.

Edith Prescott and Doc Garrett and Art Dwyer were waiting for us in that little adobe-walled house of Doc's. As Pete met Edith Prescott's eye, he sort of bristled up. "What's the meaning of this?" he snapped at her.

"Pete," Edith said, "you're in an awful tight place. I want you to listen to Old Man Coffee."

He turned on me, looking like a buck deer that the dogs has brought to a stand.

"Son," I said, "I've certainly made it easy for you. Chamberlain was killed by one of two men. I can't say which it was. But, Pete, *you can*."

"Name them, then," he said.

I got out the little hunk of lead. "About an hour ago Art Dwyer come to me with this Thirty-Eight slug. According to Doc, here, it's one of the bullets that killed Chamberlain. Art's idea was to try to find out what gun this bullet come from, by comparing bullets through a microscope.

"Art Dwyer also had with him a gun. It was a Thirty-Eight gun, one that some folks thought had been used. We tried that first. Well, sir, this here bullet was from that same gun."

"Whose gun was it?" Crabtree demanded.

"Now naturally," I said, talking him down, "you'll ask how I know that Art Dwyer didn't kill Chamberlain. Because, after all, the next place anybody seen that gun, after the murder, was in Art Dwyer's hands. But look! If Art Dwyer had killed this man with this gun, would he make it his first act to get it proved that the death bullet come from that gun? I doubt it. Therefore, Art Dwyer didn't do it, and that answers your question."

"I didn't ask no such question," said Pete. "I asked whose gun it was!"

"Now you look here, Crabtree," I said. "We got you up here because it's your rightful place to solve this murder . . ."

"*Whose gun was it?*"

"It was your gun," I said.

When Pete finally spoke, I thought he was going to make a grab at me. "Are you accusing me?"

"I'm asking you where that gun was?"

"That gun was in my room . . . it couldn't possibly have killed that man. I heard the shots that killed Homer Chamberlain, and that Thirty-Eight was in my plain sight when I heard 'em!"

"That sure makes it very simple," I said.

"Simple? How does it make it simple?"

"Pete," I said, "I ask you one straight question, and then I'm through. Did you kill Homer Chamberlain?"

"I did not!" said Pete.

"And there you are," I said.

"And where is who?"

"No one," I said, "could have killed Homer Chamberlain except you or the one other feller. Well, if you didn't do it . . . what the hell! Go ahead and arrest the other guy."

"What other guy?"

"Do I have to draw a diagram? If this Thirty-Eight of yours isn't the one that killed Chamberlain, then this bullet that Doc Garrett offers us isn't the bullet that killed Chamberlain, either."

I was watching Doc Garrett out of the corner of my eye, but I couldn't read his face. It had a set look like a man who has played poker all night, but still don't aim to quit.

"You mean to say . . . ?"

"I don't know," I said, "where Doc Garrett got a bullet once fired from your gun. But how is it that Doc hands us a bullet from a gun that wasn't nowhere near the crime?"

There was one of them all-fired shaky quiet spells, and I heard a kind of a shuffling, trampling sound, like a herd of cattle coming in. The mob was on the move at last.

"I don't know the answer," I finished up. "Why would Doc make that switch? Unless . . . ?"

"Unless," said Crabtree, "he killed Chamberlain himself!"

I wasn't looking at Doc. I had my eyes on the floor where I could watch everybody's boots. By watching a man's feet, you catch his first move nearly as quick as if you're looking him in the eye, and you have the extra advantage that he doesn't know you are watching him so good as you are.

So it couldn't have been more than a fraction of a second after Doc Garrett went for his gun that I went for mine. Only, I didn't need it. One shot banged, and Doc Garrett's gun dropped on the floor beside his boots that I was watching, and, as I looked up, Doc was bent over, his left hand hanging onto his gun arm that Crabtree's shot had busted. Pete Crabtree's gun was smoking in his hand, and all that stubborn, steamed-up look had gone out of his face, and he was smiling as he looked at Doc.

Then, in the little quiet that followed, I heard that sound of walking in the street, so near and plain that you couldn't get away from it or shut it out, a hundred boot heels coming along the board walk, and three hundred more pairs of boots a-scuffling in the dust.

"In God's name, Pete," began Doc Garrett, "in God's name . . ."

"What?" said Pete.

"Don't ever turn me over to that crowd, Pete," Doc said. "That's all I ask. I swear, Pete, I never meant to hang it on you. I didn't suppose there was anybody around here had sense enough to compare a bullet with a gun. I picked up this bullet when you was shooting targets this morning. But all I was thinking was that it was a Thirty-Eight, and everybody knows I don't have a Thirty-Eight to my name. I swear to heaven, Pete, I never meant to hang it on you!"

"Doc," said Pete, "you killed Chamberlain."

190

Doc Garrett's long face had gone slack, but his eyes was like the bowls of lighted pipes.

"What if I did kill him?" he come out. "Didn't you hate him . . . didn't everybody hate him? I tell you, I knew that man! I knew him down to the ground. Why, over in Lords-town . . ."

There you had it! Folks always look for the man who has the nearest and the latest motive. They don't take into account that there may be twenty others who have stronger motives that everyone but themselves has forgot.

"Don't worry, Doc," Pete said. "I'll never turn you over to the mob."

Art Dwyer said: "Well, what are we going to do?"

For just a moment uncertainty came across Pete's face again. Quick as he was in action, when he knew what he ought to do, that slow brain of his was with him still.

Then Edith Prescott said: "You go out there, Pete."

Pete looked at her and nodded, sober and cool, but not scared or anxious any more. He put his gun in his holster and turned to the door. I blew out the light inside, and Pete opened the door and stepped out.

I heard a big growl go up in the street, and I tell you that was a terrible sound. Then the growl died away, and we heard Pete's voice, strong and slow. "Rollie Marshall," Pete said, "a hundred men can shoot to get me from where they stand. But, by God, Rollie, if it comes to that, I'm going to get me one man. And that one man is going to be you."

Right there I kind of relaxed and put away my gun. I don't know for sure if Marshall was the leader of that mob — I kind of think it didn't have any leader. But Marshall being who he was, and singled out by Pete, I knew the rest would wait to see what Rollie would do — and, of course, Rollie didn't want to die.

But the main thing was that the mob could see now they wasn't tackling the spirit-busted man they thought he was, but, instead, they had got hold of the same Crabtree that had took Hanrahan and the Gormsons. If Art Dwyer had tried to face down that mob, they would have shot him, and if I had tried it, they would have laughed at me and maybe rode me on a rail. But with Pete Crabtree back to life again, he could do more for himself than an army could, and the mob was done.

Out in front I heard Marshall say: "Crabtree, we can't let a killing like this pass by."

"There isn't anything going to be passed by," Pete said. "I've located the man that killed Chamberlain, and I've got the evidence against him, and I got his confession. The shot you heard just now was when I took him. I had to bust his arm when he drawed."

"Who is it?" somebody yelled in the crowd.

"You'll know who it is," Pete growled, "when I get ready to tell you. This is my prisoner, and I aim to handle him in my own way. If anybody thinks different . . . step out!"

It was all over. Pete Crabtree had played out his hand pretty good, I thought — once he had had his cards read to him.

I kind of straightened up and filled my chest with air. And I was fixing to look modest and kind of laugh it off, as I turned around to Edith Prescott. But she wasn't looking at me at all. She was at the window, looking out at where Pete Crabtree was putting on his little show. Dumb adoration. Yes, sir, that's the only name for the look on her face. Dumb adoration.

Still, why should a girl like she was waste them violet-colored eyes on a lion-hunting old rip pretty near a thousand years old? If Edith had not gone ahead and given the credit to Pete, I would have had to figure out some way to make her give him credit, wouldn't I? So, after all, once I thought it over, I was real tickled that it had worked out the way it done.

Broncho Fighter's Girl

Polly Collins sat on a corral fence in Las Cruces, looking at the rodeo stock, and many a young broncho rider found it hard not to stare at her discreditably. Her soft silver-dust hair, setting off her deep olive tan, and her dark, restless eyes always made the riders highly aware of her, whenever she had been among them. But just now she was happy — not blithely, but tremulously and uncertainly, and the new, gentle, entirely wistful radiance this gave her transformed her into something very lovely, so that they thought they must have forgotten what a honey she was, in the year that she had been away.

Polly herself could hardly believe it was really a year since she had last come out of these same saddling chutes raking a contest bucker, with the roar of the crowd curiously distant in her ears. Just now, on the eve of tomorrow's rodeo opening, the big grandstand was empty, and the arena was a deserted twenty acres, but around the cattle pens and the horse corrals was gathered a high-spirited bunch of thirty or forty people who would contest tomorrow — broncho men, bulldoggers, crack ropers, all living by their occasional

194

ability to win a year's pay in one day's ride. These she had known in many contests, in all parts of the West. Polly herself had ridden often against the half dozen girl riders who were there. No one had forgotten her. They waved hats at her, whooped greetings, sought her out to ask where she had hidden herself. It was like coming home.

She had come to Las Cruces on a last moment's impulse, and partly against her will. But now that she no longer concealed from herself why she had come, every remembered voice took on a new meaning, and became peculiarly stirring. She knew that Lee Macklin was somewhere here. Presently he would seek her out, as inevitably as dust settles to dust. And then the long, unhappy emptiness of the year in which they had been separated would be ended — perhaps.

For now she was ready to admit to herself — to him, too, if he asked it — that the barrier which she had raised between them was a foolish and trivial thing compared to her need for him and his need for her. A year ago, when she had finally turned back Lee Macklin's headlong lovemaking, she had had a stubborn belief in the fairness of her side of their quarrel. That belief was gone now, lost somewhere in the dreary vacancies of the empty year. The surrender was responsible for that new and unexpected happiness — a happiness made almost tearfully unsteady by the fact that she did not quite know whether or not she was wanted any more.

Lee Macklin, completely reckless, utterly carefree, living strictly in the moment, always gave the effect of

195

having the world by the tail and making the world like it. He was a lean, long-legged, blue-eyed humorist; his loose, lazy half-swagger concealed the muscular cordings of the rough-string horseman. You could hardly think of Lee Macklin separated from bronchos. Leather and dust, and bronchos and cows, those things had set the pace of his life — almost were Lee Macklin himself. If ever they wanted to put up a statue of the spirit of broncho fighting, it would have to be a statue of Lee Macklin.

These were things Polly Collins had tried to forget. Now, with the smells and sights and noises that represented Lee all around her, she knew completely, once for all, that the effort had been a foredoomed folly. Tears were very near her eyes, just from the knowledge that he was somewhere near, but she didn't care.

A hoarse whoop went up immediately below her, and big old Rowdy Kate Hutchinson hauled Polly off the fence to half crush her in an enthusiastic embrace. Old Rowdy Kate, big and clean and rough handed, was the nearest thing to a mother most of the rodeo girls had. When Kate's own riding days had ended, she had stayed in touch with the rodeo game by marrying Jake Hutchinson, owner of broncho strings, and no rodeo seemed the real thing without Rowdy Kate's familiar whoop and bawl.

"Glory be, child! I thought you'd lost yourself! You just got in, huh? I didn't see your name checked in at the hotel. Say . . . know where you're going to sleep?"

"I don't, Kate. Las Cruces is sure full up."

"Uh-huh. Well . . . I was splitting a room with Rose Moran, but she run out on me. So I guess that fixes you up. Don't thank me! 'S pleasure! Seen Lee Macklin yet?"

"Well, no, Kate."

"That's funny. Still, of course, you just now got in. You all set to do them gals out of first money?"

"I'm not even going to ride. No," — as Kate's laughter boomed — "I mean it, Kate."

"Well, child, it's all right with me. There ain't many of your age has twisted as many cayuses as you have. How old are you, honey? Going on twenty-two? Uh-huh. And how many first moneys did I hear you had . . . ten in three years, was it? I'd give something to know why you quit the game!"

"I don't know, Kate. It looked to me for a while there as if broncho fighting was just a racket for wasting good cow folks. The boys that start in are the cream of the crop, then pretty soon they slip, and get punk . . . and they're all through."

"Like Lee Macklin," said Kate, looking at her.

Polly Collins's eyes were dreaming into the dust that drifted through the poles of the broncho corrals. If she had been looking at Kate, perhaps she would have got more out of that last remark. But she nodded. "The cream of the crop."

Rowdy Kate grunted and looked at Polly curiously. "Well, I'll say one thing for him . . . he ain't so much as looked at another girl since you gave him the gate."

"Kate," said Polly, "are you . . . you wouldn't tell me that if it wasn't so?"

Rowdy Kate studied her. "Oh, that much of it's O K. Well, say, most likely he'd come over here and answer the rest of the questions himself, if I'd flog out of the picture."

Polly said in a weak voice: "Kate, is he . . . is he here?"

"Heck, don't you even know him when you see him? He's right over there, talking to Jake."

Polly Collins turned and followed Kate's glance. And the year that she had let slip out of their lives turned on her and took its revenge, cruelly, all in a moment for which she was unprepared.

You could hardly say, first off, just how Lee Macklin had changed. He was still tall and lean and careless-looking, and though he had not shaved that day, that was true of half the cowboys there. Some might not even have seen the difference in him at first. But Polly saw it instantly, in that first glance, and her breath held still for a moment, exactly as if the head of a rearing horse had struck between her eyes. Something was missing, so that the whole picture of the man had a different meaning. She had looked for a swaggering youngster who had the world by the tail, and, instead, she saw a man who was tired, unhopeful, and — licked.

For a moment she could not even believe that this was Lee. She turned to where Rowdy Kate had stood. "Kate! That isn't . . . ?"

Then Lee Macklin turned and caught her eye. He hesitated, then came across the corral to her slowly, not swaggering, but with a sort of hitch in his walk that might have been the ghost of his swagger.

198

"Hello, Polly."

She heard herself answer — "Hello Lee." — and her voice sounded even and natural. But she felt faint and dizzy, as if she might possibly be going to fall. This was not Lee Macklin. This man that looked like Lee and answered to Lee's name was just another lanky, unshaved cowboy, reminiscent of what used to be called the malaria school. And though he grinned at her slowly, as he used to do, no trace of the old irrepressible humor was there.

He met her gaze steadily, and his eyes were the eyes of a man who looks at something fine — that he has long ago got used to thinking will never be his. "Sure have missed you from the pitchings," he said. "You aim to ride tomorrow, Polly?"

"No, I hadn't figured to ride."

"Well, you're wise, I guess. Not much in it these days, taking it all around. I . . . well . . . I'll be seeing you." He grinned again, without humor, not meeting her eyes this time, then crawled through the fence and moved on.

He had come, and he had gone. He left her with a swelling lump in her throat, and a dazed bewilderment before her eyes. Polly turned from the corral, found her car, and drove back to town, not radiant any more.

She was waiting for Kate in the room Kate had offered to share with her when Kate came in at half past eleven that night.

"Why wasn't you over at the dance, child? You sick? You look like the wrath of God!"

"Kate . . . what's happened to Lee Macklin?"

"Who? Oh, him."

"Kate! You've got to tell me! Something has . . ."

"Easy, honey. Sit down quiet, here on the bed. What's got into you?"

"*What's happened to Lee Macklin?*"

"Him? Why, he's had a kind of a bum year, I guess. What do you care?"

"What do I care? I care a lot."

"He's just proved out you were right, that's all."

"That I was right?"

"You sure knew what you was doing when you wouldn't tie yourself up to no common broncho fighter. Short hoss, soon curried. That's the average broncho rider, all right. And that's Lee Macklin."

"But how . . . how could . . . ?"

"Well, while you was away from things, Lee went down here to Tucson and got himself bucked down by a new hoss, name of Black Powder, and that was about all from *him*. He hasn't amounted to a hoot since."

"Do you mean . . . he was smashed up and can't . . . ?"

Kate's voice rose in an end of patience. "I mean he went yellow, that's what I mean! What's left of a broncho rider when he loses his guts? Nothing!"

Polly Collins's eyes blazed. "I don't believe it!"

"You don't believe what?"

"No such thing could happen," Polly said furiously. "Lee never quit in his life . . . he couldn't quit, he doesn't know how . . . not if they killed him!"

"Don't take my word for it, honey. Take a look!"

"I *will* take a look. And he'll show you you're wrong! Lee . . ."

"All right, honey, all right." Kate stood up and stretched. "They'll be drawing for their hosses pretty soon here. You feel good enough to come see them draw?"

Polly snapped to her feet. "You bet your life I'm coming to see them draw. And I'm praying to heaven that Lee Macklin gets a good tough horse. If he does, you'll see him make fools of them all!"

Rowdy Kate sighed and looked sad. "All right, honey."

At Las Cruces the rodeo runs three days. The broncho men draw for their qualifying horses at midnight, on the eve of the first day. Polly Collins had taken part in such midnight drawings over and over again, but not even the first drawing she had ever made had seemed more important to her than this drawing tonight, as she waited to see what horse would fall to Lee Macklin. On this horse he would make the first ride she had seen him make in a year.

The forty or fifty crack contest hands lounged about the big room in disorderly bunches. Polly Collins glanced over them, her eyes avoiding those which always sought her face. She located Lee Macklin, standing against the wall, talking to Bob Kennedy. After that, she prevented herself from looking at him again.

Jake Hutchinson, his big leather-seamed face genially ugly, got up to sit sideways on the edge of a table and shout at the buckaroos: "Hey, listen, you bronc' fighters! The Matagordas buckskin is off the contest list. Some of you seen him kill Dutch Iverson here last year. Matagordas ain't been in a chute since. But there's twenty-five bucks extra for anybody that wants to ride him for a special exhibition!"

For a moment a touch of cool chill took Polly Collins's mind away from the reason she was there. Dutch Iverson had turned and grinned at her just before Matagordas had bawled and come out, beginning Iverson's last ride. The buckskin was a killer, a tromper. It had been a terrible thing to see Dutch die under the crazed beast's hoofs. Though it was partly coincidence that she had not ridden since, the death of Dutch had been the last straw, the last word in her case against broncho riding as a profession.

She forgot that, though, as the drawing began. By twos and threes the broncho twisters slouched up to Jake Hutchinson's table to draw from the hat. Polly waited, hardly patient. She was hoping with all her heart that Lee Macklin would get a horse that no one else could ride, a horse on which he could show them all. Perhaps there was desperation in that hope, she so wanted to believe that what she had heard was not true.

Because he had entered late, Lee Macklin drew almost the last of all, but he finally strolled forward. For a moment or two, when Lee had drawn, there was a confused muddle around Jake's table, so that she called out to Jake: "Is this a private drawing? Sing out, will you!"

"Lee Macklin draws Black Powder!"

A fierce thrill momentarily possessed Polly Collins. The same thrill she had always known whenever she had watched Lee draw a hard-fighting horse — one that could win for him.

The new horse, Black Powder, had been ridden only once this season — and it was his first season. And it was Black Powder that had bucked down Lee Macklin himself at Tucson. Not everyone would have wanted Black Powder, but Lee Macklin would want him. She knew he would want him!

And then — she saw Lee Macklin quit. Casually, without expression, as he might have thrown in a poker hand, he turned in his slip and withdrew from the contest.

From the back of the room, near the door, Polly stared at him, but he did not meet her eye, and she could not read his face. Then she got out of there, and made her way back to the hotel through the ruin of a world.

She found Rowdy Kate Hutchinson in their room.

"Kate! . . . it's true! He *has* gone yellow! He drew Black Powder, and he folded up and quit like . . . like . . ."

"Uh-huh . . . I know. Poor child! Don't stand there staring like you was out on your feet. Sit down!" Kate forcibly removed Polly from her position against the wall and planted her in a chair. "Gosh, child, I never realized you was so plumb batty. Why, you must actually *love* that guy!"

"I suppose . . . I'll always love him."

"Well, he was certainly nuts about you. How come you to get split up so?"

"I don't know, Kate. I . . . I wanted him to quit broncho riding. I didn't see any future in it. I wanted him to make something of himself."

"And he allowed he'd decide them things himself?"

"It kind of seemed that way. But I think now . . . Kate, I think he would have quit the contests in a second, knowing the way I felt."

"Then why didn't he?"

"I didn't understand it then. But I think now that he just felt that was a commercial kind of thing for me to be specifying, in a love affair. I know that he would have wanted me, even if I insisted on spending my life as . . . as a sheep shearer. And I think it kind of hurt him that I didn't seem to feel the same way about him. And then I got stubborn."

"Well, it's too bad. But he's sure proved you was right."

"But to see him fold up and quit . . . Kate, it seems like it's more than I can bear."

Kate snorted cigarette smoke. "Well, it's over with now. There's nothing you can do, and you might as well . . ."

"No, it isn't over with. I can snap him out of it yet. I'll snap him out of it if it's the last . . ."

"And how," said Kate cynically, "is this to be done?"

"I'll show you how it's to be done! I'll do it, and you'll help me. Kate, I'm going to ride Black Powder!"

Kate stared at her without comprehension. "Who, you? When is this? *You* can't ride Black Powder!"

"Kate, you're going to fix it . . . for tomorrow, as a special exhibition. You run Jake, and Jake runs the bronchos. Don't tell me you can't fix it! You can . . ."

Rowdy Kate looked flabbergasted. "And what if I could? You think I want you killed? That hoss is green apples! This isn't the old Powder. This is the new black, right in his first prime, an', boy, he smashes 'em down in a cloud of dust!"

Polly's eyes burned with a dogged fire. "What if I'm bucked down? I've been bucked down more times than there are stickers in a salt bush. But I tell you, if I come out of the chute on Black Powder, that broncho is going to get the raking over of his life."

Unquestionably Rowdy Kate was set back. She sat for a long time blowing smoke through her nose and staring at Polly Collins. At last she said gently: "Child, maybe it might be done. Maybe there's things that can so shame a man that he'd rather take a quick die in any shape than go on as he was. I expect maybe you've got hold of one of them things. But, child, leave old Kate tell you something else. You realize that if you do this to him, he'll hate you for it . . . hate you till the hour he dies?"

"Kate," Polly said, "it's the least I can do for him . . . maybe all in the world I ever can do for him."

"And make him hate . . . ?"

"I know."

"And what," said Kate softly, "if I won't play?"

Polly Collins seized both Kate's arms above the elbow. Polly had slim, wire-hard fingers that could snap tight a latigo and tie it quicker than a man's, and

205

Kate flinched. "You've got to! You've got to fix it! I'll never . . ."

Suddenly the tears flooded Polly's eyes and ran down her cheeks, and she hid her face on Kate's Amazonian breast.

Old Rowdy Kate gathered Polly into her arms. "'S all right, honey. It's murder, maybe. But I'll fix it up."

Polly Collins spent a long night, and an even longer morning. She arrived at the rodeo arena only at the last moment and, having arrived, managed as well as she could to stay apart and alone. She was hoping against hope not to meet Lee Macklin face to face.

For an hour she evaded him. They were running off the calf roping before, inevitably, he finally managed to corner her.

"Howdy, Polly."

"Hello, Lee." It was queer to see his blue gaze filled with grave concern. He was shaved now, and he looked taller and leaner and almost as competently leathery as she had ever seen him look. But nowhere in his face was there any sign of the old reckless humor, so that he was a stranger still, and it brought the same nagging lump into her throat again.

"Polly," he said, "I just got out from town. I didn't realize until just now that you somehow fixed it to ride this Black Powder. Polly, that's the craziest fool thing I suppose I ever heard of, up to now. You can't ride that horse!"

She said almost inaudibly: "Are you telling me what I can and can't ride?"

"Look here, Polly, I know that brute. I've been on him!"

"And off him?"

"And off him." Lee nodded. "I never rode a horse that's got the plain, hard power that he has . . . and I've rode them all."

She said oddly: "You used to ride them all."

He didn't notice. "Black Powder's been ridden, and he'll be ridden again. Montana Bill rode him, before Black Powder ever saw a rodeo. But Montana Bill can't sit a horse at a common wolf trot today . . . and never will again."

She said hotly: "If you think that's the sort of thing I go by . . ."

He interrupted her. "I know you can ride, but a woman isn't built for a smashing like that. There's lots of good tough men that aren't built to ride that horse and come out sound."

"And there's others . . ." — there was a tremor in her voice, but her eyes were full of sparks — "there's others wouldn't stay it through to find out if they could."

He stared at her, and slowly all expression left his face, except for his eyes, which were bewildered. "You mean . . . why, look here . . . you mean . . . ?"

"You know what I mean, I think," she said. A bitter smile twisted her mouth crookedly, even while her lips quivered. She looked him straight in the eyes.

"Dear God," said Macklin. "I . . . I thought you at least knew me well enough so . . ."

She turned and broke away, unable to meet his eyes any longer, and headed for the chutes almost at a run.

The broncho riding was already beginning, and the loudspeakers were blaring that Gil Strick was coming out on Misfortune. In the program the women riders would be interspersed among the men. Black Powder might be hazed into the chute for her any minute.

She went off and found a secluded spot among some bales of hay, where Bob Kennedy finally found her. His moon face was tough and dogged. "You're as good as murdering this boy . . . you hear me?"

"Murdering who?"

"You know damned well who. If Lee rides Matagordas . . ."

"Wait a minute! If who rides who?"

"Lee has took them up on that special ride proposition. The announcer's pretty near crazy over the whoopee he's going to make about it. Cowboy will attempt to avenge his old pal by riding out the horse that last year killed Dutch . . ."

A queer, mixed emotion swept through Polly Collins. The death of Dutch Iverson was an enduring nightmare, and she despised the everlasting showmanship that seized upon his death for exploitation. But there was still a deep, sure thrill to the news that Lee Macklin was coming back to ride, unafraid to tackle anything that bucked.

But Bob Kennedy was rushing ahead. "I promised Lee to keep my trap shut. But you run him into this, and you got to haul him back out of it. If he rides . . ."

"Sure he'll ride!" She was suddenly exultant, blind to danger in the blessed thrill of believing that Lee was coming back — coming back like a cyclone that nothing could stop. "I know I drove him into it! And I know he'll hate me for it. But I'm glad! You hear . . . I'm glad!"

Bob Kennedy stared at her, his stolid moon face incredulous, astounded. "You don't know what you're saying," he decided. "You don't know . . ."

"I . . ."

Bob Kennedy took her by the shoulders, shook her once, and glared into her face. "You don't know," he growled at her again. "Lee . . . he's hurt. He's hurt bad."

"He . . . he's what? He's . . . ?"

"Lee's all smashed up inside. Nobody knows how bad he's smashed up . . . he won't even let them examine him right."

"But . . ."

"Powder done it, at Tucson. I had to talk like hell to get him to scratch off last night when he got the same horse again!"

"But then, how is it they can let him . . . ?"

"They don't know, I tell you!"

"But . . ." Polly's stare was dazed, bewildered.

"Last month," Bob was running on, "he was half killed by that roan cayuse, Bald Hornet, and the broncho never come halfway unwound. He liked to passed out on me when I was driving him back to town. All that night I was up with him, keeping hot packs all over his left side, and him whiter than my hat."

"In God's name, Bob . . ."

209

"The way Lee is now, not fit to ride a buckboard . . . look here! You done this! If Lee follows Dutch, it'll be on you, you hear me?"

"Bob . . . oh, dear heaven . . . Bob, you've got to stop him!"

"Who? Me? *I* can't stop him."

"Go to Jake Hutchinson . . ."

"I've been to Jake. He won't step in except on a doctor's say so. The only doctor Lee has let lay hands on him is in Tucson, and Lee won't tell what he said. You've got to stop him yourself!"

Polly Collins turned dizzy and sick. She dropped her face to her hands again, covering her eyes with those slender, wire-hard fingers. "Go away," she said. "Leave me alone a minute! I'll try . . . but . . ."

"But hell! *Right now, damn it!* For all I know they're putting Matagordas in the chute."

"All right . . . I know. But I got to figure a minute how to work it. Just a minute more."

"Well . . . pour leather into it! I'll go see if I can fix up any mix-ups and delays."

Polly Collins tried to steady herself and think it out. The judges, she knew, wouldn't take time now to call a physical exam on the demand of some wild-eyed girl. She had to go to Lee. She had to.

The loudspeakers were calling: "Chute Number One . . . Lee Macklin coming out on . . ."

Polly jumped like a quirted colt. Across the hay bales she could see the heavy barriers of the chutes, cowboys clustered along the top rails like roosting *paisanos*. The Yuma Kid was straddling Chute Number One. She saw the heave of his back as he jerked upward, tightening the bucking strap. His arms flipped up to signal *ready* — and he climbed out of the way. The lean, careless figure of Lee Macklin swung over the gate slowly, eased into the saddle. She heard the resounding crack of hoofs on wood as Matagordas let drive at the chute walls with his forefeet.

Polly Collins ran for the chutes. "Lee . . . for God's sake! *Hold up!*"

Nobody seemed to hear her. She sprang up the side of the chute. "Hold that gate! Lee . . ."

The gate was swinging. It opened slowly, as things move in a slow-motion movie, or a fever dream. Matagordas seemed to stand, as bronchos sometimes do, not aware that the wall is gone. No — he was leaning, rolling out of the chute, gathering for that first whirling jump. He swayed off balance for the jump — still slowly, all in slow motion. Polly reached out and tried to catch hold of Lee's shoulder, but her own hand was in slow motion, too.

Lee Macklin's face turned toward her, expressionless except for a faint surprise. She caught the quick flash of his grin. Then Matagordas jumped.

Watching that ride was like nothing Polly Collins had ever experienced before. She had watched a thousand rides, made scores of such rides herself, and perhaps that was why she could see and understand every detail of what was happening now. And the horrible effect of slow motion went on, so that she could miss no gather and release of the muscles of the fighting buckskin horse, no least movement of the man in the saddle.

211

And the Matagordas horse could fight. He was a horse that knew no tricks or twists — he never sunfished or shook himself or whirled to unbalance the rider. He was a horse like Black Powder, letting go a blind, squalling explosion of nerves and a thousand pounds of hard horseflesh at the job of putting the rider down by sheer smash of impact. It seemed to Polly that the Matagordas buckskin was not made of flesh and bone, nothing but steel — heavy machinery broken wild under the drive of steam — could achieve this savagery of abrupt, unloosed force.

Lee Macklin was riding as hardly anybody but Lee ever could ride. It was beautiful, in its own way. Ordinarily you only see a rider jerking crazily on top of a horse that pitches and thrashes in the midst of dust, but that awful effect of slow motion that was upon Polly made plain the flex and play of muscle, the beautiful swing of balance, the accurate swift placement of spurs. Lee Macklin rode with muscles loose and free, in an incredible unity with the explosive battling of the horse. And he was scratching, scratching on every jump. He could have ridden tight and saved himself, maybe, at least given himself a chance, but he rode as he always rode, free swinging and reckless, his spurs raking from neck to flank.

Dutch Iverson had been killed on the ground, but Polly knew that, before Dutch left the saddle, he had been blind and dazed, perhaps knocked out altogether. And now she knew the exact moment when the lights went out for Lee Macklin. As surely as if she had been in the saddle herself, she sensed by his slack, dull swing

212

the instant that the ride was ended, for all Lee Macklin knew.

The long-experienced vinegaroon, who had ridden them all, suddenly shouted: "Gosh, what a *horse!*"

Somehow Lee still rode, skillful muscles still fighting by habit in the dark. She saw Matagordas snap him like a rope.

The pickup men were answering the whistle at last. Bob Kennedy, who always rode pickup for Lee, was coming up on Matagordas with the fastest pony he had been able to borrow. He got an arm about the rider and hauled him bodily out of the saddle. He pulled up his horse and lowered Lee to the ground as he swung down. Macklin lay quiet in the dust.

Polly Collins swung a leg over the chute bars. She was starting to run across the field to Lee Macklin. Then the strength went out of her. What little could be done, there were plenty of others to do, a hundred ready hands at Lee's service now. The one thing that only she could have done was past and over with. She had been the only one in the world whose job it was to stop that ride, and she had missed out.

Up in the hospital, the room where they had Lee Macklin was cool and shadowy, very quiet. Polly could feel the desert-country grit of the arena in her fine, soft hair, and it made her feel out of place in that clean room, with its smell of formaldehyde and ether. But she was happy, for Lee knew her now and was glad that she was there, and they let her stay.

They were going to operate on him, but it was going to be all right. Maybe he would never ride again, but even so the quiet and the reassurance were like spring coming on, after what they had had before that. Lee had raved deliriously for an hour — knocked cuckoo, just plain knocked cuckoo — before they even found out what he was raving about. He had been obsessed with the idea that Polly was about to ride Black Powder! She had forgotten about Black Powder.

After that, they had let her in, and Lee had come around all right. And now she sat beside him, and he held both her hands in one of his. They didn't talk much. Lee was supposed to keep his mouth shut.

Only, he finally said: "I don't care whether you like it or not. But somebody has to stick around and keep an eye on you. Seems like nobody has been taking care of that since you turned me out on the free range. I never seen anybody so crazy reckless. You got no more notion of taking care of yourself than a new colt. From here out I aim to stand by and ride circle on you, and I aim to keep it up until you get somebody that suits you better to take my place."

Polly marveled. He might have taken the words right out of her mouth, so accurately they fitted the thought that was running in her head. How was it that he couldn't see he was the crazy, reckless one, whom someone had to ride circle on? You could hardly dare leave him out of your sight, lest he dive headlong into his come-uppance. He had no more notion of how to take care of himself than a — but those were his words.

214

"Whether you like it or not," he said again, doggedly. She bent her head, and pressed her eyes against his hand. "I guess I can make out to put up with it, Lee."

The Young Rush In

With twilight it began snowing in soft, broad flakes, salting the dark backs of the cattle. Daylight blurred out slowly, leaving behind it that odd luminous quality that night is sometimes given by a sheeted moon and the almost phosphorescent snow. The crawling dusk had a curious electric feel, a subtle, edgy warning, in spite of the stillness: the sort of thing felt before a thunderstorm sometimes, or at sea when the barometer is dropping unaccountably in the midst of a calm.

Whiskers Beck felt the unrest in the twilight as he stood hugging his sheepskin coat about him on the cañon's low rim. From there his keen old blue eyes squinted down into the bedding ground of the eight hundred white faces, a hundred feet below. He was tired, for he had worked hard in the cold, and he was old, but that odd expectancy in the air kept him from wanting to sit down.

The cattle felt it, too. He could see that. They should have been grazing, or trying to, for, although the drive had been slow, they had picked up very little forage on the way. Instead, they stood quietly, heads downcañon, in a too compact mass. Only here and there a few had

216

drawn off to tear at the scant thicket along the foot of the rock walls.

The old cowboy clawed at the ice in his white beard, wondering what they had better do in place of circle riding tonight. It was Beck's religion that virtue lay not so much in how well you did a thing as in how easily you did it well enough. The cattle were dog tired and hemmed in by the cañon walls. Three more miles of widening cañon were ahead before the cut lost itself on the prairie. Whiskers was badly tempted to mount no rider at all. Still . . . old man Rutherford, for whom they rode, was in a corner again. When he had got his full beef herd to the railroad, he had found himself without cattle cars — a circumstance foreseen but unavoided. He had been obliged to sell at a loss. The winter hay he must have was not available on his shaken credit.

He had cattle cars waiting for him now, enough cars for two or three brands. The cattle were not in them. The critters were strung out over their winter range; the ponies were scattered into the hills; the cowboys paid off and departed. To buck this bleak situation three remaining riders had set out to get a herd for those cars. And Whiskers Beck, after almost sixty years spent in avoiding that contingency, was boss.

For three men the rounding up of the cattle, strong from the summer's forage and wild from the fall roundup, had been a long, tough race against the day when the cars would wait no more. Holding the growing herd, necessarily a one-man job, had been harder yet — it would have been impossible in the day of the Sonora longhorns. The long circle rider peeled a pessimistic eye and offered fervid, blasphemous prayers. And cutting the herd, so that chiefly beef steers of their own brand should take the trail to market, had been hardest of all.

It had been a monstrous, Herculean labor for those three men. There are cattlemen who will tell you it should have been easy; there are others who will tell you it could not have been done. Under the particular combination of conditions, it was just possible, and that was all. Somehow, they had wangled through, proud that they were the boys who could tackle such a job and make it stick, too proud of their own abilities to offer other comment than complaint. Later they would tell about their feat, casually, with ever-increasing figures: "I mind once me an' two other fellers went out to get a winter beef herd, an' we picked up three, four thousand head . . ."

But if they lost another half day now, there would be nothing to tell. The cars would be missed, and their labors lost, reduced to a futile ramming about that accomplished nothing. Whiskers guessed, after all, that they would have to sit up with the cows.

Squirty Wallace, wiry little top hand, came to stand beside Whiskers on the edge of the bluff. Wrapped to the eyes in his sheepskin coat, his swerving legs in winter chaps, he looked like a big cocoon, mounted on the two halves of a furry barrel hoop. He had opinions of his own about working cattle, but he kept them to himself, lest they happen to be more exacting than orders from some other source.

218

"Tomorrow," said Whiskers Beck, "we'll prod along right smart, an' aim to make Apricot Creek. Next day we'll have to go slower, but we'll hit Spring River all right, about eight o'clock at night, an' shove right into the corrals an' feed hay. An' then is when three hired men take a rest."

Below in the gathering chill dark the cattle stood motionless, oddly quiet. There was no breeze; you could about hear the settling of the snow. The men kept listening, expecting to hear, perhaps, the munch of the grazing ponies off somewhere in the gloom. At regular intervals one lone calf blatted dismally, separated from its ma. It had no business there, in this beef cut, but that could not be helped now.

Behind Whiskers sounded the steady drone of Dixie Kane's voice as he cooked supper. The young broncho peeler crouched gracefully by his frying pan, his high, thin nose catching the firelight like the back of a knife. He wore a black and white Navajo coat, belted close about his slim body with a broad leather strap.

"That's the *young* feller of it," Dixie was saying, evidently under the delusion that Squirty Wallace still stood beside him. "Never figurin' the cost. Old fellers keep thinkin' about the time some onion got the saddle horn through him . . . they see his eyes rollin' 'round, an' the blood runnin' out through his teeth. Young fellers figure different. Take me. *I* never think about cost . . . don't even come into my head. Me, I'm jumpin' into hell an' high water, gettin' the work done. Why . . ."

Whiskers Beck repressed a snarl. "We'll ride circle same as usual," he said loudly, so Dixie would hear him and shut up. "Though o' course there ain't nothin' to do but set around at the lower end, this time, I know you been thinkin', mebbe them cattle would stay put, an' I think the same. But I got a phony feelin'. An' we ain't goin' to take any chances now, an' mebbe miss out. So, Squirty, you stay up to eleven o'clock, an' I'll take the graveyard miserableness until two, an' then it's mornin', insofar as Mister D. Kane is concerned. An' about two, three hours before daylight, here we come."

The snow muffled sound so that, even when they raised their voices, they seemed to be speaking in hushed tones.

"What's the idea?" demanded Squirty Wallace hotly. Ordinarily he moved and spoke with a low calm, but the nerves of the three were worn and jangling now. "The cows won't run out on us . . . an' steers don't stampede in a cañon."

"That's nice," said Whiskers noncommittally.

"Say!" yelped Dixie Kane. "What yuh think us fellers is made outta?"

"Glass," said Whiskers. "An' right here's somethin' else. Ever'body keep a horse tight saddled, right close. If they kin be rid tight an' live, I guess they kin stand tight for once. Now listen, riffraff. You know this here gully . . . she makes a hook up here a piece, an' curves about three miles. But there's a short cut here through the timber. It comes out on the cañon again in about a mile and a half, at a place we used to call the

220

Stepladder. You mind the Stepladder! *Dixie, you mind the Stepladder?*"

"*Ya-as!*" yelled Dixie with sarcastic emphasis.

"The cañon's pretty deep right there. But it can be got down in at the Stepladder. The shortcut will make up the ground we'll lose gettin' started, an' we kin plunk down in ahead o' the rumpus. So's we'll be out in front when we come to a place where we kin mill 'em, instead o' bein' behind an' scarin' 'em along. You hear?"

They heard. "You make me sick," said Squirty under his breath. Whiskers let it pass.

They ate wolfishly, in silence. Squirty mounted, and his pony started down into the cañon with little unwilling steps, like a cat hating the snow. Whiskers Beck retied his muffler over his bald head and rolled into his blankets under a runty piñon pine.

For a few moments he let his mind turn to smoking food and plenty of it, a bed with hay under it in the weather-tight bunkhouse of the Triangle R, and men tired but comfortable, who hardly spoke except to give something a humorous twist, so that they were better than a show. Only the weather fighters — riders, loggers, seamen — know the deep, keen savor of these plain things, just as only desert men know the sweetness of water. Food, warmth, laughter, a long postponed smoke — they are the things a man remembers after the bitternesses are gone.

"All right, midnight," he growled to himself. "I'm ready."

It seemed as if Whiskers Beck never pulled his head under the blankets without it instantly being time to get up. He did not know how long he had slept. He awoke on his elbow, listening with every nerve, while the frozen air quickly stiffened the moisture in his nostrils. Only an instant, while his ears confirmed what his unconscious mind had known! From the cañon came an increasingly ominous shuffle, swiftly rising to a murmur, a rumbling groan. *Wham!* spoke Squirty's pistol, a heavy, muffled jolt. *Wham!* His long yell shrilled through the rising mutter of hoofs.

One gnarled and buckskinned hand jammed Whiskers's hat down over his ears, the other had already found the reins where he had laid them over a piñon limb. His pony stood head up, snorting.

"Easy, boy," said Whiskers, "plenty time." He put the reins over the horse's head, mounted stiffly, and they wheeled.

They started off through the scraggly timber at a light lope, Beck holding the pony in. That cantering gait gave the blood time to start in the pony's cold legs, made him watch where he put his feet among rocks and logs half concealed and slippery under the snow. Whiskers noticed that the snowfall had stopped, that there was a dim light of moon through the clouds.

Behind them, over the ashes of the dead fire, the dark, confused figures of a man and horse whirled and reared. Dixie, who had made a sleepy rush and grab, was still trying to mount. His violent voice, excited to desperation, rang through the trees: "Haar! Stand down, you dirty . . ."

They dodged through the timber in easy bounds, leaping windfalls and brush. Five minutes, going on ten, while they drove steadily up grade. The pony blew a long, thrumming breath and took to the full gallop; it seemed almost as if he knew both the work and the trail. The blood began to course in Whiskers's arteries, waking him up. He could hear Dixie's pony crashing through the brush, a long way back and coming hard. But mostly he listened to that long mutter of the running herd. It was almost a mile away now in the bend of the cañon, but it filled the night with a distant, low roar, like a mighty wind far away. It had reached its ebb and was coming slowly nearer again, rising almost imperceptibly as the timber thinned, the drum of hoofs that must at all cost be stopped.

Whiskers put the pony into a sprint. He spoke to the horse in short yelps — "Hip! . . . Hip!" — gradually stringing him up, getting the speed without breaking that quick, clever placing of feet that kept them bounding over the tricky ground. "Hip . . . Hip!" One more rise, a break in the timber, an avoided gully — the Stepladder was a hundred yards ahead. The earthly rumble of the herd sounded close, stronger . . . stronger, a steady slow increase. He thought he could distinguish the click of horns.

Whiskers drew down the gait. In the dim light of clouds and snow he picked the landmarks at the drop of the trail — a dead lodgepole pine, with a fir tree by its side. They came hammering to the brink, hesitated, the pony's head down to pick its footing for the first jump — and the pony suddenly squatted on quivering haunches, and stopped.

Something turned over inside Whiskers Beck. His mouth partly opened, and the upper lip sucked in under his teeth. Something had happened to the Stepladder — if this was it. Where once had been a steep, barely passable zigzag trail, a footing for goat-like ponies, there now opened before the man and horse what looked to be a sheer drop, not perpendicular, but to all purposes so. The eye fell away into the dark below, found a little projection of stone that might have been footing or might not, then on down, lost in the little light, with no further suggestion of anything to break the fall. Two hundred feet to the bottom and, at the bottom, the rocks.

The shock of failure, no less than the swift vertigo of the drop before him, sent a quick whirl of sickness to Beck's head. This passed, and he slumped in his seat, feeling suddenly the accumulated weariness of his saddle years.

For a long moment he sat there, alone with his defeat, while the pony waited, quivering, and the night was alive with that rising moan of hoofs, like a voice from the deep throat of the cañon itself.

He did not hear Dixie Kane racing up until man and pony came alongside with the stiff bounding hops that a horse uses to check a thousand pounds of galloping bone and flesh and leather.

"This it?" yelled Dixie. The open mouth of the pony turned upward as it struggled to swerve this way or that from the brink, with a great stuttering of hoofs.

"I guess it is," said Whiskers.

Dixie's quirt slapped, and his pony sprang crouching to the edge. With a great shock Whiskers saw that Dixie was going to take the plunge.

He tried to yell to him, but it was already too late. The horse put its head low over the edge, its hindquarters squatting — far down the wall with braced, curving forelegs, trying to shorten by a length that ugly drop, then for an instant seeming to check, fighting gravity, as if it would have pulled back.

That moment seemed an hour, while man and horse toppled forward slowly, slowly — though no more than a second elapsed. Whiskers saw Dixie lengthen his reins, holding high the end of the swinging loop, so that the horse had a free head. He sat straight up, lithe and slim, apiece with the brute. Then over they dived — snatched out of sight as if a great hand had jerked the horse over the edge of the world.

Whiskers, bending forward, saw the horse strike once and bound sidewise, far down, in a high flurry of snow, then man and horse disappeared, catapulting over a bulge of the drop. The searing air returned to Whiskers's lungs. As the first shock of his astonishment passed, his feeling was that of a crushing mortification and disgrace. He somehow did not doubt that Dixie would make it to the bottom. He only saw that he had sat there, old and beaten, fearful to go on, while the younger man had gone slashing over, unfaltering, into the face of the impossible. He heard Dixie's words again, a bitter though unintended taunt. "Young fellers figure different . . . I never think about the cost . . ."

Two hundred yards away, at the hook of the cañon, the first cattle came streaking around the shoulder of the bluff, black against the snow like big flies. He made out Squirty Wallace, galloping hard ahead of the herd, and to one side.

An insane rage came into Whiskers Beck, a rage at the precipice, a rage at the long, grinding years that slowly bent a man, holding him up at the last a fool and a drag, shamed by the younger men. He had been a top hand before Dixie Kane was born.

"Old and beat," he muttered. "No, by gad!"

He struck the spurs into the horse, uncaring whether he lived or died. Over the edge they dropped, down and down in a roaring slide of stone and snow. An upstriking ledge ripped at his left chap, and his stomach jumped against his throat as the cañon floor rushed up to meet them. Only a moment of it — a bound, a carom, half up and down again — and it was over! Miraculously they swung in beside Squirty and his horse, at the head of the stampeding parade. Afterward, when they pointed out the scene of that mad descent, the descent that no horse had a right to make and live, listeners believed Dixie, but not Whiskers, for Dixie had broken his pony's leg.

The herd milled at last in the widening flats, resolved upon itself by their yells and fusillading shots. The cattle rotated slowly, and more slowly, and finally stopped, heads down, the vapor of their breathing going up from the mass of them as if they slowly leaked puffs of steam.

Two hours had passed since some unknown agency — a rolling stone, perhaps — had stampeded the herd. Dixie Kane was there by that time. A dozen horses of the remuda had seen fit to stampede inanely after the cattle, and Dixie, pulling himself together and watching his chance, had roped one of them and changed his saddle to it from his dead mount. But, when all was quiet again, it was Whiskers Beck who could not be found.

"Where's the old goat got to?" Squirty demanded in a queer voice. There is something uncanny about the disappearance of a man from your side. "I been singing out to him fer fifteen minutes."

"He shore ain't around here," said Dixie.

"You seen him get out in front, didn't yuh?"

"I seen a landslide."

"Well, he did. An' he helped me mill 'em when we got 'em stopped."

"Maybe that was me," offered Dixie hopefully. "I kind o' swang in on the tail end."

"This wasn't no tail end, an' it wasn't you. We gotta find the old buzzard, Dixie. Mebbe he's hurt an' down some place."

"Well . . . let's take one more swing around."

They turned and rode, and presently met on the far side of the herd with still no word of Whiskers Beck.

227

"Suppose he's under them steers," said Squirty pessimistically. "They keep snortin' in there an' edgin' away from one place."

"What'd be the use? Anyway, cows won't stand by blood. Move off an' build a fire, Dixie. I can hold 'em now."

It was another half hour before Squirty left his circle, riding for a bit to consult with Dixie at the fire. Dixie was mounting to ride back. And then, mysteriously, Whiskers Beck reappeared.

"Well, hell almighty," said Dixie. "Where you been? We had a heck of a time here."

"Oh, yuh did? Well, I was here an' you wasn't. An' yuh want to know where I been? Take a look at this here."

He hefted a faintly struggling carcass from his saddle bow, and awkwardly lowered it to the ground. It bleated, and staggered off toward the herd.

"I went back after that doggie calf," Whiskers said, "that's where I been. I figgered he'd git left behind, an' that's what he done. I don't know what'd become o' the stock if I left it to you fellers!"

Dixie and Squirty stared, tired men on blown horses.

"A calf," said Squirty at last. "Shore enough, a calf!"

"What kind of old buzzard is this? He jumps his horse two hundred feet, an' somersaults in a pile o' rocks with the horse on top, an' gets stampeded over, an' what's he thinkin' about? A four-dollar calf!"

"Oh?" said Dixie, smarting under his own mischance. "I s'pose he was lookin' for the calf when I passed him at the top o' the bluff!"

Whiskers leaned far out to look at his horse's legs. There was hide missing from the animal's belly, and a long gash on the inside of a foreleg.

"Who, me?" Whiskers said, making his horse walk away. "I was pickin' the best way down."

The two cowboys sat looking at each other, through the half transparent dark.

A Shot in the Dark

Silvertip Hughes had gone out to the stable to put up Old Snoop's horses, leaving Larry MacShane and Old Snoop alone. Even so, the young deputy would not have dared speak as he did had not the drone of the wind in the New Mexican spruce so filled the night that a man listening outside the lean-to could have heard nothing within.

"What are you doing here?" he demanded, the moment that Silvertip had disappeared into the snow. "I told you to go back down to town as soon as you had investigated the Magpie shaft."

"This blizzard . . . I figured I couldn't make it down to Underholt, MacShane. And this cabin bein' on the way, and me knowin' you'd already be here lookin' for Silvertip Hughes . . ."

"Blizzard!" scoffed Larry MacShane. "Well, what did you find at the Magpie?"

"Nothin'." Old Snoop, who would have been called Mr. Willis Jones if he had had his rights, had a scrawny figure, a scraggly mustache, a bottle nose, and an ill-preserved look. No chin seemed to have been included. "Nothin'. Except, o' course, Dad Young's corpse."

"Nothin'," MacShane mocked him, "except Dad Young's . . . you old fool! How was he killed?"

"Seemed like he might 'a' died natural, MacShane."

"Did you examine him?"

"Not to no extent. I knowed you'd never be satisfied on my say so, so I rigged a travois and brung him along."

"You brung him . . . oh, you infernal old idiot! Where is he now?"

"Here." Snoop shoved at a long canvas-wrapped bundle with his foot. "I put him here in the lean-to before I come in."

MacShane remembered now that noises in the lean-to, which he and Silvertip had attributed to wind and rats, had been audible for several minutes before Snoop's unexpected appearance at the door of the cabin itself. Rage swept him as he now flung open the cabin door and found, by the light from within, that Snoop's statement was verifiable.

"Here!" he ordered. "Help me heave him back in the corner! If Silvertip sees this . . . listen, you . . . I'm workin on Silvertip on the grounds that Dad Young is *alive*, you hear?"

"Alive?" said Snoop dimly. "But . . . ?"

"The second he finds out I've been lying to him, it's a shoot-out, d'you understand?"

"*Lyin'* to him? You been lyin'?"

"Didn't you just hear me tell you?"

"But I thought you figured Silvertip might 'a' *killed* Dad Young?"

"Never mind what you thought I figured! You . . ."

"You're the darnedest feller ever I see," said Snoop. His watery eyes, now thoroughly scared, traveled quickly upward from MacShane's high-heeled boots, over the scarred chaps and faded brush jacket, to the young deputy's lean face, burned brown by the wind, but dropped again before encountering MacShane's gray eyes.

"If Silvertip killed Dad Young, like I bet you think," said Snoop, "I'd say he has cause to know Dad Young's dead, it stands to reason. And here you want to try and convince him different . . . and with the corpse right here in the house, at that!"

"That last is your contribution," snarled MacShane. "Catch hold. Gosh, the old boy weighs a ton!"

"Fact is," said Snoop hesitantly, "there's a kind of reason . . . this . . ."

"Where's Midnight Zachary?" MacShane suddenly recalled that the Negro muleskinner whom he had sent with Snoop had not reappeared. "Didn't I tell you to keep him in sight, so he wouldn't talk? Did you let him go on back to Underholt alone?"

"I'm tellin' you," said Old Snoop with injury, "Midnight didn't like this spooky business . . . he kept takin' another drink. Finally he got so illuminated he couldn't walk, and I piled him on top of the . . . the bundle on the travois. But he kept rollin' off, and I see we wasn't gettin' no place, so finally, when a hard bump busted loose the lacin' o' Dad Young's canvas, I jest laced Midnight inside the canvas with Dad."

"Oh, gosh," moaned MacShane. "Dad Young is the only dead man in the world that could spoil my game, and I suppose Midnight Zachary is the only Negro within five hundred miles, and here you come and dump both of 'em onto me in the same sack! Say! We've got to get that superstitious fellow out of there before . . ."

"Too late," said Snoop stoically. "Here comes . . ."

"Shut up! And stay shut up, you hear? I'll do the talking here!"

The towering frame of Silvertip Hughes came stumping in as he spoke, but MacShane had to finish the cautioning command.

"All right," said Snoop. "Only . . ."

"Shut up! I sent this old fool to Clear Springs," he explained to Hughes, "to hand out a writ of attachment, but he has to get switched off and go hunting a bear he heard about. And to show what kind of an optimist he is, he borrows a mule to pack the hide and meat."

"Clear Springs?" said Snoop blankly. "But . . . ?"

"*Arrgh!*" said MacShane. He hunched his left shoulder significantly, so that his shoulder-holstered weapon shifted visibly under his brush jacket, and Snoop subsided.

"Snoop's a card, all right," Hughes agreed. He led the way into the cabin proper, flung off his sheepskin, and warmed enormous hairy hands that dwarfed to a red-hot melon the stove over which they were held. His blanket-thick woolen shirt was now open part way down the front, and MacShane saw, with a sudden keen anticipation of action, that a shoulder-holster bulge, similar to that under his own left arm, had now appeared under Silvertip's arm as well.

Silvertip was conspicuously tall in a country in which most men were tall. He had a mighty breadth of shoulder, and arms as powerful as legs. Between a tangled red beard and the shag of his forelock Silvertip's eyes were slits, sleepy looking and a little slanted. The violent beard and the veined, belligerent nose suggested that the eyes might be a fiery red.

Old Snoop fidgeted unhappily. Old Snoop might not be very smart, but he knew the makings of trouble when he saw them. Even without those unfortunate mysteries in the lean-to, which he himself had so unadvisedly introduced, Snoop could see that MacShane plus Silvertip added up to spell dynamite.

Cowboys like Larry MacShane gave Snoop a distinct pain. The faintly melancholy philosophy always present in those reckless and hell-bent riders never prevented any of them from diving into danger with glad whoops head on and without reservation, like frogs into soup. This did not endear them to Snoop. Whatever might be said against Snoop, he certainly was not reckless.

Unfortunately, Snoop's only asset was a marked flair for nosing out facts that were none of his business — this, and a natural dog-like genius for the life of a professional hanger-on. The worst possible luck had landed him in New Mexico in a day when direct action was more popular than discretion. And his temporary professional attachment to Deputy MacShane was the ultimate disaster in a life that had been one long series of winters.

MacShane's slight limp was a reminder to Snoop, if not to MacShane, that the cowboy deputy habitually put his horse headlong down steeps upon which practically no horse could be expected to live. The slight notch in MacShane's left ear was permanent testimony that he would rather try to kick a gun out of a drunkard's hand than actually have trouble. Worst of all, just now, was the speciously innocent look in MacShane's eyes — a faintly entertained, faintly hopeful, faintly expectant look — that told Snoop clearly more than a thousand probably futile explanations that any moment might produce unfortunate surprises. MacShane was not the right company for an old gentleman who had long suspected himself of a weak heart.

MacShane seemed to be waiting for Silvertip to open a conversational lead. Long minutes trailed away while Snoop fidgeted, suffering unknown agonies of apprehension, while Midnight Zachary, presumably, snored unheard in the lean-to, peacefully unaware of his peculiar bedfellow, and while MacShane smoked, apparently unconscious of them all. In the mountain cabin prevailed a silence about which the howling wind in the spruce wrapped a blanket of extraneous sound.

Old Snoop would have been horrified to know that MacShane had chosen these uncertain moments to let his thoughts wander ten miles downmountain to the little town of Underholt, and there to focus on the daughter of Dad Young. Early that afternoon MacShane had been sitting in Underholt's best and only boarding house. By letting his thoughts return there, he gave himself a big advantage in the nervous game of waiting out Silvertip Hughes.

MacShane seemed to recall that he had absent-mindedly ladled a spoon of beans into his coffee cup, and stirred them around and around. His eyes had been elsewhere. The dining room in which he sat was run by valiant old Mrs. Minsterhoff, who denied that she had been found running exactly the same place and in the same way the year that the first white man had showed up in what was now New Mexico. But table was waited on by Molly Young. Since old Dad Young had left his daughter in Mrs. Minsterhoff's care, while he and Silvertip reopened the old Magpie shaft, business in Mrs. Minsterhoff's eating department had flourished no end.

"Anybody would think," Molly Young had said, "that law officers in this part of the country would have to be alert, wide-awake, young men."

A certain sharpness of tongue, that Molly had perhaps inherited along with her turned-up nose from an Irish mother, had given the cowboy deputy a pleasant sort of homesick sensation.

"You sure have pretty eyes," he had offered. "They put me in mind of them blue flowers that come out all over the Cimarron hills in spring."

"The Cimarron hills," Molly had reminded him, "are frozen tighter than a drum under three feet of snow."

"Only bluer," Larry MacShane had said. "A feller don't know what to say about anything that's such a blue-blue as that."

"Is it necessary to say anything?"

"It ain't the sort of thing," MacShane had said solemnly, "that a feller wants to leave pass without favorable remark."

At this point Old Snoop had come in, obviously bursting with news that he could not keep, yet he was afraid to spill.

"Somethin's happened," he had said. "There's a feller waitin' to see you out here."

"Then you go keep him company," MacShane had ordered.

"But . . ."

"You lam, now!" Of course, if he had known then that Molly's future had been involved . . .

Snoop had tried a series of mysterious grimaces and gestures behind Molly's back, but MacShane had started to rise, and Snoop had lammed.

"Molly," MacShane had said, "don't you ever get tired of foolin'?"

"No," Molly had replied.

Old Snoop then had reappeared, cautiously following his extended nose.

"I guess," he had offered doubtfully, "I got to speak to the deputy alone, Miz Young."

"He'll do nothing of the kind, Molly," MacShane had declared.

"He certainly may," Molly Young had said. She had whisked out.

"Midnight Zachary's out here," Snoop had said in sibilant whispers. "He's the black packer that prods a mule of grub up to Miz Young's paw, up at the Magpie every two weeks, if sober. He's just come back. There's a dead feller up there, MacShane."

"Which one?" Larry had asked grimly.

Old Snoop had rolled an apprehensive eye toward the kitchen door.

"Dad Young," he had said almost soundlessly.

"Damn!" MacShane had said.

"Of course," Snoop had agreed, "of the two it couldn't have been Silvertip Hughes. Dad Young shouldn't have gone pardners with that feller. Who's goin' to break the news to Molly. You?"

"Not yet," MacShane had decided.

"Too bad about Molly," Snoop had said. "Left without a dime. Hughes ain't tried to conceal lately that the Magpie's worthless. His own self, he calls it the Magpie Salt."

MacShane's eyes had hardened. Somehow, even then — without evidence, and without knowledge of mining — even then he had known that Hughes had lied, and that there was something of value in the reopened Magpie shaft.

Now, as he sat in Silvertip's cabin, the job of telling Molly about her father's death remained undone. He dreaded it a lot. He'd rather get shot in eight places than call up tears into those blue eyes. Nobody but Midnight, Snoop, and himself — and possibly Silvertip? — knew that Dad Young lay dead. He was trying to find out just what Silvertip knew — that was his mission here tonight.

His mind suddenly snapped back to the present as Silvertip spoke.

"So," said Silvertip, "you seen Dad Young, did you?"

"Yes," said MacShane, "I saw him."

"Today?"

"No, yesterday."

"You sure," pressed Silvertip, "it was yesterday?"

"Yeah, it was yesterday, all right," MacShane asserted. "I was surprised when I heard he was in town, because he hasn't been down to Underholt for so long."

Silvertip grunted. Another session of waiting seemed to be beginning. Silvertip could have outwaited him two to one, MacShane knew, but for the ease with which MacShane's thoughts turned to Molly Young.

After Snoop's news had dragged MacShane out of the boarding house, the deputy had talked to Midnight Zachary. Zachary was chocolate brown, and of dignified deportment. He claimed to have been a preacher once. A scar on his neck that looked suspiciously like a rope burn perhaps explained his unnatural fear of entanglements with the law.

MacShane had led Zachary and Snoop into the deserted back room of a bar. "Midnight, what's the story?"

"This mornin', when I led my mule into the cabin up at the Magpie Mine, thar lies Dad Young daid in his baid."

"See anything else, Midnight?"

"No, suh. I come rapidly away."

"Silvertip," Old Snoop had put in, "is at the cabin in Big Cat Gulch. It's ten miles up . . . about five miles this side of the Magpie shaft. I saw him when I was huntin'. He didn't see me, though. I don't trouble folks much. That was last week."

"I expect that's right," Midnight Zachary had said. "I seen a sign of life at that shack, as I drawed nigh."

"You had to pass that shack on the way up to the Magpie," MacShane had told Midnight. "Did you see Silvertip?"

"No, suh, Big Cat Gulch is given to ha'nts, Mistah MacShane. When I seen movement at that shack from afar off, I stopped. And the Lawd said unto me . . . Mister Zachary, I wouldn't go nigh that dump, was I you. Best go 'round . . . way 'round. Mister MacShane, I so done."

"And coming back . . . did you go by that Cat Gulch shack again?"

"No, suh, Mistah MacShane. I went 'round. I ain't goin' tuh forget no such commandment as that go 'round business."

"I betcha he ain't," Snoop had said.

"Snoop, saddle up, and go up to the Magpie. Go around that cabin where you saw Silvertip, just as Midnight did. Find out anything you can up there. Midnight . . . you go with Snoop, and show him that way around you know so much about. I'm going to ask some questions here in Underholt. Then I'm going up and call on Silvertip. I'll see you here when I get back."

MacShane saw now that he had been mistaken on that last point, at least. His reunion with Old Snoop was at Silvertip's cabin, after all, and poor Midnight's dread of the trip was justified, for he was sleeping it off laced to a tarpaulin with Dad Young himself. MacShane

240

wondered nervously how soon Midnight, and consequently Silvertip, would find that out.

Once more Silvertip broke the silence, recalling MacShane to his immediate surroundings.

"I been worried about Dad's health for a long time," Hughes began tentatively.

"Somethin' wrong with him?"

"Fellers his age," said Silvertip, "is terrible suckers for ailments."

"Come to think of it," MacShane improvised, "he was looking peaked. Looked like a feller come out of the grave."

Silvertip said nothing, and MacShane, recalling that he was skating near the edge of mighty thin ice, decided it best to keep his gaze vacuously upon the stove. Certainly, he thought, Silvertip must know that old Dad Young was dead. If the deputy's suspicions were correct, Silvertip had personally seen to Dad's demise.

"Well," said Silvertip slowly, "I'm right glad to hear he made it to town. He's had a right bad cough, Dad has. Me and him was just settlin' down in this here halfway cabin for the winter, when Dad took it in his head to go down to town. We moved here from above because this is more sheltered."

"Well, anyway," said MacShane, "I was glad to hear you fellers done so well up there."

Cautious, prying words that might draw gunfire pretty soon. MacShane expelled a deep breath of pure tension. He had come to the point at last. Whether or not Silvertip had killed Dad Young was legally his primary concern, but he realized now that he did not much care. Dad Young was dead, and nothing that he or the law could do would bring him back, or make Molly Young less alone. What remained in the balance was the wealth that might or might not have been yielded by the Magpie Mine.

"There was rumors," went on MacShane, "that you fellers got fooled on the Magpie. Maybe you know some fellers call it the Magpie Salt. I certainly was relieved to hear they was wrong."

"Well," Silvertip began, apparently feeling his way, "that was a funny thing . . . and seein' as you was . . . is . . . a friend of Dad's, I don't mind tellin' you how it was. I suppose he . . . said a little somethin' about it himself?"

Silvertip paused, obviously praying for some enlightenment from MacShane that would give him his cue.

"Oh," said MacShane with just as fervent a prayer, "he did say a little something."

"Me and him," said Silvertip — now at last, something was coming out! — "me and him . . ."

From the lean-to came a peculiar noise, a sound nearer and more arresting than the impersonal whistle and drone of the wind in the spruce — a long moan, too human to be the voice of the wind, yet hardly human enough to be the voice of a man. That long, quavering moan seemed to slide under the rickety door, fill the room, and press heavily against the throats of the three. Silvertip's voice choked off, and he froze motionless.

"Oh, holy gee!" moaned Old Snoop.

Silvertip's words came with more than usual deliberation. "What . . . was . . . that?"

"I didn't hear nothin'," said MacShane nonchalantly. Silently he was cursing Old Snoop and his baggage. "What were you saying?" the deputy prompted, his voice casual.

"I," said Silvertip slowly, "forget what I was saying."

"We were speaking of the Magpie Mine," MacShane suggested.

"Was we?"

Stalemate. Once more a long silence.

"I was talking to Molly Young," MacShane began all over again. He was groping his way through a game in which his only card was the puzzlement of Silvertip over his report of Dad's impossibly continued survival. In Silvertip's mind, and there only, was the information MacShane had to get at. "She's right worried over old Dad's state of health," he said. "He's a sick man, all right."

"Seem feverish?" Silvertip suggested.

"Might have been."

"Fever," Silvertip said vaguely, "sometimes puts fellers to rememberin' things that ain't happened."

"Yeah, that's so. Anyway, all of us fellers was glad to hear that Molly won't be left penniless, if old Dad makes a die of it."

"Well, come to that," said Silvertip, cautiously now, "I guess she ain't goin' to be out in the cold at that, leastways not entire."

"That's what I gathered," said the deputy.

"Of course, it won't be *much*," said Silvertip.

MacShane could feel the scrutiny of Silvertip's hidden eyes. "Heard it would be considerable."

"You know how these old fellers are," said Silvertip. "They get a-hold of ideas. I'd jest as soon tell you how it was."

Once more MacShane stirred inwardly. Something was coming to the surface again.

"Me and him . . . ," said Silvertip, "we struck a . . . *what was that?*"

"Aw, a varmint nosing." With a great effort MacShane held his voice casual. "You struck a . . . ?"

"Snoop," demanded Silvertip, "you hear somethin'?"

It was the first time Snoop had been noticed. He visibly inflated. "Well, sir, I reckon I did."

"You're crazy, Snoop," said MacShane.

"I guess I know when I hear hollerin', MacShane."

MacShane's eyes bored into Snoop with such a force that the old fool quailed. Too late, he rallied brazenly to undo the harm he had done.

"I reckon," said the inspired Snoop, "that noise was my bear comin' to life. He was only shot in two, three places, and maybe lyin' outside in the refreshin' snow . . ."

Again from the lean-to came that long, half-human groan, but this time it broke at the end into an obscure gibbering of muttered words, half understood. The whiskey that Midnight Zachary contained was wearing off.

Silvertip leaped to his feet and snatched up his rifle. His big voice boomed. "Somethin's wrong around here!

Somethin's all-fired wrong!" There was a peculiar, ugly ring in the big miner's voice.

The big bear-like man was charging toward the lean-to door. MacShane shot up like a released spring, and passed him in the second stride. When he had passed Silvertip, and not before, his gun leaped into his hand. The cowboy deputy burst through the lean-to and hurled open the outer door beyond. Somehow . . . anyhow . . . Silvertip's attention must be distracted from the dark shadows within the lean-to.

Through the other door, as MacShane flung it open, came a whirl of snow, a deluge of cold, and the increased howl of the storm. Behind, in the cabin itself, the lantern wavered and dimmed, cowed by the strength of the blast, and the door at the front rattled as if someone were trying to break in. Half crouched, gun raised in fictitious readiness, MacShane pointed the outer emptiness with every muscle. He looked like a setter who knows exactly where the game is at last.

As MacShane had hoped, Silvertip was misled. He towered behind the deputy, rifle ready for attack upon the outer unknown. Silvertip suddenly raised his gun, aiming over MacShane's shoulder at an imagined something in the spruce. An instant panic shot through MacShane. If a rifle shot shattered the perturbed air inside the lean-to, and Midnight suddenly became aware of where he was . . .

"Wait!" shouted MacShane into Silvertip's ear.

The rifle wavered but remained raised.

MacShane pretended to raise his gun as if aiming, hesitated, aimed again, and at last lowered his weapon.

"Whatever it was is gone," he declared. He hauled the door shut. "Let's get back to the stove . . . I'm froze!"

Old Snoop was already cowering over the stove again, but a long moment's hesitation passed before Silvertip followed MacShane into the lantern-lit room. The deputy knew without looking back that Silvertip was standing, puzzled, his eyes trying to pierce the lean-to's shadows. The deputy feared that Silvertip would come and get the lantern, and with it make a successful search for the unknown, but, when Silvertip followed him into the cabin at last, shutting the lean-to door behind him, the miner only stood vaguely with his back to that door, the rifle in his two hands.

"Somethin's wrong," said Silvertip slowly. "Somethin' queer's goin' on around here."

"You're nervous, Silvertip."

"Maybe," said Silvertip, "maybe I am. Maybe it makes a man nervous to have two snoopin' spies come into his diggin's and lie, and lie, while they know they lie . . ."

MacShane looked up sharply. "What do you mean by that?" he demanded.

"I don't know what your game is, MacShane. Only that it's a damned queer one, the like of which I never see. I don't know what it is. Only, while I stand here, by God, I'm goin' to find out."

MacShane stood up. "All right. I'll lay down my cards if you will."

Silvertip stood silent, waiting.

"Ask me a question," MacShane suggested.

"What do you want here?"

246

"First," said the deputy, "I'm here to find out what Dad Young has coming from the Magpie Mine. Dad is an old man. He may never prospect again. He may or may not know what he's talking about. I'm here to find out."

"What did he tell you?"

"There've been rumors," MacShane evaded, "that you salted the Magpie before you sold Dad half share."

"Lies," said Silvertip.

"All right." MacShane knew that, but little time was left. "Then what did you do with the gold you and Dad took out of the Magpie?"

"You're a fool," said Silvertip again. "You think a shaft brings in greenbacks that a man can cart away and hide? If there was gold in the Magpie, it would mean months of hauling ore out or machinery in . . . one. What gold was in the Magpie is in there yet. But there ain't any."

"Then you did string Dad?"

"No. I bought back his share at the price he give for it just before he . . . before he went down to Underholt. He had the money on him."

"One more thing. I've been talking to the assayer." MacShane thought Silvertip's face changed ever so slightly. He dared not pause to be sure. "You've been bringing samples down. How come those samples were sand that you couldn't have got within five miles of the Magpie shaft?"

"Well, I was prospectin' 'round," said Hughes.

A terrific anger swayed MacShane. He was as certain now as anyone ever was to be that Silvertip had swindled Dad Young, or murdered him, or both. He saw through it all, the discovery of real value in a shaft that Silvertip had thought worthless. Silvertip's faking of the samples after the mine had proved good, and his forgery of a bill of sale after the death of Dad Young — perhaps by Silvertip's hand — to clear his skirts and make the mine wholly his. Yet Silvertip's alibi was watertight, as far as MacShane could see.

"I can show you Dad Young's receipt," said Silvertip slowly, "for what I paid him back. And on him you'll find . . . could 'a' found . . . what I paid him. That makes it my shaft. And, by God, no snoopin' spies . . ."

"Why," said MacShane, playing his last card, "did you leave Dad's body lying at the Magpie Mine?"

Silvertip appeared to relax. "If he turned back to the shaft, after he left me here and headed for town, and if he died up there," he answered smoothly, "then I know nothin' about that."

MacShane saw his only hope was a shot in the dark. "And why," he said softly, "did you put Dad out of the way by means o' . . . ?"

He didn't know, even as he spoke, what means of murder he was going to accuse Silvertip of using. He didn't know, either, whether he was going to be able to divert the muzzle of Silvertip's rifle long enough to draw, or whether Snoop, in case of accident, would have guts enough to plug Silvertip after the deputy was dead.

"By means o' . . . ?" He hesitated. He didn't know by what means.

From the lean-to came a formless scuffling noise, then, so suddenly and so violently that MacShane's hair stood on end, the night was shattered by a mad scream. It rang out terribly and unmistakably, and, though it came from beyond the lean-to door, it took the opposed men with an almost physical impact.

For an instant the three — MacShane, Snoop, and Silvertip — stood motionless, frozen like rabbits by sheer force of sudden sound.

Then Silvertip snatched the lantern from its hook in the upper beams. As he did so, the lean-to gave out a swift rending noise, and its outer door was heard to crash open as if charged by a steer. Silvertip shouldered into the lean-to with stiff steps, breasting the unknown. A blast of stinging snow whipped their faces, and made the lantern quiver. By the light of its wavering glow, they could see the tarpaulined bundle that Old Snoop had brought, but it was torn open now. Then the lantern crashed to the floor. In the last flash of light before the lantern died, MacShane had seen the miner's rifle swing upon him like a striking snake. He gripped the rifle barrel in the dark, and, though the smash of the rifle shot deafened him, and its flare seemed to scorch his face, he realized that he was not hurt. Silvertip's great strength wrenched the rifle from the deputy's grasp, and MacShane dropped to the floor. MacShane's six-shooter was out, now. In the moment of silence he deliberately turned his weapon to the roof, and fired twice.

Old Snoop, alone in the faint glow of the stove, and buttressed behind such protection as the hot iron afforded, heard the lantern fall, and saw its light go out. In the dark, the shock of sound exaggerated by the close walls, Snoop heard a muddle of shots — perhaps three or four. He wasn't interested in counting them accurately, just then.

After a long pause he heard two more reports, this time outside in the storm, and, muffled in the snow and wind, he thought he could distinguish the diminishing rush of galloping hoofs. Then silence for a long time, while Snoop shivered and wished he was far away.

At last a step sounded in the dark cabin. Snoop slumped behind the stove and closed his eyes.

MacShane, regarding Molly Young across the stew that she had set before him, was thinking she had stood very well the news of her father's death. She had stuff, he guessed. Because of certain investigations following the definite escape of Silvertip Hughes, MacShane had not returned to Underholt at once, and, of course, the news had preceded him.

There were a few things, though, that Molly did not yet know. "Is it true," she asked him levelly, "that Silvertip Hughes . . . killed my father?"

"I guess we're not going to know," MacShane answered. "He could have . . ." He broke off. There was no use tormenting Molly with an account of the diverse means of murder that Silvertip might have employed. "Hughes is in old Mexico by now. We have Midnight Zachary to thank for that . . . though it isn't likely that Midnight himself knows just how he turned the trick. Silvertip's run-out was pretty much luck for us all. It looks like an admission of guilt, but, if he were here, we'd be worse off than as it is. The way it is now, it's your mine, Molly, and the gold is there all right. How much, I don't know yet . . . enough to make you rich, I guess."

They looked at each other solemnly for a moment.

"There were things," MacShane continued, "that I aimed to speak to you about, before this come up. Now that you're rich, I guess they aren't suitable any more."

He shoved back his untouched stew. "I'll be seein' you sometime, I guess. I just want to say, if ever you need me, send for me. This is one *hombre* you can count on any old time, and no obligation, either."

"Why . . . where are you going?"

"Well," he told her vaguely, "I think I'll be moving on, for a little while, I guess . . ."

Molly let him get as far as the door. "Larry MacShane!"

He went back.

"I don't know," she told him, "if there'll ever be a time when I need you around any more than I do right now."

He stared blankly.

"Oh, get out!" she exploded, unexpectedly. "Go on away! I don't care if I never see you again!"

"No," he said, "I've changed my mind. I'm not going any place, not any place at all."

Lost Dutchman O'Riley's Luck

Just as a man is getting things going so that the future looks pretty good, Steve Hunter reflected, something always happens to take him down a peg. He had thought some pretty harsh things about himself from time to time, but he had never expected to be picked out as a come-on for one of the most frazzled, worn-out skin-games known to the West. Yet, there sat the man who called himself O'Riley, costumed as an old-time prospector down to the last whisker — down to the last ore sample, Hunter had no doubt, in the pocket of O'Riley's pants.

"You must have heard your pa speak of Dennis O'Riley," the old reprobate was pleading.

"Never heard of him," Steve Hunter professed, making his face look blank.

It was true that the name of Dennis O'Riley had sometimes entered the thousand tall stories that had featured the declining years of Wild Bill Hunter, Steve's father. But finding the name of someone once known to Wild Bill — someone long since disappeared — would have been easy to any impostor, about as easy as looking up Wild Bill himself, as easy as finding a white granite mountain there in the high Sierras where Steve Hunter was now running his pack outfit.

"I can't understand it," said the old man. "Wild Bill never mentioned Dennis O'Riley? Why, me and him . . . me and him . . . well, at least," the old man tried again, "you know about Lost Dutchman's gold!"

"Never heard of it," Steve declared.

The man who called himself Dennis O'Riley sat back, flabbergasted. "Never heard of . . . well, I'll be . . ." He pulled himself together. "Back in the 'Eighties," he proceeded sententiously, "a feller wandered into Buck Springs with his pockets full of the richest ore samples these here mountains ever seen. He had mountain fever . . . pretty near died. But when he pulled through, he knew that he was rich." O'Riley leaned forward. "He started back to his discovery. But Buck Springs picked up as one man and followed along, burro, pick, and pan, hundreds of 'em, and he took to twisting and turning in the hills, to shake 'em off. And in the end he did lose 'em, too. And then . . ." O'Riley hitched forward to tap Steve's collar bone with a gnarled forefinger "and then, what do you suppose?"

"He got mountain fever again."

"Eh?" said O'Riley. "No, sir! He found that *he* was lost, too!"

"You don't mean to tell me," said Steve, who had heard the story ninety times.

"Wait till you hear the next," said the old man. He drew himself up for his great effect. "I, Dennis O'Riley, am the Lost Dutchman himself!"

253

A shocked silence fell between them. Steve turned to his shaving mirror, a broken triangle tacked to the log wall. The face that looked back at him was cleanly shaved, lean and brown; from above high cheek bones comprehending blue eyes stared soberly. *So this*, he thought, *is what a born come-on is supposed to look like* . . . . He asked his visitor: "Are you of the Dublin Dutch, or one of the Amsterdam O'Rileys?"

"I admit," said the infamous wowser testily, "it's a little peculiar that the original Lost Dutchman turns out to be of honest County Kerry blood. But what does a bunch of Westerners know about different nationalities, anyway? The sun had prob'ly bleached out my hair the color of winter hay, I expect is the root of the matter."

"That explains it," Hunter accepted. "And now where is your sample of most astoundingly rich ore?"

"Right here," said O'Riley, bringing it out with a flourish. "It was considerable larger in size, but it wore down by time."

"And where," Steve pursued, "is your picture of your penniless niece?"

"Granddaughter," O'Riley corrected him. "How did you know I got her picture here?"

"Isn't that the usual play in a case like this?"

"If you keep on having these damn' fool fits of giggling," said O'Riley with annoyance, "opportunity is going to pass you by!"

"Heaven forbid," said Steve. "Get on with the description of your penniless granddaughter."

254

"Well," the old man said grumpily, "she has a sort of kind face, so she has."

"This part of your spiel isn't nearly as well worked up as the other," Hunter criticized him. "You ought to get hold of a more powerful description. Well . . . trot the chromo out."

From a pocket of his brush jacket O'Riley dug a snapshot print, showing a girl on a horse. "She's staying down here at the Two Pine boarding house," O'Riley explained.

At first Hunter thought the girl was one he had known before, for a swift, odd sense of recognition touched him as he perceived the clean, alert lift of her head, and the slim, relaxed grace with which she sat in the stock saddle. Her face, in the shadow of a big hat, was less clearly shown, but he could see that, from the camera's angle at least, this girl was lovely, too lovely to be connected in any way with the crooked old wowser who was trying to sell a mythical mine. A gust of anger stirred him.

"I don't know where you got this picture, nor who it's of," he growled at the old man, "but this I'll tell you flat . . . this girl hasn't any connection with any blue-sky mine, nor with any Dutchman named O'Riley, either, and I've a mind to see you jailed!"

"Gimme that back!" shouted O'Riley.

"All right. But I'm going to drive down to Two Pine. I'm going to find out if this girl is there. And if your story doesn't tally, this country isn't going to hold you, you hear?"

"I won't ride with you," snorted O'Riley. "I'll go back by hand, the way I come!"

"Suit yourself."

O'Riley wilted. "My story's too good," he almost whimpered. "It's so good nobody will believe it. I've got to have help, and have it soon! But if old Wild Bill's boy won't believe me, who will? I've tried a hundred fellers, and they're as bad or worse than you. God knows," he told Steve, "I'd like to haul off and bust you one. But you come very close to being the last shot in my gun." Suddenly his voice turned shrill, intense, and he shook his clawed hands before Steve Hunter's eyes. "It's there," he shouted. "I know it's there! I know right where it is. A fortune, an everlasting fortune, lost in the hills . . . and I can't get to it! I tell you, I *know!*"

He jerked from a pocket a United States survey quadrangle, folded in innumerable accordion pleats. "It's these new maps showed me the light," he declared, shaking it out. "I can stand here and put my finger on millions . . . millions, boy, you hear me? . . . right here on this map. But if I don't set my finger down, your chance is gone, and maybe mine, and maybe hers, too, and the fault is yours!"

Steve Hunter blew smoke through his nose and studied the old man. It was incredible to him that anybody could lie so well. "Well, I still figure to drive to Two Pine," he said.

"That's more like Wild Bill's boy!" said O'Riley with emotion. He led the way to Steve's battered mountain car at a shambling run.

Down in front of the Two Pine boarding house a long blue roadster stood, its chromium fittings a bright dazzle in the sun.

"That rig," said O'Riley, standing up to point, "belongs to the swivel-eared jackass that wants to stake me, and horn in on my mine. Only I won't let him. Trying to trim me! That's him at the wheel, and the other one is my granddaughter. Hey, June!"

Steve Hunter angled in beside the blue roadster — and found himself looking directly into the eyes of the girl whom he had pronounced a myth. It was the girl of the snapshot, all right. Only this time there was no intervening shadow and no hat to hide her face. It was a thin face, tanned and lively. The soft, fine hair that framed it was the color of sunlight through autumn leaves, and her eyes — Steve could not have said whether they were green or brown or blue, or sometimes all three, in changing lights, but they were gentle, humorous, and awake.

"You're Steve Hunter, aren't you?" said the myth. "This is Wally Parker."

Steve shook hands with the smooth-haired young man at the wheel without noticing him much. He was absorbed with the baffling contrast between the old wowser, with his weather-reddened nose and historic whiskers, and the slender, smiling girl in the other car. If this truly was O'Riley's granddaughter, all that preposterous story about Lost Dutchman's gold needed a different explanation than that which he had so readily supplied.

257

Wally Parker broke in. "Aren't you the Hunter who runs the Three Bar pack outfit? Can I speak to you a minute?"

"Sure." Hunter, stepping to the board walk, found himself drawn along the walk by the stranger, out of earshot of the girl.

"I suppose," Parker began, "you've heard O'Riley's story by this time. I'm the boy that drove him up to your place this morning. You didn't see me. I let him out a little way down the road."

"Where do you come in?" Steve asked.

"I," said Wally Parker, "am the boy who takes a special and particular interest in June O'Riley."

"Oh, you do?" said Steve.

"O'Riley," said Parker, "is obviously the victim of self-hypnosis. He's told the story of Lost Dutchman's gold so often that he believes it himself . . . so much so that he has even convinced his granddaughter to some extent. I'm telling you this," he explained, "so that you will not think I'm an idiot."

"Thanks. I'm glad to have it cleared up."

"The O'Rileys," Parker went on, "are . . . bankrupt. They can't seem to understand that when June and I are married there will be no cause to worry about that. Meanwhile, this gold scare is a persistent nuisance. I can't chase the O'Rileys all over the West forever, you know."

"No?" said Steve.

"No," said Parker, "and I'm not at all sure that I like your tone of voice. However, you happen to fit my plans, so we'll overlook that. The trouble is, the old

258

lunatic won't let me finance the final search, and, since nobody else is idiot enough, there the matter rests."

"Not a bad place for it."

"I don't agree with you. Didn't I mention that my plans are held up until the O'Rileys abandon this outlandish notion? Now, I want you to pack O'Riley to wherever the old fool thinks he has lost his mine. I'll pay all expenses, with a substantial bonus if June is convinced that Lost Dutchman's gold is nonexistent."

"That is to say," said Steve Hunter, "you want me to pretend to take up his proposition myself?"

"Exactly."

Steve Hunter looked Parker over slowly. He couldn't make out exactly why the man in front of him roused him to instant resentment with his every word. Wally Parker was tall, slim, blond, and clean looking. He had too small an eye, perhaps, too long a nose, and too smooth a way, but none of these things accounted for the pleasure with which Steve considered eliminating Parker with one long wallop of his right hand. He rolled a cigarette.

"Not at any price," he said at last. "I wouldn't touch it with a ten-foot pole."

Parker shrugged. "Oh, very well. I'll get somebody else."

"You think you will?" said Hunter.

He did not understand, then, what made him do what he did next. Certainly he had no belief in Lost Dutchman's gold. He could only tell himself, afterward, that it had seemed a good idea at the time.

He walked to the blue car, where June was talking eagerly to old Dennis O'Riley.

"Don't you fret, Miss O'Riley," he heard himself saying, "I'll help you find your darned old mine!"

"Oh, good boy!" said June O'Riley.

Long Thunder Mountain turned out to be old Dennis O'Riley's objective — a sufficiently inaccessible place in which to lose his gold. Not until the eleventh day did it loom over them, gaunt, black, and austere.

"This is it," Dennis O'Riley exulted, "this is it! It all comes back to me plain. I'd know that hill from the floor of hell!"

For an hour they pressed upward across the deeply carved face of Long Thunder. And there, incredibly, half an hour before dusk, they came upon O'Riley's ancient stope. One thing, at least, was decided for Steve Hunter in that moment. If he had any further doubt as to the sincerity of either the girl or the old man in their quest for Lost Dutchman's gold, it vanished here. No one could doubt the reality of the tears which the old man tried to hide as they trickled into his beard, or the overwhelming emotion of June O'Riley as she hugged her grandfather close in her arms.

The old man snatched a pick-pointed hammer from a pack and rushed into the dark mouth of the stope. For ten minutes, while Hunter unsaddled his pack animals and made camp, he could hear the ring of steel on stone. Then, finally, O'Riley came running toward Hunter, both hands filled with fragments of rock. He pressed ragged chunks into Steve's hands. "Look at that! Look at that!"

Steve looked, turning the fragments over, holding them close to his eyes in the failing light. He saw a dark volcanic-looking rock, which he could not immediately name, marked with innumerable small irregular inclusions of a steely gray, something like the wings of a Plymouth Rock hen, and his spirit dropped heavily.

Now, Steve was no geologist. He didn't know a lot of things that there were to be known about the vast sheers of rock among which he lived. Yet he had spent his life in these hills, and he knew gold when he saw it, and this was not it.

"O'Riley," he said, "this isn't the rock you got your sample from."

For just a moment Lost Dutchman O'Riley let his embarrassment check his enthusiasm. He coughed twice and shifted his feet. "Now that we've actually found it and you can see that it's rich," he said, "I suppose I may as well admit that the sample I showed you didn't come from here. I know as well as anybody," he said, "that there's nothing quite so exciting as plain, free gold, so I just run in that other sample to make my story more interesting." O'Riley's enthusiasm surged up again magnificently. "You know what that is?" he shouted. "You know what that is?" He extended the gray and black rock fragments to Steve once more in hands that shook with excitement. "That's *graphite delirium*. Graphite delirium, man!"

"Graphite . . . what?" said Steve. A curious anger was upon him, an anger that somehow made him want to

261

laugh, yet left him without energy for laughter or anything else.

"Graphite delirium," cheered O'Riley again. "Rich in gold, rich in silver, and there's a million tons of it under the hill. We're rich, man, rich!"

"I see," said Steve. He didn't know all the geology there was to know, but he was not impressed by graphite, and he knew that delirium was a state of mind. The painful thing was that June's hopes would now be riding high upon the old man's mad imagining. He turned his back upon O'Riley and the worthless stope.

Next morning, putting on as cheerful a face as he was able, Steve Hunter set to work. That day he spent in digging and chipping little pot holes in the rock, systematically, in lines radiating from the abandoned stope. He sketched a rough map of the location with his pot holes marked upon it, and from each digging he took a sample which he carefully put away in a little bag marked with its map location. Yet all day long he saw not one trace of the yellow color for which he hoped against hope. He was only going through the motions that he would make if the discovery was real, and he knew that he was stalling, unable to make up his mind what he was going to say to June.

People think what they want to think, he told himself. *She'll never believe me against the old man. We'll take back the rock samples and get them assayed. She'll have to believe the assay. There's nothing I can do here.*

The next day they started back.

Steve Hunter kept to himself quite a bit during those two weeks of the return. When spoken to directly concerning the Lost Dutchman's mine, he always grinned, but answered briefly, without committing himself. Sometimes June reproached him for his apparent indifference. Once, when they sat in front of a campfire, while O'Riley slept, she turned to him.

"Don't you realize what's happened, Steve?" she said. "Why, we're rich, Steve! All three of us. Don't you realize this is the mine that Granddad had been hunting almost all his life?"

"I don't exactly rate a share," he said soberly. "All I've done is lend you some mules, June, and come along for the fishing. I was glad to do that, June. That you should know."

"Of course, you own a share!" she insisted. "A half share, just as Granddad said to begin with. Nothing else will do!"

He whispered to himself: *Graphite delirium. Oh, good Lord!* He wanted to caution her not to believe too strongly, to prepare her for what he knew must come. But, when his eyes met the dancing firelight reflected in hers, he could not.

"I've made a thousand plans," she persisted. "I suppose there'll be some delay while the mine is organized and all that, but, after that . . . first of all, I'm going to have tons of pretty things to wear, like Mother and I used to have before Dad's business went smash. Oh, wait until Wally Parker hears about this! You know, he never believed in Granddad at all."

"Well," Steve commented, "that was mutual."

"Granddad doesn't understand Wally, and that's a shame, too. Wally Parker is a peach in every way."

"Are you going to marry Parker?"

He had surprised himself by asking that. But somehow in the high, thin air of the pine forest, with its close stars, they seemed very near together.

"Marry him? I don't know," she answered. "If Dad's business hadn't crashed, I suppose I would be married to him now."

Steve Hunter said nothing.

"I suppose I'm foolish," she went on presently, "but you see Wally's family has so much money I couldn't possibly think of marrying anybody like that when we had nothing at all."

"Must a million marry a million?" Steve asked.

"I don't mean that. But, Steve, you don't realize how completely, utterly broke I was before we found the Lost Dutchman mine. When Dad died, he left nothing at all. Even the insurance had lapsed. I put every last dollar . . . literally . . . into coming out here with Granddad to take just one more look for his lost mine. It was a wild, crazy thing to do, I know. Do you know how broke we were when I first saw you in Two Pine? We had just enough to pay our board bill for two more days. As close to the edge as that!

"So . . . you see . . . it wasn't a question of millions at all. If I had married Wally any time after Dad's crash, someday he would have got to thinking I had married him only as a rescue, not because I loved him at all. If I had had anything at all . . . enough to carry on with and hold my head up for a little way . . . it would have been different, but I didn't, and I couldn't marry him even when I wanted to. Do you see?"

"And now?"

"It's all different now," she said, and her voice seemed to sing in his ears. "I feel as if I had escaped from some terrible trap! Steve," she said, her voice very low, "do you realize that we owe everything in the world to you? If I hadn't come out here, if we hadn't found you . . ."

"Shush, child," said Steve. He didn't dare look at her; he kept his eyes deeply on the dying embers.

"You're nice," she said unexpectedly, and for a moment laid her hand upon his. And still he sat motionless with his eyes on the coals.

"Good night, Steve. Excuse my talking so much."

"Good night."

By the time he had delivered the O'Rileys at the Two Pine boarding house, he had made up his mind what he was going to do. He went first to Harry Weir, the local assayer, and dumped his bags of rock rubbish on Weir's floor.

"You've got to do something for me, Harry?" he said.

"When the best trout guide in the country says that, there's only one answer, Steve."

Steve thanked his stars he had friends. "All right. Assay this worthless rip-rap first. Then you're going to buy the O'Rileys' right in the mountain this junk came from."

"With whose money?" said Harry Weir skeptically.

"Mine," said Hunter. "Only, my name is going to be kept out of the deal."

"Sounds like a shenanigan," said Weir.

"Call it what you like. You ought to know me well enough by this time to take a chance." There was a short wordy struggle, and an explanation or two. But in the end Weir, indebted to Steve for more than one free pack to his favorite streams, agreed to all Steve asked.

Next he went to Abe Cramp — a slouching, unshaved figure always to be found at Cramp's Two Pine corral. Just as Steve Hunter made a business of supplying transportation upon the mountain trails, Abe Cramp made a nice thing of horse trading with the trail men, who owe their whole existence to horses and mules.

"Abe," said Steve, "if you still know where you can sell the Three Bar, you can have her now . . . lock, stock and barrel, name and brand, and I guarantee not to set up another pack outfit within a hundred miles in the next five years."

"How much?" said Cramp.

"Six thousand cash, today."

Abe Cramp studied him. "I won't horse trade you, Steve," he said at last. He masticated his straw, devouring it slowly. "I could easy beat you down, but I won't. I'll offer six if you want."

There was a silence. Then: "Sold," said Hunter. The word came hard, but he had decided what he was going to do.

The straw dropped from Abe Cramp's mouth. "You mean I've bought the Three Bar for six thousand?"

"You heard me, Abe."

Cramp took off his two-gallon hat and slammed it on the ground. "Then you're a fool!" he shouted. "You're a fool, you hear?"

"Maybe I am," said Steve.

"You've built you up the best pack outfit in the best stand this side of the backbone of the Rockies. You've got the best stock and the best equipment of any packer I ever saw, and I've seen them all. You get the cream of the fishermen, the cream of the deer hunters . . . they know your name, and they come to you, more of them every year. A few years more and you'll own this country, Steve! Don't you do it, don't you sell!"

"I'm set on it, Abe."

Abe stared. "You'll cuss hell out of yourself for this, Steve, someday." He led the way to the house.

It took all day to get that deal straightened out, but there was a certified check for six thousand dollars in Steve Hunter's pocket when he pulled up in front of the Two Pine boarding house again. It was dusk, and in the unpainted board houses that line Two Pine's hundred-foot-wide-street, warm yellow lights were beginning to show. But no light showed in Steve Hunter's future as he sought out June O'Riley. When, at last, she sat beside him in his parked car, he knew that he had reached the moment he had dreaded, that he could no longer put off telling her the truth, as he knew it, about the Lost Dutchman's gold.

"Look here," he said, "look here . . . I've got to tell you something. I've got bad news."

"Steve, what's the matter?"

"The mine," he said, "the mine . . . it isn't as good as you've been thinking, June, you and your grandfather."

"Are the assays finished?" she asked, almost inaudibly.

He rushed over that, anxious to be finished with what he was trying to do. "You remember," he said, "we staked three claims on the Lost Dutchman ledge, one in your name, one in mine, and one in the name of Dennis O'Riley?"

"But the understanding was," she said, "that we were to pool all three claims."

"I know," he said, "but I'm pulling out of that agreement."

"You mean you're selling out separately?"

"Yes." He made his face expressionless and hard lest it give him away, for at this point he had to leave the narrow path of facts as he saw them, and launch into the fiction for which he had sold his packs. "Now, as to the claim that is in your name . . . Harry Weir represents Catlin Mines, Incorporated. He's going to offer you six thousand for your rights."

"Six . . . but I thought . . . ?" June pressed the back of her hand against her mouth and stared at him wide eyed.

Never in his life had six thousand seemed so small, so foolishly inadequate. "I'm sorry, June," he said. "God knows, I'm sorry, but listen, June. Do you believe that I shoot square, and that I know these hills?"

"Of course, Steve," she said in a small voice.

"Then sell," he told her. "The six thousand seems like nothing, I know, but it's every cent your claim is

268

worth, and more. And if you can bring yourself to think that it's anything at all" — unconsciously he slipped into her own remembered words — "anything at all, enough so that you can carry on for a little way . . . then maybe, after all, it wasn't a wasted trip."

They sat in silence while a great sense of vacant weariness overwhelmed Hunter.

"One thing more," said Steve. "Forget this million-marry-a-million stuff. It's all wrong. I'm sorry we didn't find a mine that would put us all on the same money level as Wally Parker. I don't know how many millions he has, and I don't care, but get this . . . if he owns all there is, he still isn't good enough to saddle your horse. If you want him, take him, and never let the thought come into your head again that where you're concerned money counts."

Once more they sat silently. Steve, his hands on the wheel, was looking straight ahead. "I've got to take some fishermen into the upper basin after steelhead," he said. "I've got to go now, I guess, and, if I don't see you any more, God knows I'm sorry this thing came out like this. That's all I can say."

Somehow he could not bring himself to look at her. After a moment she left him, without a word, and still he did not look after her, but only sat there, staring at the dusk. Presently he smashed into gear and drove down to the assayer's office where Harry Weir was working in a crowded little room full of bits of rock, retorts, and acidulated smells.

"I've been looking for you all day," said Harry Weir.

"Listen," said Hunter, "this morning you promised to help me. Now I'm ready to tell you what you have to do."

"But first . . . ," began Weir.

"Listen to me," Steve snarled at him. "I have here a certified check for six thousand dollars. You're to take that check. You're going to buy the girl's claim from her in the name of an imaginary company . . . Catlin Mines, Incorporated. Get that? I've already talked to her. You . . ."

"If you'll let me get in a word edgewise . . . ," begged Harry Weir.

"Listen! Above all, she's not to know I'm back of this. I'm out. I've . . ."

"I'm trying to tell you . . . ," said Weir, raising his voice.

"Will you listen?" shouted Steve.

"No," yelled Harry Weir, "you big jug-head! These samples of yours are rotten with sylvanium!"

"And what the devil is sylvanium?" asked Steve.

"Gold, silver, telluride, you big ignoramus. Those little gray marks are twenty-four per cent gold and thirteen per cent silver!"

The breath went out of Steve Hunter as if by the kick of a mule. Harry Weir, enjoying himself hugely, rolled a cigarette in acid-stained fingers and sat back to watch his news soak in. If this was true, Steve Hunter was thinking, then June O'Riley and her old wowser of an ancestor had found Lost Dutchman's gold in truth.

"Some call that type of deposit graphic tellurium," Weir was saying. "Ever hear of it?"

Hunter had no trust in his luck. It was incredible that the senile old wowser had by a weird freak of chance — *or was it?* What if it was no freak of chance at all? Certain of Weir's words had a strangely familiar ring. Could it be that old O'Riley . . . ?

"You mean . . . you mean to say . . . ?"

"I mean to say you've stumbled into something. Of course, if it's only a small intrusion . . ."

"There's a big long ledge of it," said Hunter faintly. "If there isn't ten thousand tons . . ."

"You're overestimating," said Weir.

"I was there, wasn't I? I know what . . . ," he broke off abruptly. "Good Lord," he whispered under his breath.

For the first time he saw exactly what he had done. June O'Riley was in possession of invaluable holdings, and he, through the name of an imaginary company, had tried to buy her rights for six thousand dollars. He stood silently while the blood drained from his head and a slow, cold sweat appeared upon his forehead.

"Don't take it so hard," said Weir. "You should have seen how coolly O'Riley took it, just as if he'd been sure all along."

"He was here?"

"He left just before you came in."

So, then, they knew all about it already — his trivial offer, and the true value of the Lost Dutchman's deceptive gold. He knew what June must be thinking of him now, and he wondered if Wally Parker was at her side.

"If it's an extensive ledge," he heard Weir saying, "I guess you've hooked into your millions, all right."

"Oh, he has, has he?" said a voice from the door. In the whirl of the moment they had not noticed Wally Parker's long blue car slide to a stop in front of the assayer's office. "So you've made your millions," Parker repeated. "Now, isn't that odd! That explains the rumor that you sold your outfit for six thousand dollars, Hunter, and it explains," he added deliberately, "why you offered Miss O'Riley six thousand dollars for her rights."

O'Riley pushed in past Parker's elbow. His voice was shrill and enraged. "Trying to trim me!" he shouted. "Trying to trim me! Why, you damned . . ." Words failed him, and he shook furious fists under Hunter's nose. "Graphite Delirium!" he got out at last. "Graphite delirium! And you made out you didn't know what it was!"

"So," said Steve, "that was what you meant. Graphic tellurium! Well, I'll be . . ."

It was worse than he thought. The discovery was not even the accidental coincidence he had supposed. Old Dennis O'Riley, however he had garbled his scientific terms, had yet known what he was about, and Steve Hunter had been the only one of them all who had been dead wrong, a fool who had made himself look like a crook.

"I suppose," raged Dennis O'Riley, "that there's the check for six thousand that you was going to buy me and June out with?" Hunter had forgotten that the check was in his hand. He stared at it stupidly. "Oh, you big horse thief!" yelped O'Riley. "Oh, you big . . ."

Steve Hunter rolled the check into a little ball and shoved it down into his pants pocket. "Out of the picture," he mumbled to himself. "Out of the picture, once and for all." Dazedly, without a word to the others, he turned to the door. Wally Parker still stood in the doorway, however, and made no move to get out of his way.

"Stand aside," said Steve, his voice very thick and low.

Parker did not obey. "I've had my eye on you," said Parker slowly. "The first time I saw you I recognized you for what you are . . . an ignorant, shifty, hill-billy crook."

Hunter stared at him. Perhaps he was still dazed by the overpowering significance of the assayer's report; perhaps he had not comprehended that Wally Parker was there at all.

"And yellow, too," said Parker. "I'd knock a man down who said that to me."

Steve Hunter said: "For once you're right." Parker suddenly started back, throwing his arms in front of his face, but all Steve's unexpressed bitterness against the turn of the luck was in the right hand that he brought crashing through. Parker's feet flew from under him, so that he seemed to pivot in mid-air with the shock of the blow, and he lay where he fell, in the doorway, a stertorously breathing heap. Hunter hardly glanced at the fallen man as he stepped over him and out into the night.

Ordinarily it was not in this man to evade his fate, but it may be that he would have avoided June O'Riley then if he had seen her in time. He did not. A breathless figure came racing along the board walk to collide with Hunter with such force that she would have fallen if he had not caught her in his arms. For a moment or two June O'Riley clung to him, out of wind.

"Steve, what's happened?" June gasped.

Hunter cast a despairing glance at the door of the assayer's office. Too many explanations of what had happened were already waiting for her there — versions he was not going to be able to dispose of, he was sure. But Weir and old Dennis O'Riley had carried Wally Parker inside, and for the brief present June and Steve were alone on the Two Pine board walk.

"It isn't so," he said inanely. "June, it isn't so."

June O'Riley disengaged herself. "Steve, Granddad said he talked to the assayer, and that you were wrong . . . that Lost Dutchman's gold is real!"

"June, that's true."

"Then . . . you were wrong all the time!"

"Yes, I was wrong."

"What makes me mad," said June, "is that Harry Weir tried to buy us out for next to nothing, when he must have known . . ."

"No," said Steve; "that wasn't Harry Weir. I just used his name."

"Steve! Are you trying to tell me that you were buying my share yourself? It's true you sold the Three Bar so that you could offer me six thousand for my claim?"

274

"Yes," he said.

"And what," she asked queerly, "have you got to say for yourself?"

He hesitated, then looked her in the eyes. "Nothing," he said. "Not one word!"

There was a silence in the Two Pine street.

"I think," she said slowly, "that you are the most generous man in the world."

Steve Hunter was struck dumb. For a long moment they stood looking at each other through the starlit dark. "You didn't think, then . . . ?" he got out at last, "you didn't believe? . . ."

Suddenly he saw that she was laughing at him, and he paused. And now it occurred to him for the first time that he might have misread the light he had been seeing in her eyes, that his greatest error might have been in supposing that she would ever disbelieve in him at all. Inspiration swept him, overriding his insistent distrust of his luck.

"You come here a minute!" he said, and caught her in his arms.

Dennis O'Riley came stamping out of the assayer's office. "Graphite delirium!" he was yelling. "Tried to trim me! Tried to trim me!" He checked abruptly, and, as he spoke again, his voice was as if the unbelievable had seized him by the beard. "Well, I'll be . . . Well, of all the . . ."

"Oh, shut up," said June O'Riley.

Spanish Crossing

You've heard how Emmett Corbin stood off twenty men at Mokelumne, and walked alone into the fire of Saul Bassett and his brothers at Steamboat Springs. You know how he made a name for himself as a peace officer all up and down the gold frontier, until at last he became a real power in his state.

But I've seen Emmett Corbin when he didn't have enough spirit left to prod a skunk out of a brush heap. Yes, I saw him in the lowest moment of his life.

Emmett Corbin was eighteen years old, and had got smashed up by a killer horse, so that he had to lay off riding. Tough luck stuck with him like a brother — he like to starved. And then he drifted into Spanish Crossing.

Here he stuck for a while, seemingly because of a girl named Virginia Mead, and here his hard luck took a final whack at him.

Emmett Corbin was standing in the Silver King Saloon, and near him at the bar stood Bill Andreen. This Andreen was a pretty tough *hombre* who herded with the gambler crowd. He never fooled with gun-quick men, but he sure liked to jump us common people, for he was fast, and had killed four men.

Bill Andreen was fairly well into his liquor and talking freely, and pretty soon I heard him mention the name of Virginia Mead. I don't know what he said, or what Emmett Corbin took offense at. But anyway, young Corbin spoke up now.

"I'd sooner," he said, "you wouldn't use that name."

Andreen couldn't believe it. "You spoke to me?" he asked.

"I did," Corbin said. "I told you to stop using . . ."

"Dear God," said Andreen. Another man might have looked at Corbin and seen that he was just a half-starved kid. But not Andreen. "Why, you little squirt . . ."

I never heard any man take such a dressing-down as Corbin got before Andreen was through. Corbin turned green and sick, and his hand moved toward his gun, but stopped, and kind of hovered, uncertain, over the butt. We ducked out of line, expecting to see gunsmoke drifting, and Corbin lying on the floor. Then Corbin's hand came away, slow, without the gun.

Andreen laughed, very ugly. He said: "I'll give you ten seconds to get out of my sight!"

Corbin went. He moved slow and unsteady, but he went.

We had a gun-toting law in Spanish Crossing, not enforced very much, but often used to head off trouble already begun, and Dogtown Smith, though a partner in the Silver King, was deputy marshal. So now Dogtown made Andreen check in his gun, and Dogtown put it on the back bar, with some others.

After Andreen was gone, Dogtown Smith sent for Corbin.

"How come you not to fight, Emmett?" Dogtown asked.

"Empty gun," Corbin said. "Swapped my lead for grub."

Dogtown Smith looked around the bar, and only one or two of us was there, and not a one but what hated Andreen. "Emmett," said Dogtown, "there's a yellow streak in Bill Andreen. I've got a scheme for bringing that yellow streak out. If it works, Andreen is through in Spanish Crossing. If it don't . . . no harm done. Either way, you get ten dollars."

"I'm listening," Corbin said.

"I have Andreen's gun. I'll unload it. Then, when he comes in, I'll send for you. As you come in, I'll pass Bill his gun. You tackle him. His gun will seemingly miss fire. You step in with your own empty, and bend the barrel over his head."

"It won't work," Corbin said.

"Why won't it? In the confusion I'll put the load back in Andreen's gun. When he comes to, you'll be the boy that bucked his draw and downed him . . . with an empty gun."

Corbin didn't like it much. But he sure needed the ten.

"I'll send for you," Dogtown said, and told him where to wait.

Bill Andreen came back to the Silver King about three in the afternoon. "You've hit into it now!" Dogtown told him. "This morning that boy didn't have any lead in his gun. But now he's borrowed some. And he's on the hunt."

"Let him hunt!"

Dogtown Smith looked at Andreen with pity. "It's your funeral," he said, kind of queer.

Bill Andreen stood there at the bar, drinking by himself. Then we saw Emmett Corbin moving across the walk toward the door of the Silver King.

Dogtown Smith made a quick grab at the back bar, and slid iron across to Andreen. "Quick . . . holster your gun," he said. "By God, watch yourself! Or he'll kill you where you stand."

Andreen obeyed, and shoved the gun into the leather.

Emmett Corbin had slouched up to the door, looking terrible hopeless. But now, as he saw the gun go into Bill Andreen's hands, it seemed like something woke up. His face turned hard. He walked to within six feet.

"Draw, Andreen!"

Andreen had a poker face, and a good one, but, looking at Corbin again, I saw what had delayed Andreen's draw. I've seen some good, sure-handed gunfighters go into action, but I swear I never saw anybody look so confident, so deadly sure as Corbin looked now.

A second passed, two seconds — then five. Andreen said, kind of peculiar: "You gone crazy, kid?"

"Draw," Corbin ordered, and there was plenty quiet. Then Andreen said: "I don't want to kill you, kid."

Emmett Corbin stared. Then suddenly he laughed. "Ten seconds to get out of my sight . . . ten minutes to get out of town!"

I believe Bill Andreen took more than ten seconds. But he swung around slow, and went out the side door, walking very stiff. At the door he kind of lurched, as if he was dazed drunk, which he was not. And I never saw him again.

We turned to Dogtown, and I was fixing to praise him up on how good his little scheme had worked — better than anybody could have expected, better than it could possibly have worked. But now I saw that Dogtown Smith's face was a pale green color, and all sprinkled over with beads of sweat. "Good God!" he said.

"What's the matter?"

"I near got Corbin killed," he said, so shaky his teeth chattered. "I . . . I give Andreen the wrong gun!"

My hair kind of raised, and I felt a cool breeze on my back.

But now — Emmett Corbin grinned! "Yes, I knew that."

"You *knew* . . . ?"

"I saw you pass him the wrong gun . . . a loaded gun. But . . . I thought I'd go through with the play."

That was the turning point for Emmett Corbin. The week after, as a deputy marshal, he walked into the Steamboat Springs fight, alone against four guns, and made the beginning of his name.